THE QUEEN OF WAR

THE NORSEWOMEN

BOOK SIX

JOHANNA WITTENBERG

SHELLBACK STUDIO

BOOKS BY JOHANNA WITTENBERG

The Norsewomen Series

The Norse Queen

The Falcon Queen

The Raider Bride

The Queen in the Mound

The Queen of Hel

The Queen of War

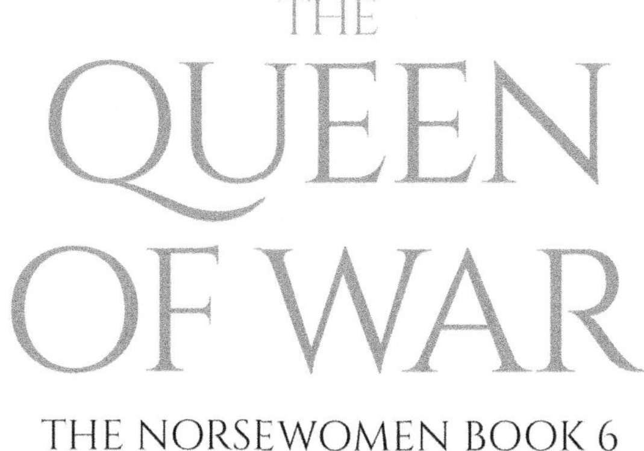

THE NORSEWOMEN BOOK 6

JOHANNA WITTENBERG

THE QUEEN OF WAR
The Norsewomen Series Book 6

ISBN 978-1-7345664-6-8

Published by
SHELLBACK STUDIO

Cover design by Deranged Doctor Designs
Cover art by Bev Ulsrud Van Berkom

Author Website: JohannaWittenberg.com

CONTENTS

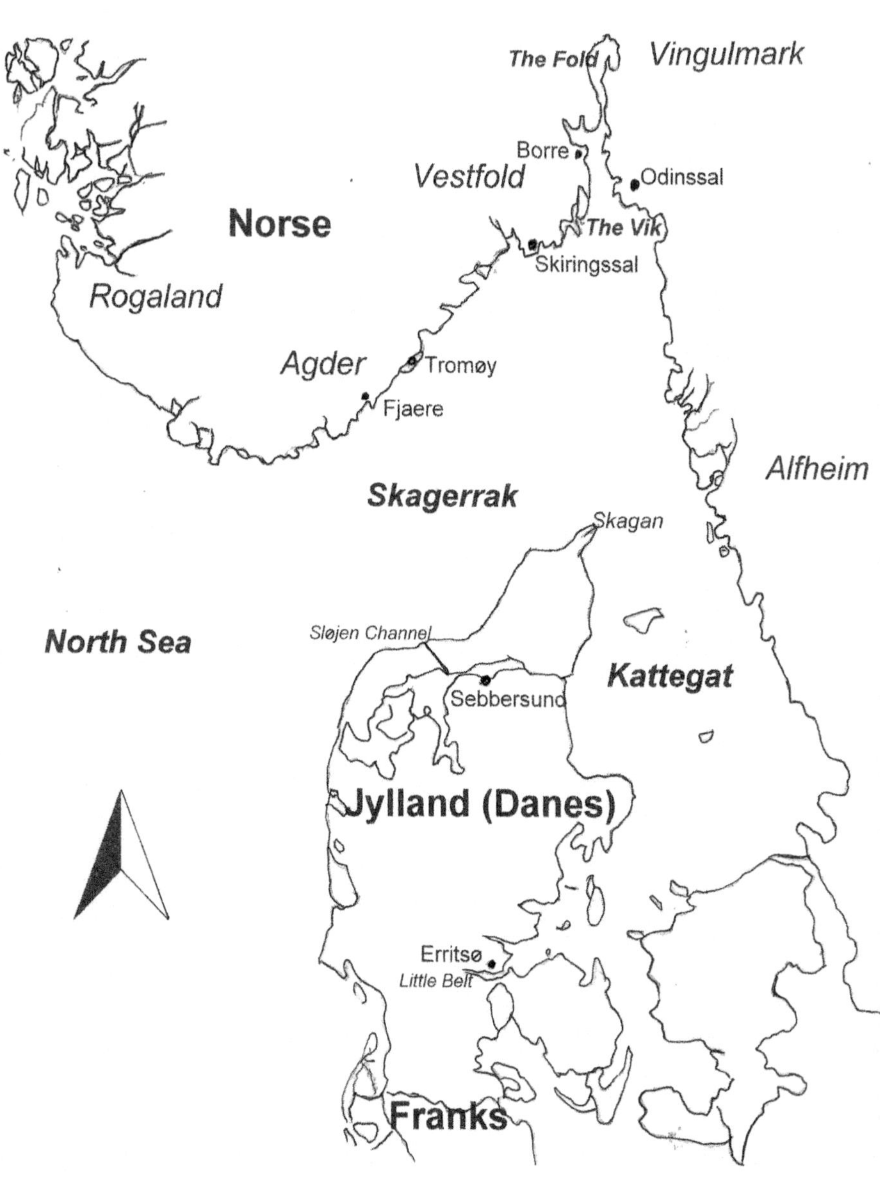
The Fold
Vingulmark
Borre
Vestfold
Odinssal
Norse
The Vik
Skiringssal
Rogaland
Agder
Tromøy
Fjaere
Alfheim
Skagerrak
Skagan
North Sea
Sløjen Channel
Kattegat
Sebbersund
Jylland (Danes)
Erritsø
Little Belt
Franks

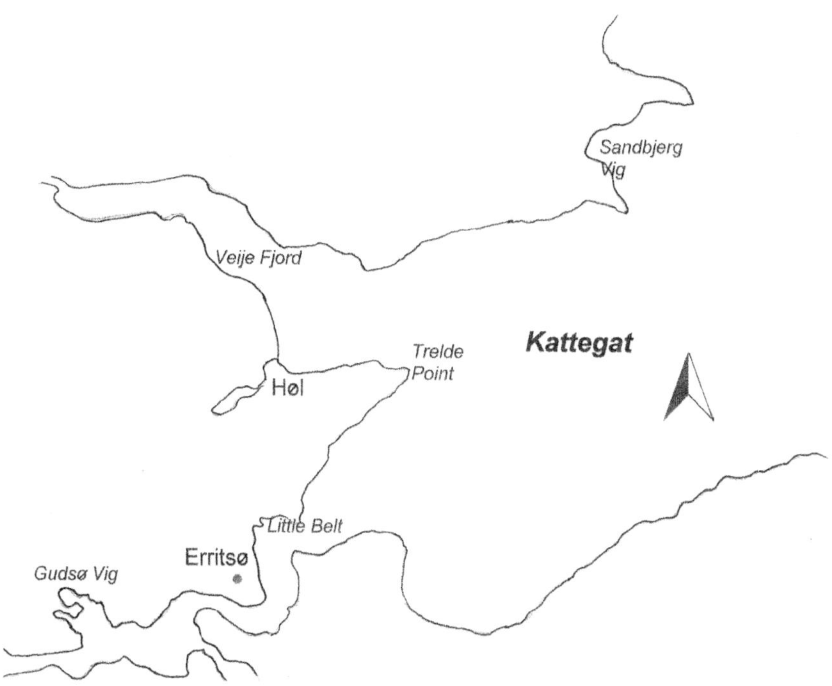
Sandbjerg Vig
Veije Fjord
Kattegat
Trelde Point
Høl
Little Belt
Erritsø
Gudsø Vig

Bright one, they called her when she came to the houses
The seer with pleasing prophecies, she charmed them with spells
She made magic wherever she could, with magic she played with minds
She was always the favorite of wicked women.
—Voluspa

CHAPTER 1

Tromøy
June, AD 825

Tromøy celebrated Halfdan's sixth birthday with a feast and games for the children. Benches had been brought out of the hall into the yard to allow the adults to bask in the summer sun while they watched the youngsters compete. The sky was a deep, endless blue, and a gentle breeze tickled beards and braids. In the distance, the sea glittered in invitation.

Åsa sat between Eyvind and the smith, Ulf, watching the children anxiously. Halfdan's raven-black hair stood out among the brown and blond more common among Tromøy's children. Åsa cringed as the others lagged behind her son at the end of a race, even those whose legs were much longer than Halfdan's.

Next came the wrestling tournament. Halfdan's opponent had him pinned to the ground, then mysteriously lost his hold, throwing the match. It was obvious to everyone but Halfdan himself that the others deferred to the queen's son.

An uneasy feeling roiled in Åsa's gut. These easy victories were dangerous. Halfdan needed to be tested, challenged. Otherwise, he would not survive long as a king with powerful enemies like the Danish king, Horik, who was determined to put this entire coast under his rule.

"He needs to come up against someone who won't let him win," she murmured.

"Nobody on Tromøy is likely to teach him that lesson," observed Ulf. "We all want him to win." The smith paused, then cleared his throat. "I expect you'll be sending him to foster with Olaf soon."

"Olaf and Kalv will make sure he learns," said Eyvind.

Åsa sighed and nodded. "Yes, I suppose." It was time for others to teach her son. After all they had been through together, Åsa dreaded being separated from Halfdan. She had nearly lost him more than once, first to her homicidal husband, then to the vengeful Hrafn. And last summer when Åsa went astray in the darkness of Niflheim, it was Halfdan who reached out with his mind and guided her safely home. There was a connection between them that transcended the normal mother-and-child bond.

Perhaps Halfdan was ready to be away from her, but what would she do without him? "Jarl Borg and Olvir still have plenty to teach him." Her words sounded lame to her own ears.

Ulf nodded but said nothing. Eyvind wisely held his council.

She sighed again, knowing the old smith was being diplomatic and trying not to pressure her. Halfdan needed to be fostered away from his home and family. He needed the experience, the exposure to others, and training in a place where he was not the doted-on heir. In Skiringssal, Olaf and Sonja's three-year-old son, Rognvald, held that position. Olaf's second-in-command, Kalv, would give Halfdan expert training without the favoritism the boy experienced on Tromøy. And Olaf was Halfdan's father, though very few knew this. Most thought that Olaf and Halfdan were half-brothers, both sons of the late King Gudrød.

Olaf deserved the opportunity to get to know his eldest son.

Åsa took a deep, ragged breath. "I'll send word to Skiringssal tomorrow."

Eyvind put a consoling hand on her shoulder. "Skiringssal is but half a day's sail. You'll be able to visit him often."

Åsa gazed into his glacier-blue eyes, set in a face tanned from years at sea. The crinkles around his eyes made him look as if he was always laughing.

"True," she admitted. But it would not be the same as having her son growing under her gaze each day. She would miss so much.

The games ended and the feasting commenced. More than one hundred people crowded the yard to celebrate the young heir, from fieldworkers and sheepherders to the elite warriors of Åsa's hird. Ale flowed freely and the aroma of cooking meat wafted in the air. Halfdan's face gleamed with happiness and excitement as the community toasted him.

Åsa wished he was a normal boy who could stay with his mother and not a royal heir who had to be fostered. She tried to smile as if nothing was wrong, but Eyvind kept sending worried glances her way.

The feast continued throughout the long summer twilight. Nobody wanted to go indoors. After a winter of darkness, the sun was a magnet that drew the Norse. Even the children were allowed to stay up late to revel in the waning light. After they'd eaten their fill, Halfdan led the youngsters back to the playing field where their shouts and laughter filled the evening air.

At last the sun dipped behind the forest, glinting amber through the trees. The children were rounded up with cries of protest. Halfdan's fóstra, Brenna, presented her charge to bid Åsa good-night. Halfdan was filthy from head to toe, his black hair dusty. His teeth and eyes gleamed bright in his dirty face as he gave his mother a peck on her cheek.

"It's a bath for this one," said Brenna before she swept the protesting boy off to the bower.

Åsa and Eyvind retired to their chamber. As soon as the door closed, he swept her into a bear hug. "It must be hard to part with your only child," he murmured into her hair. "But it has to be done for his own good. It's part of becoming a man."

Åsa nodded wordlessly, breathing in his earthy scent of pine-tar and the sea. She let his caresses distract her from her worries as she shed her linen gown and pulled his tunic over his head. Their lips and hands found each other's skin in tender caresses, and soon she forgot everything but Eyvind's touch.

In the morning, Åsa rose early and set to work with the other women out in the yard, dyeing wool yarn in preparation for weaving. The stench of rotting cabbage filled the air as she stirred the vat of woad dye, but the evil-smelling stuff turned the wool the color of a midsummer sky. While she stirred, she debated in her mind how to tell her son he would be leaving.

While she was pondering this, Halfdan appeared with a tear-stained face.

Åsa stepped away from the dye-vat. "What's wrong, son?" she asked, drying her hands on her apron.

"I don't want to go away," he said.

Åsa was thunderstruck. Had he overheard her talking with Ulf? No, he'd been competing on the field. When she'd discussed it with Eyvind, Halfdan had been tucked away in his bed in the bower with the other children. She knelt down and looked him in the eye. "How did you hear about that?"

Halfdan hesitated. "The lady in the tree told me. She came to me when I was dreaming and said she'd miss me when I was gone."

"What lady in the tree?" Åsa spluttered.

"You know, the lady who lives in the big ash tree by the hall."

Shock coursed through Åsa. "When did you meet her?"

Halfdan looked at her as if she'd taken leave of her senses. "She's always been there, since I was little."

"Does she talk to you often?"

Halfdan nodded. "Sometimes she visits me when I'm dreaming and tells me things."

Åsa stared at him. "Are there others?"

He nodded again. "One man lives in the waterfall, another lives in that big rock in the field. But the tree lady comes most often."

"Why didn't you tell me about them?"

"They said I shouldn't tell anyone that they visit me."

"Why are you telling me now?"

Halfdan looked a bit exasperated. "Because you asked. I have to tell you the truth."

"I'm glad to hear that," she said, putting her arms around him. "I'll tell you a secret. I don't want you to go away either. But it's time for you to be educated to become a king."

Halfdan laid his head on her shoulder. "Why can't I be edu—edu—taught here? I don't want to leave my friends. I don't want to leave you."

Åsa's heart clenched. She kissed the top of his head. "I'm sorry, son. But you won't be far away. I'll come to visit you often. You'll make new friends." She dangled a bit of bait. "Rognvald will be there." Halfdan adored Olaf's three-year-old son, who followed him like a puppy.

He set his jaw. "I don't want to go."

At a loss for words, Åsa just hugged her son.

A troop of children appeared, calling Halfdan's name. He broke into a smile at the sight of them.

"Go play with your friends," said Åsa. "We'll talk about this later."

After Halfdan had scampered off, Heid approached her, a

serious look on her face. "I heard what Halfdan said. I knew the boy had special abilities, but not to this degree. If the landvaettir are visiting him in his dreams, that's significant."

Åsa nodded cautiously. There had been signs of Halfdan's abilities in the past. His blind wolf, Fylgja, had once been the familiar of an evil magician, but Fylgja had shifted his alliance to Halfdan and saved the boy's life. When Åsa was trapped in Hel, her son had reached out with his mind to help her when no one else could. There was no doubt Halfdan had abilities, but speaking to the land spirits was altogether different.

"His power will have to be developed carefully," Heid continued.

Åsa stiffened. "I won't have my son labeled as ergi." Magic was the domain of women, and men generally kept their distance from it, at least on the surface. A man who had been tainted by using the wrong kind of magic was considered unmanly. Few men had ever lived down the stigma of ergi, despite the fact that Odin himself was a practitioner. The thought of her son being labeled this way was unconscionable. It could even prevent him from being elected king.

Heid laid a claw-like hand on her shoulder. "Halfdan is a very special boy. If he's being visited by the landvaettir, his power is strong. If he is not trained properly, his abilities will manifest anyway, but he will not have control over them. Ungoverned magic is very dangerous. It's imperative that a talent like his be developed with care."

Åsa nodded, considering. "He's going to be fostered with Olaf —how will we manage it? I don't know how Olaf would feel about him being trained in the völva way. He has little to do with magic, nor does Sonja."

"He doesn't have to learn völva magic. Ulf can teach him rune magic. His knowledge is great, but no one would ever accuse him of being ergi."

Åsa gave this some thought. It was true—the smith was

adept in rune magic, though few knew the true extent of Ulf's expertise. He imbued every weapon he made with it, and there was no taint of ergi on him. Ulf had proved himself in battle, had served Åsa's father for years before he served her. She trusted him. She had grown up spending hours by the forge, watching Ulf work and listening to his tales. Halfdan had already discovered the delights of the smithy and Ulf's stories. No one would be better to teach her son the ways of magic with a strong foundation while avoiding anything that was considered unmanly.

She thought furiously. "I can send Ulf to Skiringssal to train Halfdan in the art of smithing. Of course I want him taught by the best." It was well known that Ulf was the greatest master of the craft in the region. Gudrød had considered Ulf quite a prize when he captured him along with Åsa. Smithing was a high-status skill, befitting of kings and jarls, like hunting and falconry. Kings were known to be buried with their blacksmith tools. "Olaf will be glad to have Ulf teach Rognvald as well." A niggle of guilt rose in Åsa. "But I could be putting Ulf in a difficult situation with Olaf and Sonja."

"I am certain Ulf is equal to the task," said Heid. "Besides, what choice do we have? The boy must be trained. And how can Olaf and Sonja object? It's not a crime."

Åsa knew the völva had the right of it. She hoped Ulf would see it the same way.

That evening she visited the smithy. The sweetish smell of hot iron sent Åsa back to childhood hours spent by the forge, listening to Ulf's tales.

The smith was forging a blade. Sparks flew from the red-hot metal as he brought down his hammer with a familiar clang. Ulf wielded the hammer with a power that belied the gray strands that flecked his beard.

As she entered, he looked up with a smile and set aside his hammer. He plunged the blade into the quenching liquid, sending steam hissing into the air. "Good to see you, Lady," he said. "What brings you here?"

"I have something special to ask of you," Åsa said.

Ulf wiped his hands on his leather apron and gestured to the bench. She sat, and he took his place beside her. "What can I do for my queen?"

"Halfdan is visited by the landvaettir in his dreams."

Ulf nodded, unsurprised.

"Heid tells me he needs to be tutored in magic to learn to control it."

Ulf gazed into the fire, stroking his beard thoughtfully. "Yes, I agree. But how will he be taught if he goes to foster with Olaf?"

"I've come upon a solution, if you're willing."

Ulf stopped stroking his beard and looked at her. "Me?"

Åsa nodded.

"I'm no sorcerer," he protested.

"That's why you are the perfect choice. You've been by my side all of my life, and all of Halfdan's life. There is no one else I would entrust with my son's training. He's close to you, and I trust you to teach him rune lore and the ways of magic that are appropriate for a king. But the question is, would you be willing to go to Skiringssal with him?"

"How will King Olaf and Queen Sonja react?"

"I was hoping to keep it private," Åsa said. "I don't want any taint of ergi on his reputation. I would send you to teach Halfdan the art of smithing."

"What if they find out?"

"Then you must refer them to me. You won't be teaching him anything a king should not know. I will take responsibility and make them understand. But I have faith that you will be able to keep it confidential." She eyed the smith. "Will you do it?"

Ulf furrowed his brow. At last he gave a slow nod. "If King Olaf and Queen Sonja will have me, I would be honored."

"Fine, I'll send word right away. I'm very grateful to you, Ulf."

The smith bowed his head. "Glad to be of service, Lady."

Åsa left the smithy and found her son chasing about the yard with three other children. She called him to her, and he ran up, grinning and breathless. "Would you feel better about going to Skiringssal if Ulf went with you?"

Halfdan thought for a moment, catching his breath, then nodded. "If I must go, it would be good to have a friend there."

Åsa kissed the top of his head and gave him a fierce hug.

First thing in the morning, before she could lose her will, Åsa sent a messenger to Skiringssal.

The reply came back in a day, far too quickly for her liking. Olaf and Sonja would be delighted to welcome Halfdan and Ulf.

CHAPTER 2

Two days later Åsa's long ship, *Ran's Lover,* was ready to make the short trip north up the coast to Skiringssal. Halfdan led Fylgja, up the boarding plank. Despite his terror of water, Fylgja followed his young master onto the ship. Ever since the blind wolf had saved Halfdan's life, the two could not be separated. Fylgja crept over to the shelter of the stern, where he cowered, shivering. Åsa noted with dismay the gray on his muzzle. The wolf was getting old. She tucked a pelt around him, glad Fylgja would accompany her son to his fostering. Who knew how many years they had left together?

A crowd of children had gathered to see Halfdan off. Far too excited to be sad, he waved a cheerful good-bye from the railing as the crew shoved off.

Ulf's tool chest had been carefully stowed, and the smith stood by the rail, gazing at Tromøy.

"I'll miss it, and you," he said to Åsa. "But I'll enjoy the adventure and the opportunity to teach the boys. Olaf's a good man."

"I know he'll be thrilled to have you."

With a favorable wind, they would be in Skiringssal by evening. If they had to row the entire distance, they would arrive after midnight. Either way, it would be ideal training for the new sailors. For many of them, this was their first sea voyage. The previous year, a smallpox epidemic had taken a ferocious toll on Tromøy's population, leaving them short of sailors and fighters. But last fall many young folk had come to Tromøy from the mountains and the inland farms where times were hard, looking for a livelihood. Åsa had recruited the likeliest among them, and they had spent the winter being trained in combat by the old warrior, Jarl Borg. In the spring, Åsa and Eyvind drilled them in rowing and sail handling in Tromøy's harbor.

The newly minted sailors sat eagerly with their oars held high while Åsa strode down the ship's centerline, greeting each one by name. They beamed with pride and excitement as the crowd shoved the longship off the beach, and Åsa gave the command to lower their oars. They brought their oars down in perfect unison and began to row in a steady rhythm.

Åsa brought out Halfdan's harness and lifeline. At the sight, he danced away from her.

"I can swim like a whale!" he protested.

"That is true, my son, but we cannot spare the time to come back and pick you up if you fall overboard," said Åsa, taking a firm grip on him. "When you are tall enough to see over the gunnels, then you may dispense with the harness." She strapped him firmly into his harness and tied off the lifeline to a cleat.

Halfdan's sulk evaporated as the ship left the harbor, and soon he was running from stem to stern, straining the limits of his rope. Åsa took the tiller and watched her son.

The boy was still too small to man one of the ship's long oars, but when the crew raised the vast sail, he fell into line with the others, heaving on the halyard with all his might.

"Halfdan loves the sea almost as much as he loves battle," Åsa remarked to Eyvind as they watched the sail belly out in the breeze. The ship surged forward like a goaded racehorse.

"He's born for the sea," Eyvind agreed. "I promise you, we'll make many trips up the coast to visit him."

Åsa nodded, trying to put aside her gloom.

The wind held fair, and *Ran's Lover* scudded across the sea. Excitement bubbled up in Åsa and her spirit was light as the breeze. She scanned the new faces in the crew as they chattered among themselves with broad grins and sparkling eyes. They loved sailing as much as she did. She set aside her worries and reveled in the day.

Once the sail was set and the ship was on course for Skiringssal, she gave the tiller to Eyvind and called Halfdan for his latest lesson in seamanship. The new recruits gathered around, eager to learn.

"Which direction are we heading?" she asked.

The boy faced forward as she'd taught him and paid attention to the lay of the land. He held up his left hand and considered. "The coast is on our larboard side. We're heading north."

"That's right," she said. "Now, what if we crossed the Vik? What direction would we need to go?"

Halfdan squinched up his face and looked across the water. "We would head east."

"How do you know it's east?"

"The sun rises in the east. It sets in the west. It's still morning, so the sun is in the east."

"How else do you know?"

"East is to steerboard of north." Halfdan referred to the side of the ship that the steering oar was mounted on.

"And once we arrived on the east side of the Vik, and turned north again, where would the land be?"

Halfdan held up his right hand. "To steerboard!"

"That's right! Where is the wind coming from this afternoon?"

Halfdan looked at the sail. He licked his finger and held it up to feel the wind, as she had taught him. "It's coming from behind us—south!"

"That's right!" Pride coursed through Åsa as her son demonstrated his understanding of the general directions. Later she would teach him the finer nuances of the sun's progression through the seasons. "That's enough for one day," she said. Halfdan ran off to the bow, the wind ruffling his dark hair.

Late in the afternoon they fetched Skiringssal's harbor. The crew dropped the sail at the entrance and manned the oars, threading their way through the treacherous skerries and islets that littered the bay.

The pier was crowded with merchant vessels unloading, so Åsa steered *Ran's Lover* toward an empty stretch of beach. The hull carried enough way to run the prow gently onto the sand while the crew shipped their oars and hurried forward. The youngsters vaulted over the side into the shallows and heaved the ship high on the beach where the keel wedged itself firmly in the sand.

The crew planted an anchor on the beach and lowered the boarding plank over the side. Halfdan scrambled down, followed by Fylgja. The boy murmured encouragement to the blind wolf, who crept along the plank on shaking legs.

The bustling trading port teemed with merchants, their booths displaying wares from all over the known world. Åsa's eyes feasted on lumps of uncut amber, vats of honey, fine silverwork, furs and walrus ivory from the far north. Woodworkers shaped cups and bowls. Men and women called to each other in many languages while their children ran in troops. Halfdan's eyes lit up at the sight of new playmates, but then his gaze found a target that stopped him in his tracks.

Sonja and Olaf, mounted on splendid horses, waited on the shore. Released from his harness, Halfdan ran to Olaf, who swept the boy up onto his saddle. Åsa stared at the pair, struck by how much Halfdan resembled his father, despite the boy's raven hair. Halfdan's features were resolving themselves into a miniature of Olaf's, his eyes the same shade of blue, the same set to the jaw.

Sonja's gaze met Åsa's. It was clear she was thinking the same thing.

Olaf nudged his horse into a canter. Father and son rode up the hill to the Shining Hall, Halfdan shrieking with delight. Fylgja loped along behind, tongue lolling, thoroughly recovered from his ordeal and obviously thrilled to be back on dry land.

A cart waited for Ulf's tool chests, and the smith supervised the loading. He climbed up on the seat next to the driver and they started up the hill to the smithy. Åsa and Eyvind mounted the horses that had been brought for them and followed Sonja at a more sedate pace while the rest of the crew climbed the trail on foot.

At the hall Olaf and Sonja's three-year-old son, Rognvald, ran up to greet Halfdan with shrieks of delight.

"Halfdan! Halfdan!" Rognvald shouted, jumping up and down. "Hyndla has puppies!"

Halfdan struggled against Olaf's grip, and he let the child slide to the ground. In an instant the two boys were running off toward the corner of the hall, where the mother dog lay with her new batch of pups. Fylgja followed, hunkering down to give each pup a polite sniff. Their mother let him, seeming to sense he meant them no harm. Then the old wolf curled up, covered his nose with his tail, and took a well-earned nap.

"Rognvald has really shot up since we were last here in spring," observed Åsa. "Soon he'll be as tall as Halfdan."

"Yes, he's a stout lad," said Sonja.

"It won't be long before Rognvald can join Halfdan in the smithy."

"Yes, we are so grateful that you have sent Ulf to us."

"He'll be teaching Halfdan the runes as well." Åsa broached the subject delicately.

"Rognvald will benefit from that."

"I've asked Ulf to school Halfdan in their more advanced aspects."

Sonja's eyes widened a bit. "I see."

Satisfied that Sonja grasped her meaning, Åsa changed the subject. "Halfdan is used to being the doted-on heir at home, and it's something he must get away from. Others let him win, giving him an unrealistic idea of his abilities. That kind of treatment will not serve him well in the future. He may take not always winning hard at first, but I trust you and Olaf will guide him through his initial adjustment."

"Of course," Sonja agreed.

All heads turned to a slim figure silhouetted in the light of the door. As the newcomer approached, Åsa caught her breath, recognizing his stride. "Knut! It's good to see you. You're looking well."

The old poet bowed to her. Though the lines on his tanned face had deepened, and his unruly mop of hair had gone dead white, he still stood straight as a willow-wand and moved with lithe grace. He studied her with clear gray eyes. "You are looking well yourself, my queen. You grow more beautiful each time I see you, and wiser too, I have heard. As for me, I've given up my traveling ways. King Olaf and Queen Sonja have graciously taken me on as tutor. I will teach these young lads their history and lore of the gods, their kennings and the rules of skáldic poetry, as I did all of you when you were young."

"I'm so happy to hear that," she said. "I know that with your training, Halfdan will grow up to be a poet and historian as well as a warrior." These skills were important for all young people, but even more vital for those of royal blood. Skálds imparted the lineage of kings as well as the history of the land. Åsa and her brother, Gyrd, had been taught during Knut's periodic visits to Tromøy. "Ulf is here to teach blacksmithing and runes as well."

"Ah, I look forward to spending time with my old friend," said Knut.

Everyone took their seats to partake of Sonja's excellent ale accompanied by roast pork, fresh-baked bread, and good conversation. When the food had been consumed and the company settled back with their ale, Knut rose from his bench. Silence fell as the old skáld took his place at the head of the longfire. His sonorous voice reverberated in the hall as he performed their favorite tales of gods and heroes. For a time, Åsa almost forgot that she must part with Halfdan in the morning.

But when Knut's stories ended, she said good-night to Halfdan and watched the fóstra lead him away with Rognvald. It all came rushing back, grief forcing her spirits down.

She trailed Eyvind into their private chamber in the guest-house, head down and shoulders slumped. He turned at the door and swept her into his arms, eyes sparkling. "I can see you need distracting." He planted a kiss on her forehead, then one on her nose, and another on her cheek, before finally settling on her lips. He lingered there, his hands caressing her back.

Åsa sighed and let him pull her down onto the feather mattress, giving herself over to bliss.

~

IN THE MORNING AFTER BREAKFAST, Åsa bade her son a reluctant good-bye. He and Rognvald were playing with the new puppies, and Halfdan barely returned her hug. He'd already forgotten her.

Åsa trudged toward her horse, her spirits as sodden as wet wool. She'd have to get used to it. Her son was growing up. A boy had to be independent of his mother.

Running steps sounded and a solid force barreled into her, sending her staggering. Little arms clung to her legs, and Halfdan buried his face in her tunic.

"Bye, Mama!" he snuffled into the thick wool.

Then he was gone. When she looked back, he was already tussling with the pups.

Sonja gave her a hug. "Don't worry, we'll treat him like Olaf's own son," she whispered in Åsa's ear with a chuckle. Åsa was relieved that Sonja could laugh about Halfdan's parentage. The discovery last year had nearly destroyed their friendship, but Sonja had overcome her shock and come through when Åsa needed her most.

Olaf escorted Åsa and Eyvind down to the harbor where they boarded *Ran's Lover*. A cart arrived carrying goods from Skiringssal's craftsmen for Eyvind to take on his next trading voyage. Åsa distracted herself by directing the loading, giving instructions where none were needed, but the crew did not complain. They seemed to sense her sadness and her need for distraction.

Skiringssal's folk launched *Ran's Lover* amid shouts of goodbye. Åsa returned Olaf's wave as they rowed out of the harbor. They cleared the entrance onto the Skagerrak Sea, where the water was a dull gray and a chill mist thickened the air. The wind was too light to fill the sail, so the crew rowed. They were silent, reflecting Åsa's glum mood. She gripped the gunnel, trying not to look back. Everything looked dead to her.

Eyvind put his arm around her and pulled her close. The lump in Åsa's throat prevented her from speaking. She buried her head in Eyvind's broad chest and let him stroke her hair.

"We'll visit as often as you like," he reassured her. "I'll bring you here whenever my queen commands."

A breeze finally cut through the mist, and the crew's mood lightened as they hauled up the sail. Åsa tried to smile but the effort made her want to cry.

That afternoon when the ship entered Tromøy's harbor, a wave of loss engulfed Åsa as she gazed at her people waiting on the shore. She was overwhelmed by the absence of one small person.

Ran's Lover's prow nudged the beach. Brenna, Jarl Borg, Olvir, even Heid and her apprentices hurried to greet her. Åsa smiled and brushed away the tears that crept out of the corners of her eyes.

CHAPTER 3

Skiringssal

Ulf was pleased enough to be in Skiringssal. He missed his smithy and the folk of Tromøy, but he was honored to teach Halfdan and Rognvald. Skiringssal had a vast workshop that was vacant, for Olaf did not have a smith. When he needed repairs or simple tools, Olaf relied on the itinerant smiths who came to ply their trade in his port. His weapons he got from Ulf, trading Skiringssal's wealth for fine swords, axes, and spear-heads. With the best smith in the area so close by, what was the point in housing and feeding his own?

As Ulf put his tools away, Olaf ducked under the low door-way. Ulf regarded him with approval. The awkward, unsure boy had grown into a fine king, strong and capable.

Ulf bowed his head. "Greetings, my lord."

"Ulf, I'm so glad to have you here! It will be wonderful to have the boys trained by the greatest smith in the land."

"I am honored to teach them. By the looks of him, Rognvald will soon be big enough to wield a hammer."

"And you will teach them the runes as well?"

"Of course, Lord. Halfdan already knows his runes, and he can help Rognvald." Ulf stifled a flicker of guilt at his omission, even though he knew it was the wisest course of action for all concerned.

"Excellent. I would like Knut to join you to teach them their history."

"I would like that very much," said Ulf. He and the skáld had been friends for many years. The two respected each other's skills and knowledge, and there was quite a bit of overlap in rune lore and history. Ulf knew he would not be able to keep his secret from the wise skáld for long. Eventually he'd have to take Knut into his confidence about Halfdan's training.

"I am most grateful," said Olaf. "You will be well rewarded. Anything you need, just ask and you shall have it."

Again Ulf stifled his misgivings. His responsibility was to Åsa and Halfdan. He would teach both boys to cut and color the runes, and to read and write with them. But as for the other uses of the runes, cursing and curing and foretelling the future...

For these things, Ulf and Halfdan would have their own private lessons.

KNUT ARRIVED at the forge first thing next morning, Halfdan and Rognvald right behind him, trailed by the blind wolf. Fylgja immediately made himself comfortable on a warm spot next to the forge. The wolf sighed and closed his eyes in bliss.

Ulf laid down his hammer. "Well, who have we here?" Rognvald ducked behind Halfdan. Ulf could see that the younger boy was shy and Halfdan was homesick. He sat down on his bench and took both boys on his knees, one head raven-dark, the other bright as silver.

"How would you like to carve the runes?"

Both boys nodded vigorously.

Ulf got up, and from a lumber pile brought out a flat board of soft pine. For this lesson he had whittled a short, pointed stick. He handed a board and stick to Halfdan. "Rognvald, do you know how to cut the runes?"

The three-year-old shook his head no.

"Halfdan, can you show Rognvald how to carve the first rune?"

"Yes," said Halfdan proudly.

The boys bent their heads together over the board while Halfdan showed Rognvald how to carve the first rune in the soft wood.

"That's very good carving," said Ulf. "Can you tell Rognvald the name of the first rune?"

"Fehu," said Halfdan.

"That's right. Do you know what it stands for?"

"The letter F."

"And what else?"

Halfdan thought for a moment. "Cattle, and wealth."

"That's right. The first aett belongs to Freyr and Freyja," said Ulf. "They're the twin children of Njord. They are all gods of the Vanir, who came to the Aesir as hostages to end the war between the Vanir and the Aesir."

Ulf nodded to the skáld, who took up the tale while Halfdan carved.

"Long ago, Freyr was king of the Svea, and all the years he ruled, there was peace and prosperity in the land. When Freyr died, his household pretended he was still alive, and buried his body in a great mound. Folk continued to pay tribute to him through three holes in his mound. They poured gold through the first hole, silver through the second one, and copper coins through the third.

"The prosperity continued even though Freyr was dead. Eventually the folk discovered the truth, but they believed that peace and prosperity continued because of his presence. That is how Freyr became a god. And that is why some very special people are not burned when they die, but instead buried in a mound with all their belongings, so that they will continue to bless the land. They remain with us as the álfar and the dísir, the ancestors who watch over us.

"Freyr is king of the álfar while his sister, Freyja, rules the dísir.

"Both of you boys are descended from Freyr," Knut continued. "He founded the Yngling dynasty, and your forefather King Gudrød was descended from the Ynglings."

"Gudrød was a bad king," said Halfdan. "Mama killed him."

Knut nodded. "She killed him to save your life. And then she took you away to her kingdom on Tromøy."

Ulf and Knut exchanged satisfied looks. Halfdan showed promise and mental discipline. Teaching the younger boy gave him pride and purpose. It was clear that Rognvald idolized Halfdan and was thrilled by his attention.

After another hour indoors, the boys were getting restless. Ulf was relieved when Kalv, the captain of Olaf's húskarlar, appeared at the smithy.

"Would you boys like to do some fighting?" Kalv asked, displaying a pair of wooden swords and miniature shields.

Both boys cheered and ran to the warrior, who led them down to the training yard.

Knut smiled and shook his head. "Well, old friend, the young need their exercise and the old need a nap."

"Have a good sleep," said Ulf as he watched his friend depart. He welcomed the solitude. He was eager to do some forging in his new smithy.

Olaf joined Kalv to train the boys in swordcraft. The yard was already filled with a dozen other boys and girls of varying ages, mostly the offspring of Olaf's húskarlar. Today they would practice with sword and shield, though they learned wrestling and spear handling on other days.

Rognvald was too young to learn much yet, though he brandished his wooden sword with great energy as he chased around the yard with the younger children. Halfdan already displayed some skill with his sword and shield. His stance was good, and he knew to keep his shield up.

Olaf remembered how he'd felt when his father watched him spar. Gudrød had ignored his son when he won and shouted criticism at him if he made a mistake, making Olaf burn with shame. He vowed not to make those mistakes with his own sons.

When an older boy named Eirik knocked him down, Halfdan's jaw went slack in shock. He looked up and met Olaf's gaze. For a moment Olaf tensed as he watched his son's lip quiver, and he gave Halfdan a nod of encouragement. The boy's expression turned to one of determination. He clambered to his feet and went after his opponent, screaming a war cry.

The older boy ran. Halfdan scowled when he could not catch the long-legged foe. He slowed, appearing to give up the chase, but when Eirik came at him again, Halfdan was ready. As soon as the older boy came into range, Halfdan attacked, managing to land some solid blows on his opponent's shins. Eirik's long legs tangled in Halfdan's wooden blade. The older boy went down, taking cover under his shield beneath Halfdan's furious blows.

"That's enough," said Kalv, intervening before tempers flared out of control and someone got seriously hurt.

Olaf walked over and laid a friendly hand on each boy's shoulder. "Well done, both of you." Halfdan's scowl broke into a proud smile.

He walked Halfdan and Rognvald back to the hall, where they tumbled together with Hyndla's pups in the corner. Worn out from the afternoon's tussle, the boys fell asleep instantly. The blind wolf, never far from Halfdan, settled down nearby.

Olaf could not tear his eyes from Halfdan's raven hair, the perfect skin, marveling that this boy was his son. His and Åsa's. And now Olaf had him for the next few years, to teach and care for.

"I'm glad to have him with us," said Sonja, coming up beside him.

Startled, Olaf turned to his wife and nodded.

"The boys are good together."

Olaf smiled at his wife, filled with an inner joy. He'd married Sonja out of pity, but he'd chosen wisely after all. She had brought him more happiness than he'd dreamed he could find with any woman but Åsa.

Ulf and Knut met with the boys in the smithy the next day. While Halfdan cut the runes with his pointed stick, Knut launched into another tale.

"I told you that your royal dynasty, the Ynglings, originally ruled the Svea. But they had enemies, men who would rule in their place. When a rival king attacked with forces far outnumbering Ingvald's, he burned himself in his hall with all his húskarlar rather than suffer defeat. Ingvald's son, Olaf, fled the land of the Svea to the vast forest at the Fold. There he began clearing the forest and building a settlement he called Varmland. He cut so many trees he soon became known as Olaf the Treefeller. Many Svea folk fled the new king and joined Olaf. But so many came that the land could not support them all. When the people began to starve, they blamed Olaf for it and they burned him in his hall, as an offering to Odin for prosperity. But after Olaf's death, prosperity did not return. The folk realized that they were too many for the land to support, and Olaf had not been to blame. After that they made Olaf's son their king—Halfdan Whiteleg, your namesake. Halfdan was a mighty king and went on to conquer Hedemark and Tote, Hadeland, and much of Vestfold. When he died, an old man, he was buried right here, at Skiringssal."

Halfdan looked up at Knut in awe. "He's buried here?"

Knut nodded, giving Ulf a meaningful look. "He was buried on an islet. One day we will take you to his mound."

When the boys grew restless, Ulf set them to tromping on the foot bellows.

But in the afternoon, after Knut had gone and Rognvald's fóstra had taken him away for his nap, Ulf gave Halfdan a special lesson.

"This is not to be shared with anyone, not even Rognvald. It is a secret between you and me. Agreed?"

Halfdan's eyes widened, and he nodded. He became quiet as snowfall, listening.

Satisfied, Ulf spoke. "Do you know who the landvaettir are?"

The boy nodded. "They are the folk who live in rocks and trees, even in waterfalls."

"Do you know what the vaettir do?"

The boy shook his head.

"They work for the god, Freyr. They take care of the land, the plants and animals, even people. Your mother tells me you have met them."

Halfdan nodded. "They come and visit me in my dreams and tell me things."

"And you know not everyone can see them."

"I always thought they could, but Mama says most people can't."

"That's right. We all know the landvaettir are there, but they appear to few. It's very special that you can see them and that they talk to you. Have you met any here?"

"I've seen them sometimes, but none have spoken to me. Can you see them?"

Ulf shook his head. "I can't, but I feel their presence. A few times they have come to me in dreams." Ulf thought for a moment. Then he decided. "Do you know what utiseta is?"

Halfdan shook his head no.

"Well, it's where you sit outside all night, to speak with the vaettir. Tonight, you and I could try that, so you can meet the vaettir who live here. Would you like that?"

Halfdan broke into a smile. "Yes!" He jumped up as if to go that moment.

"I will tell the fóstra that I need you to help me in the forge tonight. But you must promise not to tell anyone what we are doing, not even Rognvald."

Halfdan nodded solemnly.

After the evening meal, Ulf walked Halfdan back to the bower. He explained to the nurse that he was going to do some forging in the evening cool, and he needed Halfdan to tread the bellows for him. "I'll keep the boy with me tonight. He can sleep in the smithy when we are finished."

The nurse was only too happy to have a night with one less boisterous royal boy to settle into bed.

Back at the smithy, Ulf and Halfdan packed up their hudfat and waterskins. In the long summer twilight, they set out on the trail that led away from the steading and past the assembly site where sacrifices were made. A little farther on they came to a lake that was a holy place. It was referred to as "lake of the vaettir." If Halfdan was going to make the acquaintance of the land spirits, there could be no better spot.

Ulf followed the sound of cascading water until they came to a waterfall in a rocky outcropping, not much taller than a man. Behind the curtain of flowing water lurked the black mouth of a cave.

They spread their hudfat on the spongy moss beside the falls. Ulf searched until he found what he knew had to be there—a rock with a shallow depression carved in the surface—an álf-cup. He poured a little ale in it.

"Let them come who wish to come, let them go who wish to go, and do no harm to me or mine," he chanted.

As if in answer, a cool breeze sprang up and caressed their faces. The hair on Ulf's neck stood up.

Ulf and Halfdan crawled into their hudfat and lay snug, waiting while the sky darkened to indigo and the stars came out. The waterfall hissed its soothing music, sending up a soft mist that settled on their skin.

Ulf's eyes began to blink. His lids seemed to stick together. A snort woke him, and he realized the noise came from him. He glanced over at Halfdan. The boy lay on his back, his heavy-lashed eyes closed, breathing regular. All seemed peaceful and safe.

Ulf could not stay awake. He slid back into sleep.

He was walking along the curtain of water that cascaded over the rocks. The moss was soft and cold on his bare feet, and the air smelled fresh. Mist beaded on his beard. Beneath the waterfall the shadowed gap beckoned. Ulf stepped onto the slippery rocks and entered the space behind the flowing water. The air was chilled and thick with moisture. It was too dark to see anything but shapes that flitted in the gloom.

In their midst he saw Halfdan. The boy's dark hair was slicked to his head, contrasting against his white skin. He walked deep into the darkness behind the falls. Ulf reached out to stop him, but the child slipped out of his grasp like a fish. He followed Halfdan until the boy vanished into the shadows. Ulf tried to call out but could not form words. Ahead he could see nothing but darkness. Fearing for Halfdan, he tried to follow, but his feet were stuck in the mud. Ulf struggled for a long time, trying to escape the sucking muck.

The dawn poked cold fingers into Ulf's eyes. He lay wrapped in his hudfat. His face and beard were wet, and he was cold and soggy. To his great relief, his gaze fell on Halfdan. The boy was awake, sitting up in his hudfat with a big smile.

Ulf sat up with a groan, his old injuries stiff from the damp cold. "I am glad to see you. Did the vaettr of the waterfall come to you?"

Halfdan nodded, his eyes large. "She did."

"And what did she have to say?"

"She made us welcome. She spoke to you too, but you didn't hear her."

Ulf sighed and nodded. "I hope the vaettr was not offended."

Halfdan shook his head. "She said you were too old and thick in the head to hear."

Ulf chuckled. "That I am, boy. But you are not. Did you meet any others?"

"Yes! I met a woman who lives in the big tree near the smithy. She is happy to have us, but asks that you be very careful with your fire."

"I promise to be careful," Ulf said solemnly. "I'm glad to know she's there. I will show her honor every day."

"There were other vaettir gathered around, but I didn't meet them."

"That will do for one night. Do you feel more at home here now?"

Halfdan nodded vigorously.

"The vaettir are always around, everywhere you go, even if you can't see them. Now that you're friends with them, you can call on them for help if ever you need it.

"Well, we'd best be getting back. We can warm up and dry out by the forge before breakfast." Ulf got stiffly to his feet. His whole body ached, but he was happy nonetheless. The night had been a success.

They rolled up their hudfat and hustled back to the smithy. Ulf stoked the fire and sat close to the forge, letting the warmth soak into his bones. The lad would have friends and protection with the vaettir on his side.

CHAPTER 4

Tromøy

Åsa busied herself with the chores of the steading. There was always so much to be done in the summer—brewing, cheese-making, and the ever-present spinning, but even the dairy work that had always lifted her spirits failed to vanquish her grief. In the evenings she sat on the high seat like a stone, immune to all attempts to draw her into conversation. Eyvind and Heid looked at each other with concern. Jarl Borg shook his grizzled head. Even Olvir seemed worried.

One day, after Halfdan had been gone for over a week, Åsa wandered morosely down to the shore where Eyvind was getting his ship ready for a trading voyage.

Åsa skulked around the shore while he worked on *Far Traveler*. She picked up a caulking iron and poked a little roving into a seam. She whacked away half-heartedly, then stood holding the iron and hammer, staring at the planking.

Suddenly, Eyvind put down his tools and gathered her into his arms. She glanced up at him in surprise.

He was grinning. "Why don't you make this trip with me?"

When she began to protest, he hurried on. "You need a change of scenery. Sail with me to Sebbersund. It's just across the Skagerrak. We'd only be gone a week or so. We can stop at Fjaere to take on a load of soapstone pots and whetstones, and maybe some iron to trade."

"I can't leave Tromøy," Åsa faltered.

"Sure you can. Between Jarl Borg and Olvir, they can take care of things while you're gone. Other rulers make voyages during the summer."

Eyvind was right. It was rare for a king to remain at home during the raiding season. Åsa had been afraid to leave her little island kingdom, but she had to admit they had fought off every attack. Tromøy had gained a reputation that made would-be raiders keep their distance. And Borg and Olvir were more than capable of defending the island in her absence.

Eyvind persisted. "It's been four years and the Danes have not moved against you. You've proven Tromøy is not an easy target. And Horik has worries of his own with two exiled brothers and Harald Klak breathing down his neck."

It was true—the powerful Franks supported Harald Klak, contender to the Danish throne, against his nephew, Horik, and Horik's exiled brothers were always looking for an opportunity to oust him. This intrigue had kept the Dane king in a constant state of unrest and distraction.

But misgivings still niggled at her. "Sebbersund is a Danish port. I'm not sure it would be wise for me to go anywhere near their waters." Åsa had defeated the Danes twice. The second time she'd killed their King Rorik in battle, and Tromøy's warband had decimated his forces. The Danes were now ruled by Rorik's brother, Horik. His vengeance had long been a worry nagging at the back of her mind.

"Sebbersund is closer to us than it is to Horik's fortress. How would he even know you were there? If you come along as my wife...an anonymous trader, you'd be safe. People see what they expect to see. They won't look for a queen sailing as a merchant's wife. And think of the information you could pick up from talking to the traders from all over. You know they are notorious gossips."

Åsa's pulse quickened. This was an opportunity not only to see a place she'd never been, but also to gather information about her enemies. It was tempting, but she had to consider every angle. "We killed most of the Danes who invaded Tromøy. There's few left alive to recognize me," she admitted. "The odds that any of them would be in Sebbersund are small."

Eyvind pressed home his point. "Horik has his headquarters far to the south. Even if by some mischance he's in Sebbersund while we are, he's never seen you in person."

Åsa smiled up at him. "I could no doubt pick up some interesting information at the market. I think it might work."

"You are courting disaster," Heid said when Åsa announced the news that evening in Tromøy's hall. Though the völva had recovered from last year's sickness, her time in Hel had aged her. That was a journey from which she had not planned to return. Since then, the sorceress had lost weight and her hair turned stark white. Her face bore new furrows. Her raspy voice had become a croak, and now she raised it in protest. "Firstly, you're a fool to leave Tromøy during the raiding season."

"Jarl Borg and Olvir are perfectly capable of defending Tromøy without me."

"The sickness last year depleted your warband," the völva persisted.

"Our new recruits have had a full winter's training, and we still have plenty of experienced warriors to guide them."

Jarl Borg cleared his throat. "I agree with our queen. We are ready for any attack. There's no reason she can't be gone for a week or two if she wishes."

Heid snorted. "And what if something evil befalls her on her travels?"

Eyvind bristled. "My crew is more than capable of protecting Åsa."

"Your crew was decimated in the sickness last year," Heid reminded him.

Eyvind's eyes hooded in grief for a moment. "Yes, but I've filled my ranks."

"With raw farmers," Heid said.

"They've been training for eight months," Eyvind argued. "And enough well-seasoned sailors survived to supervise the new recruits. It's not like they've never stepped foot on a boat."

What Eyvind said was true. Though few of his recruits had crossed the Skagerrak, no Norse person was a stranger to boats. Their mountainous land was strewn with lakes, rivers, and fjords that connected far-flung settlements where land travel was arduous.

Åsa stared at the völva. Heid still looked sour. "Have you foreseen something?"

The sorceress sighed and shook her head. "I see nothing specific. Just a general feeling of dread. Something is amiss."

"And if I remain here this summer?"

The sorceress gazed into the distance in contemplation. Her eyes went out of focus as if watching something far away. After a while she drew a deep breath and shook her head. "Nay, my stomach is just as unsettled if you stay. We are doomed no matter what you do."

Åsa snorted. "I can't live my life based on your digestion. Perhaps you should eat less meat."

Heid glared at Åsa. "My guts have never given you reason to doubt them in the past."

"Perhaps we can change the subject from bodily functions to logistics," Jarl Borg suggested.

"Very well. Don't say I didn't warn you." Heid hoisted herself out of her seat and hobbled off to the bower hall.

Olvir looked to Åsa. "When will you depart?"

Åsa nodded to Eyvind with a smile. "Ask the captain."

Eyvind returned her smile. "At my queen's pleasure. My crew can be ready to depart any time."

"It's settled, then," said Åsa. "Let's go as soon as possible. We'll stop in Fjaere for a load of soapstone and bog iron, then cross the Skagerrak Sea to Sebbersund."

Eyvind sat back with his ale, a smile on his lips.

No one noticed the faint scratching of talons on the roof, nor the rustle of feathers near the smokehole as a goshawk lofted into the sky and took wing, heading south.

CHAPTER 5

Erritsø Fortress, Land of the Danes

The goshawk soared over the Skagerrak Sea and across the Jylland Peninsula to the south. Below lay a vast expanse of land cut off from the north by a long, narrow lake that fed into an even longer river. The southern shore was separated from the mainland by a serpentine waterway known as the Little Belt, forming a vast island. Scattered across its confines stood a shipyard, a blacksmith complex, and other workshops.

Far to the south, on the highest point overlooking the Little Belt, a fortress rose above a treeless marsh. In its center loomed a great hall, its roof ridge bristling with spears, the gable ends defended by carved dragon heads, silver-gilt and glinting.

The hall was surrounded by a moat as deep as a man was tall. Behind the moat rose a high timber palisade. From the fighting platform that ran along the wall, the lookouts could survey the countryside and waterways for miles. They could see anyone approaching by land or sea.

The goshawk soared over the courtyard to the women's bower, where she alighted on the gable end. It opened into a small chamber lit by a pole lamp stuck in the earthen floor. Bundles of herbs hanging from the rafters scented the air. The hawk flew in and perched on the crossbeams.

A bed dominated the room, its headboard carved with a corpse knot. A thin, middle-aged woman lay on the down mattress, deep in a trance. Her dark hair, streaked with white, spread out over the pillow and framed her starkly lined face.

The hawk fluttered down to perch on the headboard and sat, waiting for her mistress to rouse.

The woman rasped in a deep breath and her eyes blinked open. She struggled to a sitting position, propping herself against the headboard. After a few ragged breaths, the woman lurched out of bed and threw on her cloak. She grabbed her iron staff from its spot by the door and stumbled outside.

Crossing the yard to the great hall, she addressed the húskarl who guarded the side door in imperious tones. "I must see the king. I have news for him."

The guard did not question her, but rather opened the door and ushered her into the cavernous hall. Its depths were lit by a crackling longfire, as well as guttering fish-oil lamps hanging from iron brackets on the wall that gave the air a fishy smell. Tiny squares of amber glass set in the walls let in thin shafts of daylight, more decorative than illuminating. In the smoky haze, warriors lounged on the benches that lined the room, drinking ale and dicing.

King Horik sat on his high seat, playing hnefatafl and sipping Frankish wine from a silver cup. The woman entered, bringing a gust of fresh air with her that made the lamps flicker. Horik glanced up from the gaming board and frowned. His opponent, an Irish slave, shrank into the shadows and melted into the depths of the hall.

Staff in hand, bejeweled cloak shimmering in the firelight, the woman stood silent before the high seat, waiting for her king to speak.

He glared down at her. "What have you to report, witch?"

The woman bowed low, leaning heavily on her staff. "My lord. Åsa, queen of Agder, is sailing to Sebbersund."

The king stared at his völva over his cup with barely suppressed anticipation. "You're certain?"

The sorceress nodded. "I heard them discuss the voyage. Her völva advised against it, but the queen is determined. They are making preparations. She will sail on a knarr called *Far Traveler,* posing as a trader's wife."

The king broke into a grin. "This is an opportunity I have been waiting years for. Your vigilance has paid off. Well done." He tossed the sorceress a silver arm ring. Her hand snaked out from beneath her cloak and caught it in mid-air.

Horik signaled the captain of his household guard, who rose from the bench nearest the high seat. "You will send men to Sebbersund. Seek out the knarr *Far Traveler* and capture the woman posing as the trader's wife. Do what you must to take her, but do not harm the woman. Bring her to me."

"It will be done, my lord." The captain saluted and departed.

The king stared into the silver cup. In the Frankish wine his face appeared to be floating in blood. "Long have I waited for Agder's little queen to leave the safety of her coast and enter my waters," he said to the völva. "I will take vengeance for my brother's death at last, and then I'll take Tromøy. The island fortress will be the perfect refuge from the Franks, and from my treacherous brothers. From there I will command the Skagerrak and access to the North Way, to the riches of the lands to the west. I'll expand and take Vestfold from Olaf. I will be the most powerful king in the North."

He smiled at his reflection in the dark red wine.

The Irish slave shrank farther into the shadows. Whoever this queen was, he did not envy her.

~

Åsa allowed herself to be swept up in preparations for the journey across the Skagerrak to the land of the Danes. Thoughts of Halfdan clutched at her heart, but there was so much to do she was able to shake off her feelings.

Far Traveler was a knarr—a cargo ship—requiring a crew of twenty. Though similar in length to longships such as *Ran's Lover, Far Traveler* was higher sided, with a deeper draft and broader beam. This enabled the ship to carry loads of heavy soapstone pots, whetstones, and querns from the quarries of Fjaere, as well as raw iron and even livestock. Both the bow and stern featured planked-over decks to keep sensitive cargo like cloth and grain out of the rain and spray. Bales of wool and skeins of linen thread were wrapped in burlap against the damp. Precious walrus tusks that traders had brought to Skiringssal from the far north were carefully swathed in sheepskin. Lidded wood buckets of butter and honeycomb were wedged tightly under the decks.

When *Far Traveler* was ready to launch, every able-bodied person on Tromøy turned out. Heid and her apprentices sacrificed a rooster to Njord, the sea god, for a safe and profitable voyage. The völva anointed the knarr's stem with its blood, and flicked drops on every member of the crew.

The folk of Tromøy gathered in the shallows to heave the big craft off the log rollers where it had been braced with timbers, enabling the shipwrights to work on the keel and lowest planks. As the ship moved down the rollers and the stern floated, the timbers that had propped up the hull were removed.

The hull was buoyed by the waves and the rowers took up their oars. *Far Traveler* had only six oar slots on each side. To reach the water from the high-sided ship, the oars were much longer than that of a low-riding longship, of a graduated length to fit the varying height above the waters. The oarsmen had to stand to manage the long sweeps and maneuver the bulky ship into the harbor. A knarr could not be rowed great distances like a longship.

Once outside the harbor, a favorable breeze filled in, and Eyvind ordered the sail hoisted. Rainclouds stacked up on the horizon, and Thor blessed them with a downpour. The woolen sail, coated with pitch, shed water and held up in the strengthening wind. The ship scudded across the waves.

Pulling up the hood of her waxed linen cloak, Åsa laughed as drops stung her upturned face. It was a joy to be at sea, with adventure spreading out before her.

Far Traveler's motion differed from that of a longship. While its high sides made it far dryer, somehow the ride seemed tame, so far above the sea. The cargo ship was slower by comparison to a longship, breasting the seas sluggishly and wallowing in the trough.

Eyvind steered the ship through the tricky skerries and currents along the coast, while Åsa spent the day among the crew. She had met them all on the training field when she taught them the basics of fighting with axe and spear. Most had come to Tromøy already skilled with a bow and arrow for hunting, but Åsa taught them the art of wartime archery, an important skill in both land and sea battles.

Now she greeted them each by name and observed them as they went about their duties, stowing oars and coiling ropes. She instructed them on how to read the water for the hazards and currents that littered the coastline.

Because the knarr was rowed by just a few oarsmen, and then only to maneuver in and out of port, a crew member's size and strength were less important than the wit and personality needed in a successful trader. Along with their food and a warm place to lay their hudfat winter or summer, each crew member earned a share of the profits from every trading voyage. Most of that, Åsa knew, they sent home to their families on the hardscrabble farms to feed all their sisters and brothers.

Eyvind's new recruits included eight lively young women and men chosen for their brains rather than brawn. They were grateful for full bellies and proud of their status as sailors. A dozen strapping, experienced hands who could steer and reef and heave an oar with vigor had survived the epidemic last year, and they welcomed their new shipmates, teaching them with good humor. They were a congenial bunch, and their jokes and laughter lifted Åsa out of her slump. Making this trip was a good idea.

Two of her favorites were Svein and Thora. Thora was a new recruit from a farm family who showed leadership abilities, while Svein was an experienced hand who had survived the epidemic the summer before. The two were smarter than most and had proven adept at weaponry and strategy on the battlefield. Eyvind had wisely singled them out as leaders, making Svein his second-in-command, and—though she was a newcomer—Thora leader of the six women in the crew. Another new girl, Dagny, displayed a talent for treating wounds and a decent knowledge of herbs. Åsa knew Heid had her eye on the girl, and Dagny had spent more time with the apprentices than she had with her shipmates. Still, the girl had volunteered for this trip rather than remain at home with the völva. Such a natural healer was invaluable on a voyage.

Åsa stopped to help Dagny tie off a line correctly. "Thank you, my lady," the girl said with a bow. The crew showed her deference naturally, and she needed to get them over the habit.

"Remember, all of you, I am traveling in disguise. I'm the wife of your skipper, nothing more."

"Yes, my lady!" came the answer.

Åsa shook her head. "I can see we have some work to do."

After the short morning's run, *Far Traveler* tied up to the pier in Fjaere where they took on a load of soapstone cooking pots, quern stones for grinding grain, whetstones, and ingots of bog iron. Åsa kept up her disguise even here in her own lands. She could ill afford word to spread here in a place rife with traders from all parts, who might carry news of her travels to the Danes.

She kept her hair covered and wore her rough breeks and tunic, and stayed out of the way to ensure no one in the trading port recognized her.

Having stowed all that heavy stone and iron, the crew needed a rest. They left the knarr tied up at the pier and made camp on shore, where they spent the evening drinking ale and telling stories. Åsa settled back in the shadows, enjoying the illusion of being one of them.

Eyvind was up at first light. The rest of the crew roused, and after a quick breakfast of porridge and flatbread, they got underway. Eyvind set a course due south down the Skagerrak, a long day's sail that required little maneuvering. Several of the more promising crew members took turns at the helm under Eyvind's watchful eye, while Åsa gave the others lessons in dead reckoning. For many of them, this was their first voyage out of sight of land. Åsa taught them how to judge their speed by tracking the sun's progress, and how to determine the proximity of land by the behavior of birds and clouds.

Everyone was finding their sea legs as the knarr rolled across the Skagerrak before a favorable wind. With good speed and the long summer day, the low-lying country of the Danes hove into sight well before dark.

Eyvind cruised along the coastline. "Keep your eyes peeled for the entrance to a channel. The first one who spots it wins a bronze arm ring. The Sløjen channel connects the Skagerrak with the Limfjord so that we don't have to round Skagan Point."

Åsa had heard tales about the treacherous tip of the Jylland peninsula, where the Skagerrak met the Kattegat Strait, a narrow passage aptly called the Cat's Throat. The point where the opposing currents of the Skagerrak and the Kattegat clashed was a maze rife with shifting sandbars that had lured many a ship to its death. Åsa shuddered at the image of *Far Traveler* stranded there, pounding against the hard sand in heavy seas.

Svein spotted the entrance to the narrow channel, but it was the low of the ebb tide, making it impossible to navigate. The crew dropped the sail and hove to in the shelter of the shore, waiting for the flood tide. Eyvind kept a sharp eye on the buoy that streamed out behind them. While they waited, the sailors fished and cracked jokes.

When the buoy line went slack, Eyvind gave the order, and the oarsmen ran out their sweeps and rowed into the entrance and up the narrow channel into the Limfjord. Carried by the current, the ship reached inland waters of the Sebbersund just before dark.

The trading port was sited on flat and marshy ground, punctuated by treeless dunes and hills. The market had no docks or jetties. Trading ships pulled up on the sandy beach and displayed their wares on blankets and wood planks. A row of circular, thatched pit houses lined the shore, where resident craft folk lived and worked during the trading season. The sound of blacksmith hammers rang out, and the scent of hot iron mingled with the odor of fish drying on wood racks. Sheep, cattle, goats, and horses grazed on the sparse grass of the uplands. Pigs rutted in the midden piles. Geese and ducks strutted among the huts, adding their squawks and cackles to the calls of bartering traders.

Åsa, dressed in a plain linen tunic and breeks, with her hair braided under a linen cap, blended in with the other women.

Far Traveler's crew followed their noses to a booth redolent of pork stew and fresh-baked flatbread, which they washed down with spring ale, seated around the fire. They ate in silence, too tired from the long day at sea for stories and riddles. When the last drop was swabbed up by the fresh bread, they rolled up in their hudfat around the ship and bedded down for the night. Åsa climbed in with Eyvind. After a sleepy kiss, they both fell into a deep slumber.

The crew rose early. Åsa again wore her cap, tunic, and breeks, as a sea-going trader's wife would, and helped set out the bog iron ingots on a plank beside Fjaere's soapstone pots, quern stones, and sharpening stones. The fox furs and walrus ivory were carefully displayed on a wood table along with the other wares.

Business was brisk throughout the morning, and the crew proved themselves adept traders. At noon, Åsa filled her belt pouch with a handful of hack silver they had taken in. "I'm going to shop," she said.

"Not alone, you're not," said Eyvind, breaking off from a negotiation. He nodded to Svein to take over the transaction.

Åsa shrugged. She could take care of herself, but she enjoyed Eyvind's protectiveness. She'd left her swords safe on Tromøy. No trader's wife would carry such valuable weapons, but like everyone else she wore her seax on her belt for gutting fish and cleaning them. More tool than weapon, the long, single-edged knife was still effective for close fighting and self-defense. Its horizontal leather sheath made it easy to draw in a hurry.

She put her hand in his and slipped into the fantasy of being his wife. A trader's wife, with no responsibilities beyond the day's bartering and the evening meal.

They strolled through the crowds, peering into each workshop. Bead makers displayed goods such as Åsa had never seen, even in Skiringssal. There were glass beads with gold foil inside, chunks of amber, ivory, and crystal. Metalsmiths vied to create the most intricate amulets and arm rings.

She bartered for copper dress pins for Brenna and some of the other women. For Heid she chose a silver pendant in the form of the goddess Freyja bearing an ale horn.

They stopped at a goldsmith's booth where finely worked arm rings and finger rings glinted on a length of deep-blue wool.

Eyvind selected a golden finger ring. Åsa watched him bargain with the goldsmith, impressed by his expertise. The traders' eyes sparkled as they bartered.

When the transaction was concluded and Eyvind took possession of the ring, he turned to Åsa and took her hand, holding out his prize.

She caught her breath. The ring was beautifully wrought, something a man would present to his wife on their wedding day.

"If you are going to play my wife, you must look the part." As he slid the ring onto her finger, Åsa met his eyes and saw they glistened as if with unshed tears. Her throat was dry, and she swallowed, hard. She would never be the wife of any man, but for this trip she could live out her fantasy.

She embraced Eyvind. Eyes blurred with tears, Åsa wandered along unseeing.

They reached the end of the market, where a lone stall stood empty and apart from the other booths. She scanned the area. They were isolated, the crowds far away.

"We should get back," said Eyvind uneasily.

A group of men approached, walking toward them with purpose. As they neared, Åsa saw they were armed. She and Eyvind moved as one in the opposite direction. The men increased their pace.

"Run!" said Eyvind.

As they ran, one of the men moved to intercept Åsa and grabbed her arm. She jerked away, but the man's grip tightened like a vise. With her free hand, she drew her seax. Eyvind halted and drew his weapon as Åsa slashed at the hand that grasped her. The man let go with a curse. Two more men closed in from behind, short swords in hand. They wore no armor, but the way they handled their weapons told Åsa they were not merchants.

The man who had accosted her advanced, short sword clutched in his bloody hand. Åsa and Eyvind stood back-to-back, facing their assailants with weapons drawn.

One of the newcomers rushed Eyvind, sword aimed to gut him. Steel clanged as Eyvind deflected the thrust with his seax. Åsa kept her eye on the two who circled her while Eyvind engaged his opponent. Her seax was not a good match for her assailants' swords, but Åsa made it work, gripping the single-edged blade underhanded and poised to stab.

The two men came at her at the same time, one from each side. She ducked under their sword blades and swung her seax in a deadly arc, slashing her blade across one man's belly then driving the point into the other's midriff. With a huff, he collapsed, folding over her knife and dragging it out of her hand as he dropped to the ground. She bent and snatched the sword from his nerveless fingers, but the other was upon her. He drove his shoulder into her, knocking her to the ground, and rammed his blade into Eyvind's unprotected back. The third man seized the opportunity to bash Eyvind in the head with the butt of his sword.

Eyvind dropped like a stone. Åsa threw out her arms to catch him, but her two remaining assailants snatched her away. One of them stuffed a rag in her mouth and knotted the ends at the back of her head. The two men grappled her, swiftly binding her arms and legs with leather ropes. She kicked and struggled as they dragged her through the abandoned booth and out the back, leaving Eyvind on the ground beside their compatriot in a pool of congealing blood.

The two men tossed Åsa into a cart, where she landed hard on her back, knocking the wind out of her. She struggled to sit up, but bales of wool were heaved down on top of her. In a panic, she tried to thrash her way out but managed only to dig herself deeper, the cloying wool threatening to smother her. Her vision darkened as she struggled for air.

Åsa took charge of her panic and forced herself to lie quietly, calming her breath and trying not to choke on the wool fibers.

Eyvind! In her last glimpse of him, he lay still as a corpse, the blood spreading out around him. If he wasn't dead already, he'd bleed out soon.

Who were these assailants? What did they want with her? Rape, slavery, ransom… The ring Eyvind had given her was still on her finger. She had a purse of hack silver and the trinkets she had purchased, all untouched. Nothing to show she was worth a queen's ransom.

Unless they knew who she was. A glimmer of fear surged through her. She shook it off. How could they know?

The cart rolled on, jouncing over a rutted track that made Åsa grateful for the wool beneath her. The bales on top of her created utter darkness, making it impossible to tell how much time passed. She worked her hands, trying to loosen the bonds, but before she'd managed to loosen the hide ropes, the wagon halted. The bales were lifted, and she caught the scent of the sea. Her captors, two burly men, looked down at her. They are dead men. Åsa glared as they dragged her out of the wagon and dropped her into the bottom of a boat like a sack of turnips. She tried to spit out her gag so that she could use her galdr voice on them, but the rag was tied tight.

Åsa sat up and took stock of her surroundings. She was in a longship, much smaller than Ran's Lover, empty except for a dozen sailors. She was the only captive. Most slavers took on a full cargo of thralls to make the trip worth their while, yet they'd gone through all this effort for her alone. A chill slithered down her spine.

Where was she? Nowhere near Sebbersund, that was for certain. The longship lay on an open coastline. The land around was flat, interspersed with dunes rising out of marsh, for miles in every direction.

By the angle of the sun, it was just past noon, so they had to be on the east coast of the Jylland Peninsula. The ship was anchored fore and aft, the stern grounded on the beach while the bow floated at anchor. The crew cursed as they lugged the anchor off the beach and heaved it aboard. The hair on Åsa's neck stood up when she recognized their Danish accents.

They shoved off the beach, then clambered over the gunnels and hauled on the bowline, pulling the ship out to the deep water where the forward anchor held. When the anchor line hung straight up and down, one of them called, "Haul!" and the others hauled on the rope until the anchor broke free of the bottom. They laboriously pulled the line on board, finally heaving the muddy iron anchor on deck.

The offshore breeze moved the ship away from the beach. One of her captors took the helm while the others raised the sail. The ship skimmed over the waves, headed for open water.

Åsa's heart weighed in her chest, heavy as a bag of mud. She thought of Eyvind lying so still and pale in a pool of blood. He'd given his life to defend her.

Now, nobody knew what had happened to her. She was on her own.

CHAPTER 6

The longship turned south and sailed along the coast all afternoon. Åsa sat on the deck, slumped against the ship's side. Her hands were bound in front of her and her feet were still tied, making it a struggle to maintain her balance against the ship's movements.

Her captors were unnervingly silent throughout the voyage, barely speaking to each other except when it pertained to ship handling. She tried to memorize the ship's course changes, keeping track of the sun's position and the land masses she glimpsed when the ship rolled in the sea. The mainland lay to the west, so they must be in the Kattegat.

As the voyage lengthened into hours, Åsa squirmed—she desperately needed to relieve herself. As if reading her mind, her guard grinned and nodded to a wooden bucket. She glared at him until he turned his back, then got awkwardly to her knees and managed to drop her breeks and scramble onto the bucket.

After she'd clambered back to her spot against the hull, the crew broke out ale and flatbread. She stared longingly at them as they ate. Eventually, her guard brought her a cup of ale and a round of bread.

"If I take off your gag, Lady, you must be silent. If you say a word, I will gag you, and you will go without any food or drink. Do you swear?"

Åsa shivered and her skin prickled with gooseflesh. This man knew she had the galdr voice.

Her captors knew who she was.

"Do you swear, Lady?"

She nodded. At least they seemed bent on keeping her alive.

He pulled the gag down and brought the cup to her mouth. She guzzled the ale, the liquid running down her chin. When she'd drunk it all, he shoved the bread into her mouth before she could speak.

No sooner had she finished then her guard pulled her gag up again, seating it firmly in her mouth.

The worst of her discomforts alleviated, Åsa leaned her head against the hull and dozed, huddled against the chill evening air.

She jerked awake in the night, all senses alerted. Her guard was snoring, his head lolled on his chest, spear slack in his hand. The sail had been furled, and the creak and splash of oars told her they were rowing. She stared over the gunnel, but it was too dark to see more than the barest outline of the land around them.

Åsa gauged the odds of escape. With her hands and legs bound, she had no hope of getting over the side without making a splash loud enough to wake her guard. And swimming would be impossible. They'd catch her in a few minutes, if she didn't drown first.

Her hopes of escape thoroughly crushed, she closed her eyes and tried to send her thoughts out to Heid, but she was too exhausted to concentrate. She dozed, but thoughts of Eyvind tortured her.

Her hands and feet had swelled in their bonds and began to tingle. Her back ached. There was no comfortable position.

At last the sky lightened, though the day held little relief for her. She longed at least to arrive at their destination and discover her fate, and perhaps be released from the torment of her bonds.

After a breakfast of small beer and flatbread, the crew shipped their oars and raised sail, following a course that hugged the land, angling toward the southwest. They passed by a scattering of islands to the east and several deep bays and fjords.

The ship made slow progress in the vagrant breezes and contrary currents. For the most part they managed to keep the sail drawing, but from time to time they were forced to man the oars to keep the ship off a sandbar or out of a back eddy. Åsa focused on memorizing their course, the direction of the sun and lay of the land.

At midday, she was ungagged and force-fed another cup of weak beer and more bread. The sparse fare did little to silence her growling stomach.

Late in the afternoon, they rounded a point and turned due west into a narrow waterway that snaked through a treeless marsh. Once inside, they lost the wind completely. Grumbling, the crew lowered the sail and took to the oars, rowing the longship laboriously through the serpentine inlet.

The sun hovered low in the sky when they came to a sheltered bay on the north shore. The entrance was blocked by posts driven into the sea bottom. Åsa's captors pulled their way between the stakes by hand, calling greetings that were answered by someone she could not see.

The fading daylight revealed dozens of ships crowding the harbor, rocking gently at their moorings. Her captors used their oars as poles to fend off the moored ships as they worked their way through the fleet. When they reached the head of the bay, the harbormaster hailed them and waved his torch to indicate where to land. Armed men lined the shore, several of whom hurried to help them beach.

A cart stood nearby, with two horses hitched up and the driver waiting. In the distance, a fortress brooded.

The fortress of someone powerful, someone with even more powerful enemies. Åsa shuddered.

Her captors lowered her over the bow to warriors standing in the shallows who carried her ashore and dumped her into the waiting cart. This time there were no bales of wool, and she landed hard on the wooden cart bed. Ignoring her bumps and bruises, she squirmed into a sitting position.

The driver snapped the reins and the horses started up the long trail. The sun was low in the sky, but the trail was lit with torches mounted on poles. A half-moon illuminated the fortress on the hilltop, surrounded by a palisade twice as tall as a man. Above the palisade loomed the roof of an immense hall.

The cart bumped over the trail for perhaps an hour. As they drew near, Åsa could make out the silhouettes of warriors armed with spears along the fighting platform of the palisade. Torchlight showed a deep ditch running in front of the wall, making it nearly impossible for an enemy to reach it, except for a narrow wooden bridge that led to a stout gate.

The cart paused at the massive, rune-carved gate while the driver blew a blast on his horn. The gate swung open, and they continued up the torchlit trail toward the hall.

Once inside the palisade, the immensity of the hall came into stark focus. It was much bigger than Tromøy, bigger even than Skiringssal. The roof soared into the sky, its gable ends guarded by silver-gilt dragon heads that glinted in the moonlight. Spears bristled along the roof ridge. Massive pillars carved from whole tree trunks supported the outer walls.

Beside the hall stood a smaller building in its own fenced yard. A temple to the gods. There was no doubt they were taking her to a royal hall.

To see someone of high status.

A high-status Dane.

Horik.

A chill shot through her. If it was Horik, then he'd lain in wait all this time, watching for his chance. A cold, calculating, patient man. A dangerous enemy.

How had he known her movements? Tromøy was not a place where a spy could pass unnoticed. Everyone knew each other and their business on the small island. Strangers stood out.

She forced her panic down and marshalled her thoughts. Her captors knew exactly who she was. Horik had no doubt paid well to bring her here. He would want vengeance—her death in return for his brother's.

And after she was dead, he'd take Tromøy. She thanked the gods Halfdan was safe with Olaf. What a fool she had been! She'd been lured into a trap of her own making. Her mistake cost Eyvind's life. A picture of him lying in a pool of blood sent a piercing surge of grief through her.

Åsa forced the image from her mind and let the wave of emotion ebb. No time for that now. She prayed that Eyvind's crew had not been killed or taken. If they could get to Tromøy with the news of her disappearance, at least the island would not be completely unprepared when Horik's fleet swooped down on them.

The cart jerked to a halt at the great hall, in front of a massive oaken door carved with writhing creatures from the Otherworld. Åsa shivered, remembering the door to Hel's hall. At least there Heid had been beside her. Now she was alone.

The door creaked open. Her captors dragged her from the cart and cut her ankle fetters. Pain shot up her legs as the blood circulated. Her knees buckled. A guard grabbed her arm and jerked her upright. Once she had regained her balance, he prodded her into the hall at spearpoint.

She stumbled through the door on numb feet. Before her lay a cavernous room, lit by hanging lamps and the crackling longfire that ran down the center of the hall. In the gloom she glimpsed walls lined with benches, filled with húskarlar who paused their drinking and gaming to stare at her. On the walls above them hung painted shields, axes, spears, interspersed with finely woven tapestries and tiny squares of amber glass that glinted in the firelight.

Her captors prodded her the length of the room toward the high seat, its massive pillars carved with scenes from legend. Heroes and gods came alive in the firelight, fighting their battles eternally.

Upon the high seat a big man glowered down at her with cold blue eyes. Åsa met his gaze and quailed at his resemblance to the Danish king she'd killed in battle. Like his dead brother, this man's brown hair and beard were threaded with silver strands. His face, weathered from years at sea, bore a scar from the left eye to the left cheek. In spite of this, Åsa estimated his age at about thirty-five, for his movements were filled with vigor.

So this was Horik. The most ruthless of five brothers who ruled the Danes after their father's murder. Rumor had it that Horik had been responsible for the old king's death. Their eldest brother took the throne, but he died mysteriously soon after. Horik then teamed up with his brother Rorik to seize power, forcing their two remaining brothers into exile.

At the insistence of the powerful Frankish emperor, Horik and Rorik had accepted their uncle, Harald Klak, as co-ruler.

The brothers had long had their eyes on Tromøy. Four years ago Rorik had demanded to marry Åsa. When she refused, he invaded Tromøy. With Olaf's help, Åsa's army defeated his and she killed Rorik in battle.

After Rorik's death, Harald Klak and Horik had ruled together for two more years. Then Horik turned on his uncle, forcing Harald to flee once again to the Franks.

Now Horik alone ruled the Danes. A ruthless and cunning man.

She could show him no fear.

Åsa stood straight and raised her chin, her hands bound in front of her.

"Greetings, Åsa, queen of Agder." Horik's voice mocked her as he eyed her snarled hair and filthy, ragged tunic and breeks.

A girl stood beside Horik. She was younger than Åsa and richly dressed. Now she came forward and glared at the guard. "Where are your manners? This woman is our guest. Remove her gag."

The guard looked to Horik, who nodded in assent.

The húskarl hurried to untie her gag. Åsa shook her hair back from her face and met her captor's eyes with all the cold fury she could muster. She took a deep breath, charging her voice with galdr magic. "Horik, what is the meaning of this? How dare your creatures touch me?"

She could see in his eyes that the galdr power caught him off guard. Good. She must press her advantage. "Release my bonds at once. Restore my weapons to me and reunite me with my sworn men."

One of her guards was already moving to obey her, knife drawn. Before the man could recover his wits, she hooked her bonds over the blade and dragged them across the cutting edge, freeing her hands. The guard's eyes widened, and he backed away.

Uncertainty flickered in Horik's eyes. But he was a king, not easily influenced by magic. His gaze hardened. "Silence!" he boomed, a touch of galdr in his own voice.

Åsa faced him, flexing her hands as the blood returned to them.

"Lady, you killed my brother. Your life is forfeit."

"I killed Rorik in a fair fight after he attacked my home," she snapped. "I had every right to take his life."

Horik paused a moment, and Åsa held her breath. A rumble came from beneath his beard. It took her a moment to realize he was laughing. "And I must thank you for saving me the trouble."

Åsa was too shocked to reply, though she kept a stone face.

This was truly a family of vipers. "Well, then, your men may restore me to my ship without further delay."

Horik laughed outright at this. "Nay, my lady. For, like my brother, I want Tromøy. Your steading may not be as grand as the Shining Hall, but your location is strategic for trade and has command of the seaways. And so I will do you the honor of taking you to wife, and Tromøy will once again have the strong king it needs."

Fury burned through Åsa's veins. "Tromøy needs no king. I have proved more than capable of fighting off anyone, including your brother. I notice you were none too eager to cross the Skagerrak and try to roust me out of my stronghold."

His eyes seared into hers. "I am a man who can bide his time."

"I'll never marry you," she said flatly. "You can kill me, but Tromøy will stand against you on my son's behalf."

He gave her a malicious smile. "I feared you would say so. If you don't become my wife, your loyal retainers on Tromøy will be forced to surrender to me in exchange for your life. Furthermore, they'll hand over your son to my safekeeping. The outcome will be the same, but you will be my prisoner instead of my queen. The choice is yours." He gave his guards a nod. "Take her to Groa. She'll keep this witch from using her galdr magic."

Åsa bit back her retort and stayed silent. Let him think he has won, for now. She knew she must play for time.

Åsa's captors manhandled her through a side door.

When Åsa had gone, Horik beckoned to the girl. "Ingebjorg, prepare the wedding feast. I'll marry Queen Åsa in front of witnesses. I want my claim to Tromøy to be indisputable."

Ingebjorg scowled at him. "Uncle, you promised me vengeance for my father."

Horik leaned back in his chair, smiling in satisfaction, and murmured, "Fear not, niece, I will keep my word. Once she's wedded and bedded, we'll sacrifice her to Odin. The god will approve of our vengeance, and appreciate such a royal gift, my own wife. He'll grant us victory over our enemies at last."

The Irish slave shrank farther back into the shadows, praying the king would not notice him. His heart went out to this brave queen. He wished he could help her.

~

Åsa's captors dragged her across the yard to a smaller building. They opened its door and shoved her inside.

Her nostrils flared at the scent of drying herbs hanging from the rafters. The flickering light of a pole lamp revealed a small room, dominated by a bed. The bedposts were carved beast heads, and the headboard was incised with a valknut. The rest of the room was in shadow, but Åsa sensed a presence lurking there.

"Show yourself," she demanded, steeling the fear from her voice.

A woman emerged from the gloom. She was of middle years, skinny as a stick, with graying hair snaking on her shoulders. Åsa could smell the magic wafting off her. A völva.

"Who are you?" Åsa said.

"I am called Groa. I am the king's seer."

Åsa tried to gauge the sorceress's power, but the woman's hugr was opaque. This was a complication. Åsa realized she must hide her own abilities from one who could sense them. Heid had taught her the rudiments of obfuscation, and now she put forth an effort at concealment.

Groa smiled thinly.

So, the völva could sense her inner actions. Åsa hoped the sorceress could not read her thoughts.

Åsa had been in this situation years before. After Gudrød had killed her father and brother and taken her captive, he'd placed her under the care of a völva – Heid. But Heid had been secretly on Åsa's side.

Groa obviously was not.

But neither was Åsa the inexperienced girl of seven years ago. She was a queen who'd slain her captor in a duel and taken vengeance for her kin. She'd seized her father's kingdom and fought off two Dane attacks, and killed a Danish king in battle.

She was a queen well-schooled in magic, who'd been to Hel and back. She could manage this situation.

She would call Stormrider to her and get word to Heid.

In the shadows, wings rustled as a raptor roused. A chill ran down Åsa's spine. The völva had a fylgja. Now she understood how Horik had gotten his information about her. Groa had sent her mind out in her bird to spy on her at Tromøy.

Åsa stared into the gloom, studying the raptor. It was a goshawk, far bigger than Stormrider. Her little falcon was no match for this huge bird. If Groa's hawk caught Stormrider, it would tear Åsa's bird apart.

She'd have to come up with another plan.

CHAPTER 7

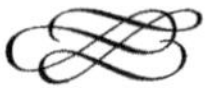

Sebbersund

F*ar Traveler*'s crew gathered at the ship for their evening meal. The trading had been brisk. Their pouches jingled with silver, and the holds were packed with goods.

"Eyvind and the queen should have returned by now," said Svein, his voice edged with concern.

"You're right," Thora agreed. "We'd better go look for them."

Svein didn't want to overreact. It could be Åsa and Eyvind were having fun and had simply lost track of time. Still, it wasn't like Eyvind to be away so long when trading was brisk.

Svein assigned seven sailors to remain with the ship, then split the remaining crew into two groups of a dozen each, placing Thora in charge of one group while he led the other.

The two parties set out in opposite directions to cover the entire market. Svein poked into every booth, questioned every merchant, beggar, and child. He found some who had seen the couple pass by, but no one had seen them recently.

"Did you notice anyone who seemed to be following them?"

he asked again and again, but the answer was always a shake of the head or a shrug. His anxiety increased.

The summer sun was low in the sky when Svein's party came to a deserted section of the market. What they first took to be discarded sacks proved to be a crumpled heap of men on the ground.

"This one's dead," said Ard, using his foot to turn the man who lay in a pool of congealed blood. He stared down at the other body. "It's Eyvind!"

Svein knelt next to Eyvind's supine form. He lay very still, covered with blood that had crusted over. His face was corpse-pale.

Svein brought his face close to Eyvind's. A flutter of breath brushed his cheek. Relief struck him like a wind gust. "He's alive."

Ard pulled the knife from the dead man's abdomen. "This is the queen's seax."

Svein surveyed the area. "Get Eyvind back to the ship. I'll search for the queen."

The sailors cut strips of cloth from the booth's display and bound Eyvind's wound as best they could. They cannibalized the booth's poles and used heavy fabric to fashion a makeshift stretcher to carry him back to the ship.

Once he was alone, Svein scouted the area. Behind the booth where the ground had not been disturbed by the fight, he found wagon tracks and fresh hoof prints. His guts roiled. Someone had left Eyvind for dead and taken the queen.

He followed the wagon tracks for an hour, but they came to an abrupt end on a deserted shore. Svein could see up and down the beach for miles, but the wagon was nowhere to be seen. All that remained was a distinctive mark in the sand where the keel of a boat had been dragged into the water since the last high tide.

Svein's hopes plummeted. There was little doubt that Åsa had been taken on that boat, and he'd never find out where she'd been taken. In desperation, he searched the area and found where the wagon tracks picked up again, leading off to the south. He followed them, hoping if he found the wagon, Åsa might be there, or he might be able to force the driver to tell where she'd been taken.

The tracks led back to the outskirts of the Sebbersund market. At the end of the trail Svein found the wagon, but it was empty, and the horses and driver were gone, their prints lost in the confused morass of many hoof and foot prints.

He questioned the nearby traders to see if anyone could tell him where the driver had gone with the horses, but it seemed that no one had paid any attention.

It was sundown when Svein returned to the ship, flummoxed.

Thora's group was already there, looking tired and discouraged. "We've questioned everyone in our path," she said. "A few remember seeing them together, but nobody saw anything suspicious."

"I found wagon tracks near where we found Eyvind. I followed the tracks to the sea, where I discovered keel marks. The wagon met a ship, then came back here. I found the wagon, but nothing more." He sighed. "It's pretty certain they've taken the queen by ship."

The crew had raised a tent to keep Eyvind out of the elements, and Dagny had done what she could with his wounds. "I think he'll survive," she pronounced, "but he needs healing beyond my abilities."

Thora looked around at the traders' rough camps. Sebbersund could hardly be called a settlement. "We'll get no skilled help here. We need to get him back to Tromøy where the völva can tend to him."

Dagny said, "He can't make a sea voyage in his condition. He's lost a lot of blood and he's dehydrated. If we get some liquids in him and a good night's rest, he may be fit enough in the morning."

Svein crawled into the tent where Eyvind lay wrapped in a

hudfat. He opened his eyes when Svein settled beside him. "Åsa?" he said faintly.

Svein shook his head ruefully and told Eyvind what he'd found. "It seems likely the queen's kidnappers took her by sea, but there's no way to tell which direction they went. She could be anywhere."

Eyvind struggled to sit up. "We have to go after her."

Svein restrained him with a gentle hand. "There's nothing more we can do to find her. I followed the wagon tracks. The cart was abandoned near here. I tried to locate the driver, but he's vanished. We questioned everyone in the market, and nobody's seen anything. We don't know where they've taken her. The ship could have gone any direction. Dagny says we need to get you back to Tromøy, where the völva can heal you, and let them know that the queen is missing. But we can't move you until you've had some nourishment and a night's rest."

Eyvind sagged back down.

"Maybe we'll hear from someone demanding a ransom," Svein said encouragingly.

Dagny came in with a bowl of broth. Svein held Eyvind's head up while he obediently sipped the liquid. When he'd drunk the whole bowl, Dagny checked his bandages and made him comfortable. "Try to sleep," she said. "You need to regain your strength so we can sail home tomorrow."

Eyvind looked miserable. "I failed her," he whispered.

"All is not lost yet. We may find her. Don't give up."

Eyvind nodded and closed his eyes.

The crew was silent as they bedded down for the night.

By morning Eyvind had recovered enough that Dagny said he would survive the trip back to Tromøy.

"But only as a passenger," she admonished. "You must remain lying down and move as little as possible."

Eyvind agreed reluctantly.

Far Traveler's crew loaded the ship with their trade goods.

They carried Eyvind aboard and made him a soft bed of sheepskins in the shelter of the afterdeck, propping him up so he could see what was going on and provide direction.

The crew heaved the big knarr off the beach and manned the oars. Under Eyvind's direction, they rowed up the Limfjord and found the opening to the Sløjen channel. The tide favored them as they passed through the narrow channel to the Skagerrak. When the ship broke into open waters, Eyvind ordered them to raise the sail to a freshening breeze. Once they were on a course for Tromøy, he sank back on the sheepskins and fell into an exhausted sleep.

CHAPTER 8

Erritsø

Åsa kept up a constant effort to veil her thoughts from Groa. She waited for the sorceress to leave, or doze, but Groa seemed to have no need of sleep. The völva sat on her stool by the brazier in an unnerving silence, working on a complicated tablet weaving. The long, finely spun warp threads were stretched between two slim poles mounted on a wood base. The warp threads were dyed red with madder, while the weft that ran through the tablet holes was the blue of woad and yellow made from heather. Silver threads flashed among the colors. This would be trim for a fine robe or perhaps a headband. It promised to be a magnificent piece.

It was a shame to spoil it.

The smooth wooden tablets clicked as Groa turned them, counting under her breath to keep track of the intricate pattern.

Åsa lay on the bed, staring up at the ceiling, trying to stay awake. Sleep would leave her hugr unguarded, and she was not in a safe place. To keep her mind occupied and obscured from her captor, she imagined a complex tablet weaving pattern of her own, mentally executing each turn.

Groa cursed and unwove several mistakes. "Stop!"

Åsa smirked. "Stop what?"

A tap came at the door. A tall, slender young man entered. He was dressed in the threadbare tunic of a slave. He bore a tray with steaming bowls of stew, rounds of flatbread, and cups of ale. The scent of food made Åsa's stomach rumble.

Groa nodded to a low table. The slave set down the tray, and the völva gave him a look that sent him scurrying off. But just as he exited the door, Åsa caught his eye for an instant. An understanding passed between them.

The door closed behind him, leaving Åsa wondering if she could somehow ally with him. He was a prisoner here as much as she.

The völva brought her a bowl of stew, and Åsa tucked into the food. She needed her strength to cope with Groa and to be ready if any chance of escape presented itself.

The stew was rich and full of chunks of pork. The fact that Horik fed her well suggested that he hadn't given up hope of winning her over. Perhaps she should act more receptive to his proposal. She needed to keep him on the hook until she could find a way to escape.

Groa took her seat and watched Åsa eat. The völva's facial expression softened, losing the irritation evident when she'd entered. The corners of her mouth twisted in what she must have meant to be a smile. "You should marry Horik." She spoke in coaxing tones so obviously contrived that Åsa had to stifle a snort. "He's a powerful king, a man in his prime. He could give you all the riches you could ask for."

Horik had no doubt ordered Groa to use her wiles to persuade Åsa to agree to the marriage. Åsa knew she needed to be careful to draw this out as long as possible, looking for a chance to escape. She must resist without making Horik completely lose patience. "I already have all the riches I desire," she said, making her tone a tiny bit uncertain, as if she could be persuaded.

"He can give you strong sons."

"I have a strong son."

"A queen needs many sons. In case something happens to the first one."

Åsa bit her lip while inwardly she fumed at the thinly veiled threat. She was glad Halfdan was safe in Skiringssal, something Groa would never find out.

The sorceress spoke slowly, as if to an idiot. "If you don't marry him, he'll kill you, and your son, and take your little island just the same."

Fury seared through Åsa like poison, and she bit back a retort. She didn't doubt that Groa spoke the truth, and Horik had put her up to it. Tromøy could never stand against Horik's fleet, even if Olaf came to their aid. They needed to gather more forces before the Danes attacked.

She had to find a way to warn them before Horik lost patience with her. Åsa lowered her eyes as if cowed by the völva's tirade.

She longed to reach out to Heid, but she didn't dare. Groa would certainly detect it if Åsa sent forth her hugr. Instead, she spent the day defending her mind against the Danish völva. She abandoned her mental tablet weaving and began to internally recite the epic poem of Hervör.

It seemed Groa was not accustomed to dealing with someone who had been trained in mental discipline. In her head Åsa was reciting the scene in which Hervör raised her father from the dead and demanded the cursed sword, Tyrfing, when she felt Groa's attention slacken. The sorceress had stopped trying to enter Åsa's thoughts and focused on her weaving. It was a victory of sorts. Åsa hoped she could find a way to use the technique to her advantage.

A brief knock, and the same thrall entered the room. To Åsa's disappointment, he bore no food. She took the opportunity to get a good look at him. He was fairly young, maybe her age, and strong enough with wiry muscles, if undernourished. His hair and beard were light brown, his skin pale and freckled, and his eyes were a shade of gray-green like the sea on a stormy day. Åsa noticed that he had unusually long fingernails.

He bowed low to Groa. "Lady," he said, "the king wishes to see you." Åsa detected an Irish lilt to his voice.

Groa did not waste any time obeying her king's summons. She rose, grabbed her cloak and staff, and hurried out the door.

As soon as the völva had gone, the slave turned to Åsa. "Lady, Horik is a desperate man, beset by many powerful enemies," he said. "He means you ill."

Åsa scrutinized the thrall, wondering if she should trust him. He could be sent by Horik to gain her confidence. She decided to play it safe. "Horik is going to marry me," she said innocently.

The slave hissed, "You don't understand. He plans to take you to wife, by force if need be, but once he is your husband and has undisputed claim to Tromøy, he…he plans to sacrifice you to Odin."

A jolt of pure terror shot through Åsa. "How do you know this?" she whispered.

"I overheard him talking to his niece. He keeps me near him at all times—I amuse him. But he knows I am powerless, and so he pays me no mind."

"Who are you?" Åsa asked.

The thrall met her gaze. He threw his shoulders back and drew himself up to his full height. He was achingly thin, but he stood as tall as Eyvind, and his eyes glowed with pride. The rags he wore no longer seemed a part of him.

He swept a low bow and said, "Lady, my name is Cian, a student of the harp from the sacred isle of Eir. I was taken by

Horik in a raid three years ago, when he attacked my school, and I have been enslaved to him ever since."

"I am honored to meet you, Cian," said Åsa. "I am Åsa, queen of Agder. I would think one such as yourself would bring a good ransom?"

Cian's eyes clouded, and he shook his head. "My father was killed, and there was no one left who was obliged to redeem me. Needless to say, Horik was not pleased, and now he's determined to take the ransom out of my hide by working me to death."

Åsa's heart ached for him. "If you help me escape, there will be a place for you in my hall, or I will give you passage to your homeland if that is your preference."

Cian shook his head. "Escape is impossible. Every fortress has an escape route, and I have found this one's, but once outside the walls, where would we go? We are far from help, and Horik's men are everywhere. We'd be captured immediately. All we can do is help each other survive for now, and wait for an opportunity."

Åsa nodded. "I understand."

"If such an opportunity arises, I will come for you. Until then, keep the faith."

The door opened and the völva stormed in, obviously displeased with her interview with Horik. Cian ducked out.

Groa said, "The king wishes you to join him in the hall this evening. He's ordered me to clean you up for the occasion."

Åsa bit back her retort and nodded, keeping her gaze lowered as if in submission.

Servants arrived with buckets of hot water and soap. Åsa submitted to their ministrations. Despite her dread, it was a relief to have her salt-encrusted hair and skin washed.

Groa brought out a gown of fine red linen, painstakingly embroidered at the hem and neckline. Åsa pulled it on and let a serving woman dress her hair into a knot at the back of her head, letting the long tail cascade down her back.

When at last she was ready, Groa ushered her to the hall. Åsa stifled a cringe and pasted a smile on her face as the völva led her to the high seat where Horik waited.

"Greetings, Lady," Horik said, eyeing her with a predatory gleam. "I am pleased to see you looking well."

Åsa gave him a brief nod as she sat on the high seat, inching as far from him as possible. She peered into the gloomy reaches, mentally sizing up the húskarlar who lounged on the benches and the weaponry displayed on the walls above them. Her heart contracted. There were so many, and they were extremely well armed.

The young woman Åsa had seen on the first day now approached the high seat and presented Horik with a chased-silver mead horn. Åsa eyed the woman curiously. She was well dressed and performed the duties of a wife with long-accustomed practice.

Horik raised the horn. "To my future bride!" he cried, saluting Åsa with the horn. He drank and returned the vessel to the woman, and she offered it to Åsa.

She held out the horn with a smile that made the hair on the back of Åsa's neck stand up. "I am Horik's niece, Ingebjorg Roriksdottir. Drink, my lady."

Alarm shot through Åsa. This was the daughter of the Danish king she had slain in battle. She took the horn from Ingebjorg cautiously. Poison? She shot a sidelong glance at Horik. He'd just drunk from it and seemed none the worse.

Ingebjorg's eyes were fixed on Åsa speculatively, a wicked smile playing on her lips. The girl was toying with her and enjoying it. She knew Åsa's ultimate fate.

Åsa smiled back and took a hearty swallow. The mead was of excellent quality, the taste of honey strong but not too sweet. "This mead is very good."

Ingebjorg gave her a malicious smile and said, "I'm glad you like it. I am brewing a special batch, just for you." Her voice, dripping with insinuation, sent a chill down Åsa's spine.

Åsa kept her smile pasted on her face and handed the horn back to Horik's niece, who bore it around the room. The girl spent time exchanging conversation with the men she served, laughing at their jests, bestowing attention upon each of them. Every man's eyes followed her as she moved on to the next.

The tantalizing aroma of pork wafted into the room ahead of half a dozen men bearing huge platters. Despite her anxiety, Åsa found her appetite piqued. She realized she'd had little to eat since her capture. She needed to gain as much strength as possible to deal effectively with Groa and Horik, and now the malicious Ingebjorg.

Beside her, Horik feasted with gusto, pausing between bites to leer at her. Fortunately he kept his mouth occupied with food and drink rather than conversation. Åsa ate as much as she could while sipping sparingly at her ale cup.

When the meal had been demolished, Horik sat back in his seat and belched. "Irishman!" he bellowed.

Cian, the slave she'd met in Groa's room, crept out of the shadows and stood before the king.

"Fetch his harp," Horik commanded.

The steward scurried to obey. He returned in an instant with a leather bag, which he placed in Cian's hands while others fetched him a stool.

The Irishman took his seat. He untied the bag's lacings and reverently withdrew a small harp. The triangular-shaped instrument was finely crafted of wood, lavishly carved and polished. The strings were of thick brass wire, glinting in the firelight. Cian closed his eyes and caressed the harp like a lover. He fitted the top of the harp against his left shoulder, holding it close to his body.

With the long fingernails of his left hand he plucked the upper strings. The rich, bell-like chord brought silence to the hall. Cian immediately damped the vibration with his left fingers while his right plucked the lower strings, sending out a mighty sound that filled the room.

While he played, no one spoke. Horik sank back in his high seat, fingers drumming to the rhythm. Cian closed his eyes, lost in the music. Tears ran down his cheeks as he played.

Åsa listened, enraptured as everyone else in the hall. The music was filled with a longing that brought tears to her own eyes. Her heart went out to this man. So sad that such a brilliant, carefully honed talent was a doomed slave in captivity when he should be a renowned harpist, showered with riches and prestige in his own land. Åsa vowed that if she could do anything to help him, she would.

But first she had to survive what Horik had planned for her.

When at last the harp strings stilled, the steward came to claim the instrument. The Irishman relinquished it with pain in his eyes, then slipped away into the shadows.

Horik turned to her. "My lady, I bid you good-night. Our wedding feast will be ready three days hence."

Åsa's heart pounded. Three days. That was not much time.

Horik nodded to Groa, who took Åsa's elbow and conducted her firmly back to her chamber.

The same female servant helped Åsa out of the beautiful gown, carefully stowing it in an oak chest. Donning a linen shift, Åsa got into the big bed and pulled the down comforter over her. Groa undressed and got into bed on the other side.

Åsa lay in the dark, her mind abuzz. She'd tested Groa's abilities, and they were formidable, but not impregnable. Perhaps there was a way she could elude the sorceress. She'd proven she could interfere with Groa's thoughts, but so far she had not gained power over her.

She had to contact Heid somehow and let her know where she was.

Åsa lay mentally reciting the long, involved saga of the

Volsungs while she waited for Groa to fall asleep. All her senses were on alert as the völva's breathing slowed and became regular. The energy of the woman's thoughts quieted. Åsa abandoned the tale and let her mind become blank.

She took in a deep breath, then opened her mouth in a deep yawn and sent her mind out, searching for Heid. She imagined the woman's frizzy head of hair, now thinning and silver, the völva's stern face, and those steely eyes that missed nothing. Heid had been with her since Åsa was a girl of fifteen. The sorceress had guided her through so much, taught her everything she knew. She'd been there to help Åsa through Hel, at great cost to herself. The journey had aged the sorceress before her time. But the woman was tough, the toughest person Åsa had ever known.

Åsa summoned all of her own strength and sent her thoughts toward Heid.

And got no response.

Fear nipped at Åsa. Heid's near-death experience had weakened her, no doubt diminished her power. Had it left her unreachable?

Desperate, Åsa tried again. She summoned all her energy and sent out her need urgently, until the power shot out of her like a lightning bolt.

CHAPTER 9

Skiringssal

Sonja woke to the sound of screams. The cries were coming from the bower where Halfdan and Rognvald shared a bed under the watchful eye of Rognvald's fóstra.

Sonja threw on her cloak and hurried out the door to the bower. The fóstra was already bending over the bed where Halfdan was screaming in his sleep. Rognvald sat hunched under the covers at the far extreme of the bed.

Sonja sat on the bed and put her arm around the crying boy. "Shh..." she whispered, smoothing his sweat-soaked hair back from his tear-stained face. She held him in her arms until his eyes opened. "What's wrong, Halfdan?"

"M-Mama," he murmured, punctuated by a hiccup.

"What about Mama?" said Sonja.

"Mama's in t-t-trouble," Halfdan stammered.

"What kind of trouble?"

"She's afraid," he said. "She's in danger."

"Oh, I'm sure she's fine," Sonja soothed. "I know she misses you." It was natural for a boy to fear for his mother when he'd never been separated from her.

"No!" Halfdan insisted, struggling to get down. "A bad man captured her! He's going to kill her."

Sonja stroked his cheek and spoke in soothing tones. "Go to sleep now. It was only a dream."

Halfdan snuffled. "A bad king has her. He hates her. He's got her locked in a room, far away, across the water. A bad witch is watching her."

"You were dreaming, dear. If anything were wrong, we would have heard," Sonja said soothingly. "Your mother is safe."

Halfdan snuffled a few times and then hiccupped. "Promise?"

"Promise." Sonja smoothed the boy's hair and crooned a lullaby. Halfdan took a deep breath and sighed it out. In his corner, Rognvald's eyes blinked. Soon both boys were asleep.

She returned into the chamber she shared with Olaf. He was sitting up in bed, blinking owlishly. "Halfdan has had a nightmare about Åsa," she told her sleepy husband.

"Homesick?" he asked.

She snuggled into his arms. "It's only natural. He's never been away from her before. He'll adjust."

Tromøy

Far Traveler ARRIVED in Tromøy's harbor just in time for the evening meal. Olvir and Jarl Borg waited on the beach. Their expressions turned grave as they watched the crew hand Eyvind over the side on a stretcher.

"Where is Åsa?" Borg said, apprehension heavy in his voice.

Eyvind tried to speak, but his lips seemed glued shut.

"The queen has been kidnapped," Svein told them. "She's been taken on a ship. I tracked them and questioned the locals, but I could not find out where she was taken."

They carried Eyvind up to the hall where Heid waited. He was grateful for their care not to jostle him, but when he tried to say so, he found he could not form the words.

"Well, that couldn't have possibly gone worse," Heid growled when she heard Åsa had been taken. She looked at Eyvind. "Bring that fool to the bower," she ordered tersely.

Eyvind breathed a sigh of relief. Despite her unfriendly tone, he knew Heid would heal him if it was possible.

Once he was safely inside and transferred to a bed, Heid bade her apprentices strip off his filthy, bloodstained clothes and wash him. When he was clean, Heid palpated his wounds and searched his body for hidden injuries. From a steaming cauldron she brought a cup of pungent brew smelling of herbs, leeks, and onion. She made him drink the broth, then sniffed the wound in his back. Eyvind knew if she could smell the strong odor of the broth at the wound site, it meant his innards had been punctured, and he was certain to die.

Heid went over every inch of his body, sniffing with a wrinkled nose. Eyvind held his breath as she sat back and nodded to her apprentices to cover him with a down quilt. "You did a good job," she said to Dagny, who colored at the praise. Heid turned back to Eyvind. "The blow on the head did you no lasting harm, and it looks as though the blade missed anything vital. If we can stave off infection, you'll live." She fixed him with a furious glare. "How could you lose her? If you weren't already at death's door, I'd make you sorry."

Eyvind stared at her miserably. "What if she's…" He could not bring himself to finish the sentence.

Heid's expression softened to something akin to sympathy. "I think I would know if she's left this world. But I will search the pathways of the dead. If she's there, I will find her."

Eyvind watched apprehensively as Heid bade her apprentices to make ready. If Åsa was dead...he couldn't think of it.

"Are you sure you should risk this?" Vigdis asked the völva, her voice fraught with anxiety. "You almost didn't come back to us the last time."

The previous year Heid had nearly died from the sickness that killed so many on Tromøy. The völva had not regained her former vigor.

"That is no concern of yours," Heid growled. "Tend to your duties, girl."

Vigdis strode off to gather what was needed, her face furrowed with worry.

When a rooster had been sacrificed and its blood sprinkled propitiously, the apprentices helped their mistress onto the seidr platform that stood in the center of the bower. The völva hobbled to her chair of prophecy and sank into its cushion, plump with hen's feathers. From her belt pouch, she took up her strike-a-light to start a fire in the brazier. Her hands shook ominously as she struck steel on flint. Sparks landed on the tinder and winked out. Everyone held their breath as she fumbled with the flint. No one dared to help her. After half a dozen tries, a spark caught and the völva coaxed a blaze.

Heid reached into her pouch and withdrew a handful of cannabis seeds, which she cast on the flame. The seeds sizzled and popped, sending fragrant smoke into the air. Inhaling deeply, the völva took up her Sami drum and beat a ponderous rhythm with a reindeer's leg bone. The apprentices encircled the platform, chanting the vardlokkur to call the spirits to protect their mistress on her journey. The hair on Eyvind's neck stood up as the eerie chanting grew.

Gradually Heid's drumming stilled. The reindeer bone fell from her hand and her eyes closed. Her head lolled back. For a long while only the chanting apprentices could be heard while the völva's hugr traveled deep beneath the roots of the World Tree.

Eyvind fell into a feverish doze.

It was late when Heid roused from her trance. Eyvind woke with a start when the apprentices suddenly fell silent. Vigdis climbed onto the platform with a cup of ale. They waited while the völva drank and came fully back into this world.

When she finally spoke, her voice grated like a rusty lock. "I came to the roots of the World Tree, and there I saw the Nornir weaving their tapestry of life. I asked if the queen Åsa had passed that way, but they said they had not seen her since she had come out with the Irish necklace. They told me it was not her time, though they gave me leave to search for her in case she'd come by another road. And so I went on." She paused and took another sip of ale.

"Svartfaxi met me beneath the root of Helheim," said Heid, speaking of the horse Åsa had ridden through the underworld. "He carried me on the Hel road, but we did not see Åsa. After a long journey through the dark valleys, we reached the gold-roofed bridge where the jotun maiden, Modgud, stands guard." Heid was seized with a coughing fit. The völva took a long sip of ale, and finally her coughing stilled. When she had recovered her voice, she continued. "I asked Modgud if she had seen Åsa pass across the bridge, and she replied, 'Not since she came out with that Irish necklace. Åsa is not in Helheim.'"

Silence fell over the bower.

Hope and desolation filled Eyvind in equal measure. "Then she is alive, but we have no way to find her."

Heid said, "I will search the world over for her."

"No," said Vigdis. "You cannot go again so soon. You must rest."

The sorceress's face was haggard, but she shook her head. "I can't wait. Time is of the essence. Anything could happen to her."

Vigdis spoke firmly. "I share your urgency, but you've weakened yourself too much in the journey on the Hel road. We can't lose both you and Åsa."

Heid raised her head, determined. "I must try now. I will get no rest until I find her."

Eyvind's hopes rose. He mentally sent a prayer to Freyja to give the völva the strength for one last try.

"Promise you will rest after this," Vigdis pleaded.

"I give you my word," said Heid.

Tight-lipped, Vigdis fed twigs into the dwindling fire of the brazier and made the völva comfortable on her cushions. Then she stepped down and joined the other apprentices as they raised their voices in the vardlokkur yet again.

Heid cast a seed of henbane on the fire and inhaled deeply. Her head drooped to her chest, and she sat like that for so long Eyvind feared she had passed out.

But at long last her head lifted partway. Her lips moved, though no words were audible, only a rasping whisper. Heid's chant built until it became a furious hiss. Then her shoulders slumped and her head sagged back to her chest.

Vigdis clambered onto the platform and rushed to her mistress's side. With soothing words she coaxed the sorceress out of her trance. Heid uttered a few words that Eyvind could not hear.

Vigdis bade the apprentices come up on the platform and carry the völva to her bed, where they bundled her in quilts.

"She must rest," said Vigdis. "Heid could not discover where Åsa was being held or by whom. Now let her be."

Eyvind lay awake, worrying. If Heid couldn't do it, how would they find Åsa?

Deep in the night, the völva stirred and groaned. Eyvind held his breath, not wanting to wake her.

"I know you're there," the sorceress rasped. "I can hear you thinking."

"I'm sorry to disturb you, Lady," said Eyvind.

"Never mind. I can't sleep either. I'm worried about her too."

"Vigdis said you couldn't find her."

"My way was blocked. Another völva guards her."

"One more powerful than you?"

A sigh escaped the sorceress. "Not if I were in my full power. But I am much diminished."

"Is there nothing more we can do?" Eyvind asked in despair.

"There is one chance. I will send Stormrider. If anyone can find Åsa, it's her falcon. Birds have abilities beyond ours, and Stormrider has a connection with Åsa's hugr. It's a last resort. It could be that we will lose the falcon too, but it's a chance we must take. Now get some rest. When we find her, you need to be ready to fight for her."

Eyvind tried to obey the völva's instructions and rest, but worry pricked at him, waking him throughout the night.

In the morning, Vigdis fetched Stormrider from her perch and set the falcon on the back of Heid's headboard. She removed the bird's hood and undid Stormrider's jesses. The falcon roused, staring about her with a piercing gaze.

Heid took a deep breath and closed her eyes. "Find her."

The bird gave a powerful flap of her wings and lofted into the air. She flew out through the smokehole, taking Eyvind's hopes with her.

~

Erritsø

"You will be a lovely bride," said Groa in coaxing tones. She held out a gown of fine blue wool trimmed with elaborate tablet-woven bands at the hem, cuffs, and neckline. Silver thread glinted among the colors.

Åsa gazed at the lavish gown with dread in her heart. As soon as she was Horik's wife, she would be as good as dead. The thought of the wedding night with her murderer filled her with horror. She shuddered as she remembered her bridal night with Gudrød, after he'd slain her father and brother and burned Tromøy. She'd tried to kill him as he attempted to rape her. Both had failed, with disastrous results.

She needed to find a way to delay this wedding.

"That gown will never fit me," she complained. "It's way too large. I'd be a laughing stock if I appeared at the wedding wearing that. Horik would be furious." A sidelong glance at Groa told her she'd hit the mark. Horik would never forgive a public humiliation.

Groa sighed in defeat. "I will call the women in to alter it tomorrow."

That would buy her a few more days. But what could change for her in a few days? Åsa's shoulders slumped. She needed a plan. Or a miracle from the gods.

Åsa lay on the bed, listening to the click of Groa's tablets as she wove. A flurry of wings at the gable end caused Åsa's eyes to open. With a jolt she recognized Stormrider perched in the opening.

She quickly averted her gaze, but Groa glanced up at the ceiling and frowned. Åsa held her breath, peering sidelong at the gable, but the falcon had gone. Had the sorceress seen Stormrider?

Groa leaned back against the wall. She opened her mouth and yawned loudly. Her eyes rolled back in her head.

In the shadows, wings beat and a dark shape flew out the gable end.

A chill shot through Åsa. The sorceress had called her own bird and sent it after Stormrider.

Åsa sent her thoughts rushing after them. She caught up with Stormrider and slipped into the bird's mind. After so many times, it was as easy as putting on a familiar cloak.

In the instant's hesitation it took the falcon to let her in,

Groa's hawk gained on her. The goshawk was larger than the falcon and shot forward like an arrow. Stormrider swooped and stalled, desperately evading her pursuer. But for so big a bird, the hawk was nimble.

Despite her smaller size, Stormrider had the greater wingspan. She watched Groa's hawk soar toward her across the open field, and saw her chance. With a powerful flap of her wings Stormrider shot above the goshawk, spiraling higher and higher, positioning herself to stoop on the larger bird. The hawk, unsuited to hunting at such heights, could not match the falcon's rise.

When Stormrider was high above the field, she folded her wings and dove, hurtling down on the goshawk in a killing stoop.

At the last moment the hawk dodged aside, and Stormrider plummeted toward the earth. She flipped upright and spread her wings, pulling up just before slamming into the ground, but the hawk was upon her. Groa's bird seized Stormrider in her talons, ready to tear her apart. The falcon fought to survive, but she could not break the bigger bird's iron grip. Stormrider ceased her struggles and sagged, inert. With a triumphant cry, the hawk opened her beak to rip at her prey.

The goshawk was about to feed when she tilted her head as if listening. Then she opened her talons and released the falcon's limp body. She spread her wings and took to the air.

Tromøy

EYVIND HAULED himself out of bed. Even after a night's sleep, his body was sore and his wound ached. A groan escaped him as he doggedly began to dress.

"Where on earth do you think you're going?" Heid demanded.

"I need to get to Olaf and tell him Åsa is missing. Maybe he can help find her."

Heid crossed her arms over her chest. "You're in no condition for a sea voyage."

"The best thing for me," Eyvind declared. "I'll heal better at sea."

"Let Olvir go."

"It's my responsibility," said Eyvind. "I lost her. Now I need to get her back."

Heid scowled. "You're no good to her dead."

Eyvind turned on her. "I have to do something. You can't find her."

The völva turned pale. Eyvind stifled his feeling of guilt for his callous remark and finished dressing. Heid was silent as he left the bower and made his way painfully to the hall.

The sound of people eating breakfast emanated from the hall. As he entered, the conversation and clatter of bowls and cups halted abruptly. Every eye was on him.

Trying not to wince, he took his place at the head of his crew as if he hadn't just risen from his deathbed. A servant shook off her trance to fetch him a bowl of porridge and a cup of small beer. He took a sip and looked at Svein. "We sail today to Skiringssal to tell King Olaf that Queen Åsa is missing."

"I will go," said Olvir.

"You will not. I will go." The words came out with more force than Eyvind intended, but Olvir took a look at him and made no protest.

After breakfast, *Far Traveler*'s crew gathered in the yard to load their sea chests onto the cart. Eyvind mounted his horse, biting back a groan. He was more than grateful that, as captain, he didn't have to heft his own sea chest. He clucked to his horse and led his crew down to the ship.

At the shore, he dismounted, and a shock of pain shot through him from heel to head. He gripped the horse's bridle as the pain receded, then made his way more gingerly up the boarding plank onto *Far Traveler*.

Eyvind took a seat in the stern, wrapped in furs despite the warmth of the summer day, while Svein manned the helm and Thora directed the sailors. Eyvind leaned back and closed his eyes, glad the weather was fair and he had a day's journey to recover.

~

Skiringssal

HORNS SOUNDED JUST after the evening meal. From the door of the hall, Olaf recognized *Far Traveler* as she entered Skiringssal's harbor. The stable boy hurried to saddle Olaf's horse and one for the guest captain.

Olaf mounted up and led the guest horse down to the shore to meet the new arrivals. At the dock, he dismounted and strode onto the planks.

"Greetings! I'm surprised to see you," Olaf shouted as the ship came alongside the dock. He caught the spring-line a sailor tossed him and held it while *Far Traveler*'s crew clambered over the sides with mooring lines.

Eyvind was at the helm, guiding the knarr in. Olaf noticed he moved stiffly and awkwardly. It was obvious the man was in pain.

"Åsa is missing," Eyvind said urgently. "She disappeared at the market in Sebbersund. It looks pretty certain that she was kidnapped. We suspect the Danes, but we can't be sure."

A shock ran up Olaf's spine. "Halfdan had a dream that Åsa had been kidnapped. We thought he was just homesick for his mother."

Eyvind stared at him.

"You'd better come up."

The shore patrol helped the crew secure the ship while Eyvind mounted the horse Olaf had brought for him. Eyvind winced as he climbed into the saddle, though he said nothing. Olaf pretended he hadn't noticed. He clucked to his horse and set off up the trail to the steading at a slow walk.

In the yard, Olaf waited, gaze averted, while Eyvind let himself painfully down from the saddle. Olaf gritted his teeth in sympathy and stifled the urge to help him.

Once they were both safely on the ground, they hurried to the bower hall and burst in the door. Sonja sat on the floor, playing with the boys and the puppies. Her gaze riveted on Eyvind as they entered the room.

Olaf said, "I think Halfdan's nightmare about Åsa was more than a dream." He didn't want to say she was missing, for fear of upsetting Halfdan even more.

Sonja's eyes went wide as she realized what he was implying.

Eyvind eased down to the floor beside the boy. "What did you dream, Halfdan?"

"Mama's in danger," Halfdan said. "Bad men tied her up and took her away on a ship."

At the words, Eyvind gripped the boy's shoulder. "Is she hurt?"

Halfdan shook his head. "No, but the bad king wants to kill her."

Olaf and Eyvind exchanged looks of alarm. "Can you tell us where the men on the ship took her?" Olaf asked.

The little boy squinched up his face, looking inward. "To a big place with high walls. It has dragons and spears on the roof."

"A fortress. But whose?" said Olaf.

"Can you remember where the sun was in the sky when they took her?" asked Eyvind.

Halfdan's face cleared. "The sun was in the west."

Olaf nodded. "Good job. You know your directions well. Do you know which direction they sailed?"

Halfdan considered. "They sailed south."

"They took her from Sebbersund in the afternoon, and they sailed south." Eyvind looked back to Halfdan.

The boy nodded.

"How long was the voyage? Did it last all night?"

Halfdan thought, then nodded. "All night and all the next morning until after noon."

"Good boy. Then what? Did they change directions?"

Halfdan nodded again. "They turned west into a fjord. Then they tied up the ship and put Mama in a wagon and took her to a fortress. A bad king has her. He's going to kill her. Mama's afraid."

The urgency in the boy's voice sparked terror in Olaf. He struggled to regain his composure and focus on what he needed to know. "You must think very hard and help us find her. Now, was it dark when they landed?"

Halfdan closed his eyes, calling up the vision. "The ship turned into the sunset."

Eyvind nodded. "She was taken around noon, to a well-fortified royal hall, a day and a half's sail from Sebbersund." He looked at Olaf. "Erritsø."

Olaf's eyes widened. "Horik's hall."

"Between us we don't have a big enough fleet to take on Horik," Olaf said. "I've heard that he's got fifty ships. I don't know if I believe it, but even so, his fleet is far bigger than ours."

Eyvind nodded glumly. "If Horik's going to kill her, we have to get to her right away. There's no time to go to Ragnhild in Gausel. The voyage would take a week each way, and there's no guarantee Ragnhild's ships would be available and ready to sail."

"There is one other possibility," said Olaf. "I don't relish it, but it may be our only option. I could ask my grandfather."

"Would he come?" asked Eyvind.

Olaf shrugged. "Alfgeir has sold me out before. There's no

reason to think he'll help me out of family loyalty. All I can do is ask. I could be there and back in a day."

"We'll ready Tromøy's fleet while you're gone," said Eyvind.

"Won't you stay the night?" asked Sonja.

"No, I'd better sail back right away. Thank you." Eyvind rose stiffly.

Olaf found himself beginning to take a liking to the trader. He was glad Åsa had someone who cared for her so much. She deserved it. "It will take Kalv a day to get my fleet ready to depart. He will have them ready by the time I return from seeing Alfgeir. I'll bring them to Tromøy."

"At least have something to eat before you sail off," Sonja insisted. "We have plenty left from the evening meal. Get your crew up here."

Relief showed in Eyvind's eyes. "Thank you, Lady. I will take you up on your kind offer." Eyvind called his crews to the hall where they ate a hasty meal.

CHAPTER 10

Sonja was not well pleased.

As she packed Olaf's sea chest, he could tell by the set of her shoulders she was upset.

"I must go." He put his arms around her. "Åsa's life depends on it."

Her shoulders slumped. "I know. I just wish you didn't have to go to war. You're so outnumbered. It's foolhardy to go against them."

"You know I have to. We must come to each other's defense if we are to survive the Danes."

"Damn those Danes!" she said, and gave him a fierce hug. "Why can't they leave us alone?"

Feeling torn between his obligations to Åsa and to his wife, Olaf rode down to the shore and boarded *Sea Dragon* with his crew. They sailed out of the harbor and headed north up the coast, past Gudrød's former hall at Borre, and across to the eastern side of the Fold to arrive at his grandfather's steading in midafternoon.

Alfgeir's kingdom of Vingulmark had been Olaf's mother's dowry when she wed Gudrød. After she died, Gudrød had retained the dowry. Alfgeir had probably been loath to go to war with his powerful son-in-law. But when Gudrød was killed, Alfgeir took the territory back from Olaf. As an untried new king with few allies, there had been nothing Olaf could do at the time. Since then, he'd gained support and attracted followers, but he did not want to challenge his powerful grandfather.

The old king's lookouts were good, for Alfgeir was waiting on the pier, mounted on a splendid Frankish warhorse, several hands taller than most Norse horses. The silver-gilt bridle mounts glimmered when the beast tossed its head.

Alfgeir himself was tall and fit, the only signs of age being his weathered face and the silver streaks among the blond. "Greetings, Olaf, king."

Olaf ignored the hint of mockery in Alfgeir's voice. "Greetings, Grandfather. It's been a long time."

His crew made fast to Alfgeir's impressive pier and disembarked. Olaf mounted the horse Alfgeir had provided and rode beside his grandfather up to the massive hall, the place where his mother had grown up. Odinssal rivaled both Skiringssal and Borre in size and magnificence, its massive roof shingled with wood, the four directions guarded by carved dragons.

Alfgeir pushed open the carved oak door and ushered Olaf into the hall, where the longfire burned. Ale and meat awaited them.

They toasted with excellent mead, redolent of honey and fall apples. Olaf was impressed with the preparations. His grandfather's young queen, Gudrun, looked to be a few years younger than Olaf. She seemed quiet and shy, but obviously efficient. When Olaf complimented her on the mead, she blushed and ducked her head.

"My wife knows her place," said Alfgeir. "Not like that Sonja of yours."

Olaf did not rise to the bait. He knew his grandfather thought him gullible and loved to lead him into verbal traps. He cast a sidelong glance at Gudrun and caught the young queen rolling her eyes. Alfgeir had outlived at least three wives, including Olaf's grandmother. He had sons younger than Olaf, and the old man showed no signs of slowing down.

Olaf ventured, "Grandfather, I am happy to see you looking so well."

Alfgeir bristled. "Are you surprised, boy? I'm old, but not yet in my dotage."

Just the reaction he'd hoped for. "You look strong and mighty, and ready for battle." Olaf could lay a few traps of his own.

"The pity is, I've bested every man in these parts worth fighting," Alfgeir bragged. He gave Olaf a disapproving glance. "Peace ages a man, makes him soft."

Olaf ignored the implied insult. "You could never go soft."

Alfgeir grinned at that remark.

After Gudrun poured the second cup of mead, Alfgeir got down to business. "What brings you to Odinssal, boy?"

Olaf took a deep breath and came right to the point. "I'm going after Horik."

Alfgeir spluttered into his cup. "The king of the Danes?"

Olaf nodded.

"Have you lost your mind? He's got the biggest fleet on the Skagerrak and the Kattegat combined."

"I know. But I fought his brothers and won."

"And he's killed them all or run them off. Horik is a ruthless bastard who murdered his own father. What possesses you, boy?"

Olaf took a breath and risked the truth. "He's taken Åsa." He cringed beneath his grandfather's glare.

"You're going to war over a woman?" Alfgeir exclaimed incredulously. "She's not even your wife! She turned you down!"

"She's my ally," Olaf said quietly.

Alfgeir continued to stare, mouth open. "And you want me to send my fleet with you?"

Olaf dangled the bait. "It's a good opportunity to go against Horik."

"Do you think I'm insane?"

"I think you're a strategic battle commander who recognizes an opportunity when it presents itself. I know you'd risk much to defeat Horik."

"If I could defeat him, I wouldn't be holed up in this cow-byre," Alfgeir scoffed. "What you are suggesting is suicide."

Just what Eyvind had said. Olaf shrugged. "Nevertheless, I am committed."

"You're a fool. I'll have no part in your reckless scheme."

Olaf set down his mead cup. "I didn't realize your liver had turned white." Silence fell in the hall at the insult. Alfgeir's face was purple.

"I'll take my leave, and trouble you no more." Olaf rose and bowed to Gudrun. "Lady, I thank you for your hospitality," he said, and walked away, aware that his early departure was as much an insult to her as his remark had been to his grandfather.

As he strode toward the door, his crew rose from the benches, abandoning their food and drink, and fell in behind him.

Gudrun escorted him to the door as befitted a good hostess. Her gaze met Olaf's, and he was glad she had apparently not taken insult. "My lord, I wish you protection and success in your brave venture."

Could that be approval he saw in her eyes? He bowed to her, then marched out the door and down to the ship where his crew wasted no time in casting off.

With a favorable wind, they made good time under sail across the Fold. Olaf stared morosely at the setting sun. He'd wasted a whole day for nothing.

They arrived at Skiringssal around midnight and found the hillside ablaze with torchlight.

Kalv was waiting for him on the pier with his horse.

"What's all this?" Olaf asked.

"Halfdan is missing. The entire steading has been out looking for him all day."

"When was he last seen?"

"In all the confusion of your departure, nobody realized he was gone until midday."

Olaf's stomach twisted as another worry piled on. Where could the boy be? It was not uncommon for Halfdan to spend the day away from the hall, usually with Ulf, but he was always back by evening. "I must go see Sonja and join the search. How are preparations going with the fleet?"

"We're ready to sail at first light," said Kalv.

Olaf nodded, relieved. He put a hand on Kalv's shoulder in gratitude. "Good man. My grandfather won't be joining us."

"It was well worth a try."

Olaf mounted his horse and rode up to the hall to find Sonja.

When he arrived, the yard was bright as daylight with folk carrying torches, scurrying about calling Halfdan's name.

Sonja rushed up to him. "Halfdan is missing!"

Olaf dismounted and took her in his arms. "Kalv told me. Don't fear, love," he said. "I'm sure he's wandered off and fallen asleep. We'll find him." He shook off his exhaustion and joined in the search.

Ulf was beside himself. "It's my fault," he said.

"How can it be your fault?" said Olaf.

The blacksmith hung his head. "I took him out one night for utiseta. I introduced him to the land spirits."

"You what?" said Sonja ominously.

Ulf did not meet her furious gaze. "He has displayed powers, and he must learn to control them. Spirits appear to him. I promised Åsa I would teach him. But now I fear it has gone awry."

"Do you think the vaettir have taken him?" Sonja's voice rose an octave.

Ulf looked as miserable as a man could look. “I don’t know. I never would have imagined they’d do such a thing.”

Olaf pitied the smith. He’d only been trying to do right by the boy. He laid a hand on Ulf’s shoulder. “Come, I’ll help you search.”

For hours they roamed the steading, calling Halfdan’s name, to no avail.

When the summer twilight had darkened so they could not see their way, Olaf called off the search.

Ulf came to Olaf with slumped shoulders. “I’ll sit out tonight.”

Olaf started to object, but he could see the smith was determined.

“I’ll try to contact the vaettir,” Ulf said. “Perhaps they will tell me where he’s gone.”

Or where they’ve taken him, thought Olaf. Sonja was red-eyed and exhausted. “We’ll have more luck in the daylight,” he said. “The boy will no doubt come when he’s hungry.” *If he’s alive.*

He led her to their chamber, where they tried to salvage a little sleep. He woke repeatedly throughout what remained of the night, Alfgeir’s mockery interspersed with worries about Halfdan.

When the boy did not appear for breakfast, Olaf’s fears reignited. Sonja was beside herself.

While they were poking at their porridge, Ulf dragged in and slumped on a bench.

“Did you have any luck?”

The smith shook his head in defeat. “The vaettir will not speak to me.” He stared at the floor for a while, then said, “Has anyone asked Rognvald where Halfdan is?”

The household left their breakfast in search of the younger boy. He’d been put to bed, but everyone had overlooked him in the search for Halfdan. Olaf feared his three-year-old son might be missing too. But they found him in his bed, hiding under the covers.

"Son," said Olaf. "Do you know where Halfdan is?"

Rognvald shook his head vigorously. "No! He said not to tell."

Olaf took the boy into his arms. "Your mother is very worried about him. He could be in danger. You need to tell us what you know."

The three-year-old stared at his parents, his lip quivering.

"Please tell us, Rognvald," Sonja pleaded. "I'm so afraid for him."

Rognvald burst into tears. "He went to save his Mama," he blurted.

"What? How? How did he go?"

"He went…on a boat."

"What boat?"

But Rognvald was crying in earnest now and would say no more.

Olaf and Sonja mounted up and rode to the harbor, where they turned the ships inside out, though each one had been searched the day before. There were few places a boy could hide on a longship.

A horrible thought struck Olaf.

It was far easier to hide on a knarr.

"He may have sailed with Eyvind. He could have hidden in *Far Traveler*'s hold to join the search for Åsa."

Sonja stared at him. "That sounds like exactly what Halfdan would do."

"I must go to Tromøy."

"The fleet is ready to sail," said Kalv.

Sonja nodded. "Go. We'll continue the search here. If you find Halfdan, send word to me. Then go rescue Åsa." She captured Olaf's gaze. "Be careful." She threw her arms around him.

Olaf closed his eyes and held her tight. "I know I leave Skiringssal in your capable hands."

"Come home to me!" she cried.

Olaf's throat thickened and he could not get words out. He nodded and kissed her.

He released her and strode to *Sea Dragon*. He boarded and took his place at the helm. "Raise oars!" he ordered.

The oars on every ship shot straight up in the air.

"Row!"

The oars came down, and the fleet rowed out of the harbor.

Olaf turned back for one last glimpse of Sonja, standing on the shore, watching him go.

HALFDAN KNEW there was nothing he could say to convince the grown-ups to take him with them. His mother needed him. Sometimes a boy had to take matters into his own hands.

While Sonja and the kitchen staff were busy feeding Eyvind and his crew, no one had noticed Halfdan slip out of the bower, followed by his blind wolf.

Keeping to the cover of the trees, boy and wolf had crept down the trail to the beach. They hid in the tall sea grass and watched the ship, making sure the entire crew had gone up to the hall.

All was quiet. Halfdan bade good-bye to the land spirits, making them promise not to tell anyone where he'd gone, then slipped past the watch and boarded the knarr. Fylgja followed, though the wolf was shivering with fear at the sound of the lapping water.

There were plenty of places to hide on the cargo ship, with its high sides and decked-over bow and stern. Halfdan crawled under the forward deck and burrowed into some bundles of sheepskins, and coaxed Fylgja in beside him. Halfdan stroked the wolf's head and murmured, "It's all right. We have to save Mama."

Fylgja's furry body was big and warm. Halfdan snuggled up

close. The sound of water lapping against the hull lulled boy and wolf to sleep.

Halfdan woke to the sound of footsteps thudding. For a moment he didn't know where he was. Then the ship rocked and he remembered. He was on *Far Traveler*, off to save his mother.

More thuds, and voices. Fylgja whined, and Halfdan stroked the wolf's soft fur. He reached out to the wolf with his mind. *Quiet, we must be very quiet.* He felt Fylgja settle under his hand.

Thudding feet sounded, as well as ropes being dragged aboard and coiled on the deck. Eyvind barked an order. Oars creaked in the tholes. The halyard rasped through the block as the sail was raised. Halfdan felt the ship surge forward as the sail caught the wind.

Soon the vessel gained a steady, rocking motion. The sound of water trickling against the hull soothed boy and wolf back to sleep.

~

Tromøy

Far Traveler arrived in Tromøy at dawn. Olvir and Jarl Borg called greetings from the beach. "What news?"

Eyvind said, "Halfdan had a dream about Åsa that confirms our suspicions. She's been taken by Horik. I'm sailing for Erritsø now."

"Alone?"

"I'm sailing ahead," said Eyvind. "Olaf has gone to ask his grandfather to join us against Horik. He'll bring his fleet here to join you."

Olvir shook his head. "Let's hope he succeeds. We have no hope of beating the Danes without his fleet. The ships will be ready to sail when he arrives, regardless. How will we find you once we get there?"

Eyvind said, "There's a beach market to the north of Erritsø called Høl where I may be able to find something out. Dozens of ships arrive in that market every day. Horik has many craftsmen there who produce fine goods, and they are traded for by merchants in knarrs just like mine. I'll blend in with the others. Nobody has better information than traders. If there's any news of Åsa, they'll know."

"I've been to the market at Høl," said Olvir. "I'll wait for Olaf to arrive with reinforcements, then we'll follow you and meet you there."

"We can meet at Høl, but hide the fleet in the deserted bay to the north, Sandbjerg Vig." Eyvind described the entrance to the bay. "Come to Høl with just one ship. These are Horik's waters, and I know he has spies among the merchants. If a fleet of foreign ships appears in Høl, word will get to him. After that, you must travel fast. Once you round Trelde Ness and approach the Little Belt, you'll be within Erritsø's sight. Horik can see a fleet coming for miles in every direction. There will be no element of surprise. He'll be ready for you."

Olvir said, "Let's hope Alfgeir comes through."

"If he doesn't, you'd best not come. If Horik's fleet is half as large as the rumors have it, you'll be vastly outnumbered. I have a better chance of sneaking in and spiriting her out of there on my own."

"If we arrive with a fleet of any size," said Olvir, "we can draw Horik out of his stronghold and give you a chance to rescue Åsa."

"Without Alfgeir's reinforcements, that would be suicide!" protested Jarl Borg.

"What choice do we have? Horik's going to kill her."

"You'll be leaving Tromøy undefended," said Eyvind.

"You forget," growled Jarl Borg. "I'll be here with my húskarlar. I may be an old man, but I'm not dead yet."

"I meant no offence," said Eyvind.

"It's suicide either way," said Jarl Borg. "If Olvir stays here, we're just waiting for Horik to attack us after he's eliminated you and Åsa. It's always best to take the initiative. This way gives us our best chance."

"There's no time to lose either way," said Eyvind. "Find me at Høl, and we'll make plans."

"The gods go with you," Olvir said.

"And with you," Eyvind replied. "Back water," he called to the oarsmen.

~

HALFDAN WOKE WITH A START. He was bundled in thick layers of sheepskin. Fylgja shivered beside him.

The ship had stopped moving. The trickle of water running along the hull had been replaced with shouts and the sound of the sail rattling down. Oars splashed in the water, and the ship began to move again, with a different rhythm than sailing.

Halfdan moved a sheepskin aside and peered out of his hiding place. The sky was just becoming light. *Far Traveler* had sailed all night. He recognized Tromøy's harbor. He was home! But Mama was not here. She was in danger.

Footsteps came closer, and Halfdan shrank back into his sheepskins. Eyvind shouted orders, telling the rowers to bring the ship into the shallows and hold there.

Fylgja whined. "Shh," Halfdan whispered, stroking the wolf's fur. "It's all right. We're going to find Mama." Fylgja ran a long tongue across Halfdan's face.

He heard Eyvind talk to someone on shore. "Halfdan had a dream about Åsa that confirms our suspicions. She's been taken by Horik. I'm sailing for Erritsø now."

Halfdan listened to the men make their plans.

The oars splashed as the rowers reversed their stroke away from the shore. The ship turned.

They were on their way to the land of the Danes, to find his mother.

Erritsø

GROA SAT IN HER CORNER, concentrating on her weaving. The goshawk preened on her perch. Åsa lay on the bed, held fast by the trance. Groa had barely been able to stop her hawk from killing the prisoner's fylgja, which would mean Åsa's death as well. Now the falcon was lost somewhere in the forest, injured. Perhaps dying. Horik would not be pleased.

The door slammed open, making Groa jump. "Wake up, woman," Horik shouted at the still form on the bed. When Åsa didn't move, he grabbed her arm and shook it. She made no response, and he let her arm fall limply on the bed.

Horik rounded on the sorceress. "What have you done?" he growled.

Groa's hands trembled. "Her fylgja arrived, and she entered its body and tried to escape. Hod gave chase and disabled her."

"What do you mean, escape? She's right here!"

"But her hugr is trapped in her fylgja. Had my hawk not caught her, she could have warned her people," Groa said defensively.

"Is she going to die?" Horik demanded.

Groa kept her voice noncommittal, though her stomach roiled. "If her fylgja survives, so will she."

"Where is her fylgja?"

Groa's reply came as a whisper. "The bird lies in the forest, injured."

The king's voice rose. "Is the woman going to stay this way?"

With effort, the völva said evenly, "I can keep her alive for a while, but she will remain in a trance unless her falcon brings back her hugr." *Or dies.*

Horik's voice came out as a howl. "I can't have a wedding feast with a corpse! I need her walking and talking. You find that bird and bring it back here. And you'd better hope they both live. Now take some men and go find that bird!"

He cursed and stormed out of the bower, calling for his captains.

Groa leaned over Åsa's still form, her brow creased with anxiety. "You breathe, and so your fylgja lives." She trickled honey water into Åsa's mouth, taking care not to cause the unconscious woman to choke. "This will keep you alive for now. But how long?"

Groa bustled about the room, collecting her staff and cloak, putting items into her belt pouch. She strapped her leather pad on her shoulder and tethered her goshawk to it. "Must find the falcon," she grumbled. "The king must have a bride. And Odin must have a sacrifice."

DEEP IN THE FOREST, the falcon stirred. Her left chest muscle twinged. She tried an experimental flap, and the pain that shot through her was profound. She could not fly, that was certain.

The hawk might come back any time and finish her off. In her condition, Stormrider could not fight off an attack by the larger bird. She must hide.

The falcon struggled to her feet. She picked her way through the forest litter with painstaking effort, pushing herself to keep going and get some distance from where the hawk had left her. She took care not to leave a trail, no bent twigs or crushed leaves that could lead an enemy to her. She was no longer bleeding, that was a blessing—at least she could not be tracked that way.

Finally she came to a hollow tree trunk that she deemed far

enough away. She crawled inside the cavity and burrowed under the fallen leaves at the base. She longed to be higher, but that was not possible.

Her predator's instincts calmed, realizing she was safe. The falcon carried Åsa inside, and that part of her yearned to return to her human body. The bird knew where her mistress was with every fiber of her being. It was imperative she get to her. But Stormrider would have to fly to reach her, and she could not fly with her injury. Sleep was what she needed to heal, and healing was what she needed to go to Åsa.

She tucked her beak under her wing and slept.

CHAPTER 11

Tromøy

By early afternoon, Olaf's dozen ships entered Tromøy's harbor.

Olvir and Jarl Borg met him on the beach. "No reinforcements?" Olvir asked.

"My grandfather declined to join us," Olaf reported tersely. "Is Halfdan here?"

"Halfdan?"

"I think he stowed away on *Far Traveler*."

Olvir stared. "Eyvind departed for Erritsø at dawn."

"Alone?" Olaf asked incredulously.

"Yes. He's going ahead to do a little spying. He'll see if he can find out anything about Åsa." Olvir shook his head. "Why do you think the boy was on *Far Traveler*?"

"He disappeared yesterday. The whole steading spent the day and most of the night searching for him, and he's nowhere to be found. His wolf is missing as well. *Far Traveler* is the only place they could have hidden. We think he may have overheard our plans and stowed away to go after Åsa."

Olvir said, "There was no sign of Halfdan on the ship when they stopped here. If he was on board, he was well hidden. I'm pretty sure Eyvind didn't know he was aboard either, and he certainly didn't get off here."

"We'll never catch *Far Traveler* before they get to Erritsø, and even if we did, there's no time to bring the boy back to safety and still rescue Åsa. Loki knows what Horik will do to her."

"Eyvind's not going to Erritsø. He's going to Høl, a beach market to the north of Erritsø, to get information about Horik's defenses from the merchants. Halfdan should be safe enough there. When we arrive, we're going to hide the fleet in Sandbjerg Vig, a bay to the north, and send one ship in to see what Eyvind has found out, then make a plan of attack from there."

Olaf nodded. He studied the fleet. "It would be helpful to know the actual size of Horik's fleet and his forces. I crammed as many warriors aboard my ships as they can hold. I bring four hundred and fifty seasoned fighters."

Olvir and Jarl Borg exchanged worried glances. "Åsa's nine ships carry a total of three hundred and fifty warriors between them."

Olaf shook his head. It was a paltry fleet to sail against the Danes' might. Twenty-one ships against Horik's rumored forty. Eight hundred warriors to fight more than a thousand.

Olvir said, "Our attack will at least provide a distraction. If we can draw Horik and his warriors away from his stronghold and keep his forces engaged, Eyvind will find a way into the fortress, find Åsa, and free her. We'll have to stay out of Horik's reach."

"We've beaten the Danes when we were outnumbered before," Olaf reminded him. "Let's get underway." The odds were against surviving this, but they had to try. He owed that to Åsa, and to their son.

~

Halfdan woke to feel the ship bowling over the waves. Fylgja whined, and Halfdan hugged the wolf, whispering soothingly in his ear to be quiet. Halfdan's stomach growled and he had to pee. Fylgja must need that too. But he didn't dare show himself. If he did, Eyvind would take him back home. He had to stay hidden long enough that it would be too late for Eyvind to turn back. He wasn't sure how long that would be, but he thought if he waited until night, it would be safe.

He stroked Fylgja's soft fur. Just a little longer, he thought. The wolf licked his cheek with a dry tongue.

~

Far Traveler was making good time. With a fair wind, it was a two-day sail to Høl. The next few hours would be easy sailing across the Skagerrak. Eyvind sent Thora to wake Svein.

Svein got out of his hudfat. He drew a cup of water from the barrel, then ambled over and took the helm.

"I'm going to sleep for a few hours. Wake me if you need me." Eyvind crawled into his hudfat and dozed off instantly.

He was awakened from a sound sleep when the air was rent with screams. Eyvind scrambled out of his hudfat. The cries came from the hold beneath the foredeck. Motioning the crew to stand back, he burrowed in and pulled the sheepskins away, revealing Halfdan and his wolf huddled in the depths. Fylgja growled in warning.

"Halfdan!" Eyvind cried. "Never fear, Fylgja, I won't do you or your young master any harm. Let me help." He held out his hand for the wolf to sniff. Fylgja settled into tense watchfulness while Eyvind cautiously pulled away the rest of the skins. With a wary eye on the wolf, Eyvind crawled in and took the sobbing boy into his arms. "What are you doing here?"

"Mama's asleep inside Stormrider, and she can't get out. Stormrider's hurt."

Eyvind's apprehension grew. "And where is Stormrider?"

Halfdan spoke between sobs. "She's lost in the woods. She got in a fight with another bird. The other bird hurt her, and Mama is trapped inside Stormrider."

"Another bird attacked her?" Eyvind asked in confusion.

Halfdan nodded. "Yes. The bad witch is searching for her. I have to find Mama."

"You're a brave boy. We'll find your mother." He'd thought the boy safe in Skiringssal. Instead, he'd brought the heir of Tromøy within reach of Horik's clutches.

Eyvind looked around. It was late afternoon. They were nearly across the Skagerrak. If he turned back to take Halfdan home, he'd lose an entire day or more. Time Åsa could ill afford.

Halfdan and the wolf gulped down the food and water Eyvind gave them. After a second cup of water, the boy was strangely quiet as he sat beside the helmsman, Fylgja cowering beside him. Eyvind had never seen Halfdan so serious.

They made it across the Skagerrak before sunset, with enough daylight left to pass the treacherous Skagan Point, where the powerful currents of the Skagerrak clashed with the opposing ones of the Kattegat. Most ships took a safer route through the sheltered waters of the Limfjord, but that would add at least two days' travel—time they did not have.

Near Skagan Point, they hove to, trailing a buoy to indicate when the tide was slack. Two other vessels were also waiting for the tide to turn, but to Eyvind's relief they kept their distance. He had a story ready, but he was glad he didn't need to use it just yet.

The buoy line went slack, and Eyvind ordered the sweeps. They safely rounded the point under oar, then headed down the Kattegat with its treacherous waters, fraught with skerries and islets. The breeze was light enough that Eyvind risked setting the sail, though he kept the oarsmen standing by to maneuver. With a sharp-eyed sailor on the bow to point out the dangers, they picked their way through the erratic currents and hidden rocks.

They kept going until the twilight sky had darkened so they could no longer make out the hazards. Eyvind was anxious to reach the market place, but he grudgingly put into a deserted cove, where they anchored the ship. The crew was tired from the long day's sail, and they ate a quiet meal on board. Halfdan was still uncharacteristically subdued, but he seemed content to stay beside his wolf.

That night Eyvind had the awning raised and ordered the crew to sleep onboard to ensure an early start. Everyone fell instantly asleep, including Eyvind and Halfdan.

After a few hours' sleep, Eyvind woke at dawn and roused his crew. They stowed the awning and sculled out of the cove to a light breeze that enabled them to raise the sail. For a few hours they made good time, until around midday when the wind died and they took to the oars.

Far Traveler rounded Djursland Peninsula and wended through the hazards that littered the coast. Eyvind passed Sandbjerg Vig and put into Høl, a lively beach market in a sheltered hook of land, six miles north of Horik's fortress. By sea Erritsø was separated from the market by Trelde Ness, a point that jutted out into the Kattegat.

Høl was distant enough that news of him would not travel too quickly to Horik. However, the market would be teeming with traders who might have recent news of Horik. If there were any rumors about Åsa, he would hear them there.

Like most other traders with bulky knarrs, Eyvind set his bow anchor offshore, then set the stern anchor on the beach, enabling them to warp into shore for trading but return to deep water for the night.

When the ship was secured, Eyvind climbed down the boarding plank and set off toward the market. Halfdan trotted at his heels, followed by the blind wolf.

"I'm sorry, Halfdan, you can't come with me."

"I can help you find Mama," the boy protested.

"You and that wolf would attract too much attention." Eyvind's skin crept at the thought of the boy so close to Horik. There was no one here to recognize him, Eyvind reminded himself, but even so, a boy with a blind wolf for a pet would definitely raise talk that would inevitably find its way to Horik.

Halfdan's face turned red, and he blinked back tears. Eyvind knelt and put his hand on the boy's shoulder. "When I find out where your mother is, you will help me rescue her. I promise. But right now I am just talking to people. I don't want anyone to know we're looking for her. So can you stay here with Svein and Thora, and guard the ship for me?"

Halfdan gulped and nodded.

"Thank you. I'm counting on you," said Eyvind. He rose and watched the boy scramble back on the ship. He gave Svein a nod, and the sailor took Halfdan to the stern, where he gave him a lesson in splicing rope.

Eyvind set off along the beach. Traders were a friendly, garrulous lot, avid carriers of news and gossip, and Eyvind learned a great deal about the goings-on in Frisia and Gotland, but little about Erritsø. He ventured up to the boardwalk where the local craftsmen had their booths. There were the usual combmakers, beadmakers, metalworkers, and weavers.

He stopped to chat with a particularly talkative silversmith. After Eyvind bought the man a cup of ale, the smith confirmed that Horik was in residence at his hall, and there were about forty warships anchored in Gudsø Vig. The rest of the Danish fleet, which the smith could not number, was out raiding and collecting taxes, in some cases both. The division between the two pursuits was a bit blurred. "Folk pay Horik for protection, but that protection is like as not to be from Horik's own men." The smith gave Eyvind a meaningful grin and drained his cup.

Eyvind was well pleased with the smith's information. Knowing how many ships Olaf and Olvir would face was invaluable.

Late in the afternoon, satisfied that he had wrested the last bit of gossip from the craftsfolk, Eyvind headed back to *Far Traveler*. No one had mentioned a captive queen at the fortress, but he did not expect that to be common knowledge.

At the ship, Halfdan rushed up to him, holding out several lengths of rope with loops and knots.

Svein grinned at Eyvind. "The boy's become an expert in just an afternoon," he said.

Eyvind admired the various splices and knot work, exclaiming over particularly well-turned splices. Halfdan beamed at the praise, his worries forgotten for the moment.

But that night, the boy had bad dreams again. Eyvind woke throughout the night, listening to Halfdan moan in his sleep.

~

Tromøy

THE COMBINED fleets of Tromøy and Skiringssal set out across the Skagerrak early the next morning. The fair wind held, and they rounded Skagan Point and entered the Kattegat before nightfall. When the long summer twilight became too dark to navigate the hazards, they anchored in the lee of an islet for the night and set out as soon as the sky lightened. At noon they rounded the Djursland Peninsula and followed the coast south until they reached Sandbjerg Vig, where the fleet anchored, out of sight of Erritsø and Horik's spies.

Olaf continued on in *Sea Dragon,* south to the beach market that sheltered in the bight formed by the sharp headland, Trelde Ness.

He spotted Eyvind's knarr, anchored close to shore. As he drew closer, he glimpsed a raven-haired child romping about the ship with a canine at his heels. Halfdan and his wolf. Relief flooded Olaf, making his knees weak for an instant.

Sea Dragon pulled alongside the knarr and rafted up. The boy bounded up to him, excited to show off his ropework.

"You should not have run away," Olaf said sternly. "Sonja and I have been sick with worry. All of Skiringssal has been searching for you."

"I have to find Mama," Halfdan said firmly. "She's in danger."

Olaf shook his head. At least the boy would be safe here with *Far Traveler*'s crew, far from the sea battle he'd be engaging in with Horik.

Eyvind's report of the Dane's forces filled Olaf with dismay. "Forty ships. That's double our number."

"You don't have to beat him," Eyvind went on. "You don't have to storm his fortress. If you can divert Horik's forces away long enough for me to find Åsa and get her out, that will be enough. Just keep your ships out of his reach."

Olaf nodded grimly, knowing it was easier said than done.

Darkness was falling, so he decided to spend the night ashore at *Far Traveler*'s camp. He sat up late with Eyvind, planning the operation, Halfdan and his wolf curled up at his side.

Eyvind's voice was filled with optimism. "We need a signal to let you know when I have freed Åsa, so you can retreat. Something you can see from Little Belt. A fire..."

"Horik's signal fires will be lit as soon as they sight our fleet," said Olaf. "How will I know it's yours?"

Eyvind gave it some thought. "I have a length of red cloth in my hold. As soon as you depart tomorrow, I'll set out overland for Horik's stronghold. It will only take me a couple of hours on foot, then I'll hide where I can watch the fortress until you engage Horik's fleet. Hopefully once you've engaged with Horik's forces, the signal men will leave to join the battle. Once I free Åsa, I'll climb the tower and fly the red banner. That will be your signal to disengage and get out of there. I'll bring Åsa here to the ship, and we'll meet back at Sandbjerg Vig, where your fleet is anchored now."

Olaf nodded, though he did not feel as confident as Eyvind sounded. "Horik will pursue us."

Eyvind's face fell. "It's a daunting challenge. I won't blame you if you refuse."

"What choice do we have? We have to try to save her."

Both men fell silent, staring at the fire.

"We should get some sleep," said Eyvind. "Let me get you an extra hudfat." He brought a sheepskin over and laid it out by the fire. Olaf crawled in, bringing his sleeping son with him.

"Good luck, brother," Eyvind said softly as he climbed into his own hudfat.

In the morning Olaf crawled out of his hudfat, careful not to wake Halfdan. Fylgja opened one eye. Olaf stroked the old wolf's head and whispered, "Wish me luck."

He roused his crew, and they shoved off to rejoin the rest of the fleet at Sandbjerg Vig.

Olvir took the size of Horik's fleet stoically. "We've beaten the Danes when we were outnumbered before," he said, reminding Olaf of his own words. "We'll have to reduce his numbers enough so that pursuit won't be an attractive option. When we flee, if we scatter in different directions, we have a better chance of survival."

Olaf called the crews together on the shore. Taking a deep breath, he filled his voice with a confidence he didn't feel. "We're going to engage an enemy with superior numbers. It won't be the first time we've fought and won against a bigger force. We can do it again. Each one of you is worth ten Danes."

He paused while the sailors cheered.

"Our goal is to cut down the enemy forces quickly, then get away as fast as possible. The enemy will pursue us. We'll have to fight a running battle. We can't let the enemy get close enough to board. We have to pick them off at a distance and make them unwilling to close with us. Archers will be key, as will the oarsmen, and the shieldmen."

A murmur went through the crowd. The crews sounded confident and willing. Hope flickered in Olaf's chest.

They got underway, rowing the longships through the shifting currents along the coast. Though the distance was only a few hours' row, it was tense work, daylight work.

They rounded Trelde Ness in the early afternoon and entered the Little Belt.

As they passed, signal fires flared, alerting Horik of their arrival.

~

Erritsø forest

STORMRIDER SENSED the hawk in the forest, searching for her. She had to return to Åsa before her enemy found her.

She roused, testing her wings. Pain shot through her chest, but the bones and muscles felt sound.

Stormrider flapped her wings and lofted into the air. The bird was willing, but her wounds drained her strength, and she was forced to light in a treetop to rest.

When she felt her strength return, the falcon launched from the tree, the pain thrumming through her chest. She glided on the breeze as far as she could manage until she was spent, then landed in another treetop to rest again. From treetop to treetop she made her way through the forest. The progress was excruciatingly slow for a bird built for speed, and she feared she wouldn't make it to the fortress before the sorceress returned.

At last the silver-gilt dragons of the hall roof glinted among the trees. The falcon took heart and launched herself once again toward her mistress.

There was a rush of wind behind her, the flap of powerful wings. Stormrider swiveled her head to glimpse Groa's goshawk, gaining fast.

CHAPTER 12

Eyvind wound the length of red fabric around his waist, then armed himself with his seax and an axe tucked in his belt. That was all the weaponry he could carry. He was in no condition to fight. Subterfuge was his only hope to free Åsa. He must get into the fortress unseen, find her, and get her out again without meeting any men-at-arms, for he would lose the encounter.

"Let me come with you," said Svein.

"No. Thank you for offering, but I must travel alone. I have to attract as little attention as possible."

Eyvind slung a waterskin across his body and accepted a small pouch of flatbread and salt cod from Dagny. As he prepared to leave, he was relieved to see Halfdan still asleep in Olaf's hudfat by the fire, the wolf dozing at his side. Eyvind hated to sneak away from the boy, but he wanted to avoid the inevitable conflict when the child insisted on going with him. If he had to tie Halfdan up to keep him here, he would. He was relieved it wouldn't come to that.

~

HALFDAN WAS careful not to open his eyes when Eyvind departed. He forced himself to wait until he was sure Eyvind was out of sight. While the others were still asleep, he roused Fylgja, and they silently slipped away.

Once they were away from the ship, he knelt and spoke into the blind wolf's ear. "Find Eyvind."

Fylgja put his nose to the ground and searched around. After a few moments, he picked up the scent and set off.

Halfdan followed, looking carefully around him. A squawking jay perched in the shrubbery and chittering squirrels seemed to greet him.

~

Erritsø

CIAN HAD BEEN WATCHING the king ponder a losing move, and the Irish slave was worried about how to ensure Horik won without being obvious. If the king lost, Cian was dead. If Horik realized that his opponent was letting him win, Cian was just as dead. While the Danish king's was not a brilliant mind, a lifetime of the Danish court's intrigue had made him conniving and suspicious. Cian was at a loss as to how to survive this deadly game when the lookout burst into the hall.

"My lord, the signal fire is lit. A fleet of ships is making its way up the Little Belt," gasped the lad, out of breath from running the half-mile from the coastal lookout.

Horik's hand hovered above a black glass playing piece. "How many ships?"

The lookout calmed his breathing and found his voice. "Twenty-one, Lord."

Horik stroked his beard, the game piece forgotten in his hand. Cian cautiously exhaled.

Horik snorted. "Twenty-one ships against my forty. They

must be insane." He signaled his ship's captains. "Crew up our fleet. We'll make short work of them."

"But Lord, that will leave the fortress undermanned," his second-in-command objected.

"Did I ask for your opinion? They'll never get to the fortress. We'll annihilate the fools. Ready the ships." Horik rose, calling for his brynja.

Cian got quickly to his feet and scuttled away. He pitied the oncoming fleet. Horik would surely decimate them, but he was grateful that their appearance had solved his dilemma and given him the chance he'd been waiting for to escape. Groa had set out this morning with her hawk and two warriors on some mysterious mission. From the food and drink they carried, they did not plan to return soon. That meant the Norse queen was likely alone and unguarded.

He hurried to the place where the steward kept the harp. Cian grabbed the leather bag and strapped it to his back.

Now to keep his promise.

GROA'S HAWK was gaining on Stormrider. The goshawk was in her element, hunting at lower altitudes where her shorter wing-span and greater strength enabled her to dodge limbs and tree trunks as she zig-zagged through the forest.

Stormrider knew the only way to escape the bigger bird was to climb. She spiraled up in the air, seeking air currents to lift her. Each flap of her wings sent pain searing through her chest.

At some point the goshawk, unused to hunting at high altitudes, had stopped climbing. Stormrider glimpsed her enemy flying below, pacing her.

Stormrider beat her way into the clouds to hide from her pursuer. Her body felt heavy as lead. Her wing muscles ached with every movement, but she kept going, putting more distance between her and the hawk.

After flying several miles through the clouds, her instinct told her it was time to emerge from cover. As she dropped below the clouds, the rooftops of Erritsø appeared, the gilded dragons glinting in the sun.

By now the pain was so intense she feared she was going to pass out. As her vision went dark, she folded her wings and dove for the bower where Åsa lay, aiming for the smokehole. She drifted in and out of consciousness.

Stormrider jerked fully awake to see the roof coming up fast. Her wings shot out to slow her fall a fraction too late. She hit the roof hard and rolled.

The falcon tumbled through the smokehole and landed on the bed beside Åsa.

The door hinges creaked. Footsteps shuffled through the rushes to the bed.

Åsa's hugr leaped from the bird into her body. Her eyes flew open.

The Irish slave stood over her. "Hurry, we must escape now," he whispered. "An enemy fleet is on its way, and Horik has gone out to meet them, taking most of his warriors with him. Now is our chance!"

Åsa struggled to a sitting position. Pain shot through her chest muscles and made her cry out.

"What's wrong with you? Can you walk?"

"I'll be all right. Help me up."

Cian put her shoes on her feet, then helped her stand. Åsa clutched Stormrider to her chest. The falcon was unconscious, but she could feel the bird's heart patter fast. The ache in her own chest muscles told her of Stormrider's injuries.

"Leave the bird," he said.

"No. The falcon comes with us."

There was no time to argue. Åsa slipped Stormrider inside

her tunic to free her hands and followed the Irishman to the door. He opened it and peered into the deserted yard. "This way," he whispered.

They skirted the wall, staying to the shadows, but the yard was deserted.

"What's happening?" Åsa whispered.

"A fleet of very foolhardy warriors are sailing up the Little Belt, bent on attacking a force twice their size. I pity them, but they've given us a chance. Horik has ordered all his fighters out to annihilate the enemy. It won't take long, so we must hurry."

Olvir! It had to be Tromøy's fleet, perhaps Olaf's too. Fear jolted her. They were sacrificing themselves to save her.

"Come on!"

Åsa had no way to stop them. The least she could do was to escape and make sure their sacrifice was not in vain. And maybe she would find a way to save them too.

She stumbled along behind Cian, gradually regaining command of her body. The Irish slave led her along the outer wall of the main hall to the side door. They entered the cavernous room, now utterly deserted. The benches were empty, the longfire burned down to coals. The weapons and shields were gone from the walls.

Cian led her to the vacant high seat, but instead of mounting the dais, they skirted the platform. Behind it was a dark, narrow aisle between the dais and the wall.

"There's a trap door in the floor," said Cian. Åsa could see nothing in the dim light, but she heard his fingers scrabbling around for a few seconds.

He grunted in satisfaction. Wood creaked, and she heard rustling and scraping.

"I'm in a hole below you," he said. "You have to step down into it." He took hold of Åsa's foot and pulled it down. She gasped as her foot met air where the floor should have been.

"There are iron rungs on the wall. Feel this one?" He guided her foot to the first rung. "I'll stand below you and help you down."

Åsa let the Irishman steady her and guide her other foot onto the rung. She bent down and gripped the hatch framework and stepped farther into the hole. Her foot found the next rung. She climbed down, three more rungs, pain shooting through her chest as she hung on.

When her feet touched the bottom, she let out her breath. They stood in a narrow passage that vanished into darkness. As her eyes adjusted to the gloom, she could make out the stout logs that braced the earthen walls.

"Stay here a moment," said the Irish thrall. "I have to close the hatch to make sure no one follows us."

Cian climbed up the rungs again. The trap door thudded closed, leaving her in complete darkness. The air smelled musty, earthy. Her neck hairs prickled as she remembered the dark valleys of the Hel road. A spider's web brushed across her face and tangled in her hair. She tamped down the panic that rose in her chest, fighting the urge to climb back up the iron rungs and run out into the light.

Cian's calloused hand gripped hers. "Let's go!"

The contact gave her courage, and she let him lead her into the darkness. With her free hand, she felt her way along the dank, damp walls. The tunnel narrowed and twisted. In places the overhead was so low they had to walk stooped over.

Cian stopped, and Åsa collided with him. She put out her hand and felt a solid wall in front of them. Panic choked her as she remembered being trapped in the blackness of Niflheim.

"There should be another set of rungs at this end," Cian muttered, his hands scrabbling over the rough wall.

Åsa swallowed her fear and put her hands out, running them across the surface in front of her. Her fingers made contact with a rough iron rung protruding from the wall. "Here."

Cian moved her gently aside. "I'll climb up first. Wait here while I open the cover. That should let in a little light so you can see your way."

Åsa waited, listening to the rustle of Cian's feet as he climbed the rungs. She heard a scraping sound and he grunted.

More scraping and grunting. "Something's blocking the cover," he said. "I'm going to have to apply more force. You'll have to support me so I can get some leverage without falling off the rungs."

Åsa put her hands out to explore the darkness in front of her. Her fingers found Cian's calves, about chest high. She wrapped her arms around them, bracing him with her body.

The Irishman grunted as he heaved at the cover. "There must be a weight on the cover. I'm not sure I can shift it."

Suddenly the cover was lifted and daylight flooded the passage.

Åsa choked down the scream that welled up in her throat.

Groa peered down at them. "What have we here?"

CHAPTER 13

The Little Belt

Olaf steered *Sea Dragon* into the narrow, serpentine waterway of the Little Belt. Olvir's and Kalv's ships flanked him. Behind them the fleets of Skiringssal and Tromøy sailed in loose formation.

As they passed under a bluff, another warning fire flared. High above them Horik's fortress brooded, its dark timbers menacing and grim. Olaf was impressed with the Dane's choice of the site. The elevation would enable lookouts to watch the land and sea for miles around.

Sea Dragon rounded a bend, and Olaf glimpsed a mast. As he watched, ship after ship spilled out of a hidden cove until the Little Belt was jammed with a forest of spars. Olaf swallowed hard and gave the signal to continue.

In this narrow waterway, there was only enough room for half a dozen ships to pass side-by-side without running aground. Olvir brought *Ran's Lover* alongside *Sea Dragon*. Kalv, in command of *Sea Steed*, one of Olaf's best warships, came up on the other side.

"Here they come," said Olvir.

The enemy vanguard clogged the narrowing channel. Olaf's stomach twisted. There was no hope of defeating that fleet.

"This is far enough," said Olaf.

"Agreed," said Olvir. Kalv nodded his approval.

He raised his fist. "Hold!" Olvir and Kalv echoed his order.

The rowers plied their oars, backing water to keep the double-ended ships stationary.

"Loose!" came the call from the Danes. A flight of arrows bristled in the air.

"Shields!" roared Olaf. The warriors flung up their shields, forming a roof over themselves and the oarsmen. Arrows thwacked into wood as the volley hit.

The enemy ships narrowed the range, and their prow men hurled javelins. Shields shattered, men screamed. Cries rent the air as warriors fell. The injured dropped their shields, which were snatched up by others and hastily flung up to fill in gaps.

"Oarsmen, hold steady. Archers and spearmen, fire at will," Olaf ordered. "Shieldmen, maintain cover."

Tromøy's warriors sent back a volley of spears and arrows. Screams echoed from the enemy, confirming they took a toll.

Despite their losses, the Danes closed the distance. Grappling hooks flew. As the claws latched on, the Norse crews slashed the lines in a desperate bid to stay free.

"Nock!" cried the Dane commander. Olaf marked him, his brown beard and ruddy cheeks under his helm.

"Shield forts!" Olaf shouted. The warriors on the foredecks joined their shields in solid walls and roofs while the enemy missiles hailed down.

As they waited out the storm of spears, Olaf watched the Dane commander. The man looked up, and their gazes locked. Olaf stared into fierce, icy blue eyes. Familiar eyes.

Gooseflesh rose on the back of his neck. He'd seen them before, blazing with the same battle rage. Rorik's eyes.

But Rorik was dead. Olaf was facing his brother, King Horik.

The two commanders glared at each other across the expanse of water that separated them. Fury rose in Olaf's chest.

"Loose!" cried Horik.

The hail of arrows forced Olaf's crew to take cover, enabling the enemy to grapple *Sea Dragon*. Now they tried to penetrate Olaf's defenses. Danes crowded the rails and tried to climb over the gunnels while Olaf's crew jabbed spears and seaxes between their shields to keep them at bay.

The high prow of the Danish king's ship loomed over *Sea Dragon*. Enemies climbed up to their figurehead and dropped onto *Sea Dragon*'s deck. Olaf's shield wall maneuvered to face them, attempting to fend off the boarders with blades thrust between their shields.

The Danes swarmed onto *Sea Dragon*.

Erritsø forest

GROA STEPPED ASIDE, and a burly man-at-arms took her place. He reached down, gripped Cian by the arm, and yanked him out of the hole. Åsa tried to back up but before she could move, another warrior grabbed her arm, wrenching her sore shoulder as he dragged her out.

They were in a clearing in the forest. The fortress could be glimpsed through the trees, a short distance away. Groa stood dwarfed by the two big men who gripped Åsa and Cian. The völva's goshawk perched on her leather-clad shoulder. The hawk jerked her head toward Åsa and gave a cry. At the sound, Stormrider roused inside Åsa's tunic.

Groa soothed her bird with a tidbit. "Good work. You've found the falcon. Rest now, my sweet."

One of the brawny men gripped Åsa firmly as she tried to

wrest herself free. The other man-at-arms had his hands full with the wildly struggling Cian. Groa unfastened a length of rope from the belt of one of the warrior's and approached the Irishman. He thrashed against the Dane's arms like a salmon in a net, but his captor managed to hold Cian's hands together while the sorceress bound his wrists.

Groa drew her knife and cut the end of the rope. She bore down on Åsa, who bucked against the Dane's hold. Åsa twisted in his arms and glared up into his eyes. "Let me go!" she cried, lacing her voice with galdr.

The big man's grip slackened ever so slightly, and she jerked away.

"Seize her, you idiot!" Groa barked. The galdr power in the völva's voice stopped Åsa in her tracks. The Dane immediately enveloped her in an iron grasp, holding her wrists while the sorceress tied them firmly and cut the rope.

While the men-at-arms held their prisoners, Groa fashioned the remaining length of rope into two nooses with slip knots. She flung the loops over the captives' heads, lashing the two of them together in a slave chain.

"You can't escape me that easily," said Groa triumphantly, tightening the nooses around their necks. "I was looking for your fylgja, but I see you've found her already." She nodded toward Stormrider, the falcon's head peeking out of Åsa's tunic. "Horik would be unhappy that you left so early. You must come back with me."

She handed the rope end to one of the men, and he gave it a jerk. Cian was first in line, and the rope tightened around his throat, forcing him to move forward or be strangled. Åsa's noose tightened when the Irishman moved, compelling her to follow. She shoved her fingers under the rope around her throat, but her attempts did little to relieve the constriction. The other Dane brought up the rear, prodding Åsa with his spear point.

As they walked, the throb in Åsa's shoulder eased to a dull ache. The damage her captor had done did not seem to be serious, and fortunately it was her left shoulder. She could fight if she got the opportunity. But how could she make that opportunity? She eyed the Dane who led them. He gripped the rope in one hand, his spear in the other. A seax was sheathed on his belt. He wore no helmet or armor, only a padded vest with a hard coat of varnish. She could charge him from behind, grab his seax with her bound hands and draw it from its sheath. But all he had to do was yank on the rope and choke her. He would still have his spear, and she would be vulnerable to the spearman behind them. Her plan required coordination with Cian.

As if reading her mind, Cian glanced over his shoulder and cut his eyes toward the man leading them, then looked back toward the spearman who brought up the rear. Åsa gave a slight nod in answer.

They had not gone much further when Cian stumbled. Åsa lurched into him and he reached out to steady her, giving her a wide-eyed stare and waggling his eyebrows meaningfully.

The Danes recovered control, and they walked a ways in obedient rhythm. Suddenly, Cian shrieked a piercing war cry. The lead Dane stopped and turned toward him, and the Irishman lashed out with a vicious kick to his groin. The man stumbled to his knees with a cry while Cian jerked the slave-line out of his hands. The spearman behind them charged forward to help his fellow, and Åsa stuck out a foot to trip him. He collapsed on the fallen man, who was still screaming from Cian's kick.

Before their captors could recover, Åsa and Cian dashed into the forest, Groa's curses echoing behind them.

"Get after them!" she cried.

As Åsa and Cian ran, they slipped the now slack slave-line from their necks.

"Hold on to the rope," said Cian. "We may need it."

They put some distance between them and the guards, and then the Irishman pulled Åsa into the brush. The sound of pursuit grew louder.

Cian put one end of the slave rope in her hands. "Take a turn around this tree trunk."

The crashing in the brush came closer.

Cian dashed across their trail to another tree and took a turn around the trunk at chest-height. Åsa quickly looped her end around the tree beside her. She yanked the line taut as the big Dane crashed out of the brush and barreled into the rope.

At the same time the Irishman jerked his end of the rope hard, and the man's feet went out from under him. As he hit the ground, Åsa and Cian were on him. Cian kneeled on the struggling Dane's chest while Åsa yanked his seax from its holder.

The Dane had gotten his breath back, and he opened his mouth to yell. Gripping the seax awkwardly in her bound hands, Åsa brought down the sharp blade and sliced his throat before he could make a sound. Her aim was true, and arterial blood sprayed her face.

Blinking away the blood, she sawed through Cian's bonds with the seax, then handed him the knife, and he did the same for her. They crouched in the brush, waiting for the next one.

EYVIND TURNED his head at the sound of shouts and crashing in the undergrowth. He drew his sword. A man-at-arms blundered into him. The Dane thrust his spear at Eyvind's midsection.

Eyvind saw the spear, and his split-second lead enabled him to dodge the thrust. He whirled on his attacker. The Dane recovered fast and jabbed the spear again. Eyvind fended off the blow with his sword, but the pain in his back nearly felled him. A warm trickle of blood told him he'd reopened his wound. His head felt light, and his legs wobbled.

The Dane rammed his spear again, and Eyvind dodged. The spearhead glanced off his shoulder with a force that shot down his sword arm and numbed his hand. Eyvind gritted his teeth and gripped his weapon with both hands, raising it to meet the next blow. His wound burned. The Dane thrust his spear, and Eyvind blocked it again with his sword, but the force of the strike threw him off balance. He stumbled to his knees, chest heaving.

The Dane had drawn back his spear to finish Eyvind when rustling in the undergrowth made the assailant turn his head.

With a shout, Halfdan appeared, wooden sword in hand. The boy rushed the big Dane, Fylgja sticking to his side like pine sap. Eyvind reached up to stop him, but the boy ran under the Dane's guard and whacked at his legs with the wooden sword. The Dane, focused on killing Eyvind, got his legs tangled up in the wooden blade and staggered. Halfdan jerked his sword back and danced out of the way as the big man fell.

In an instant Fylgja was on the Dane, savaging his throat. The man let out a scream that dissolved into a gurgle.

"Halfdan! What are you doing here?" Eyvind cried.

"I have to find Mama!"

The brush rustled, and a gaunt, middle-aged woman emerged, a goshawk perched on her shoulder. The hawk gave a piercing cry and ruffled its feathers.

Fylgja licked the blood off his muzzle and growled.

The woman's eyes gleamed with malice. She smiled, sending a shiver down Eyvind's spine.

Her gaze fell on Halfdan. The woman cackled with glee. Terror shot through Eyvind.

"You're Åsa's son." Her voice rumbled with magic. "My name is Groa. Your mother is very worried about you. Come here, boy. I'll take you to her."

Halfdan stared at her wide-eyed, and Eyvind's heart stopped.

"Halfdan, no!" shouted Eyvind. "Don't trust her!"

Halfdan hesitated. Eyvind tried desperately to crawl to him.

Groa kept her gaze on the boy and began to croon a vardlokkur, soft and alluring. The hairs on Eyvind's neck rose.

Halfdan took one step toward her.

There was so much power in her voice, Eyvind fought the urge to crawl to her himself. "Halfdan, stay with me," he commanded.

Groa continued singing. Halfdan edged toward her.

"Stop!" cried Eyvind, struggling to rise.

The boy paid him no mind, but walked to the sorceress, who clutched his shoulder in an iron claw. She grinned at Eyvind. "It seems I have the heir to Tromøy in my power. Horik will be so pleased. He'll shower me with silver."

"Halfdan," said Eyvind, "this woman is bad. She wants to do you and your mother harm."

"I want only the best for your mother. I'll take you to her now," said the völva, keeping a firm grip on the boy's shoulder as she backed into the undergrowth. Eyvind began to crawl along the ground after them.

"Keep your distance." A blade flashed in her hand, close to the boy's throat. "I'd hate for the knife to slip."

Eyvind stopped, but Fylgja advanced, growling, teeth bared.

"Call off the wolf, or the boy dies," she ordered.

"I have no control over the wolf. Only the boy commands him."

Groa eyed Fylgja while Eyvind edged closer to her and the boy. The hawk roused and gave a menacing cry that made the wolf halt—it was a bird of prey that had taken his sight.

"Halfdan, tell your wolf it's all right. I'm taking you to your mother," she crooned in honeyed tones.

"Halfdan," Eyvind called, "she's lying. She wants to hurt your mother."

The boy wavered. The völva resumed the vardlokkur and gently pulled Halfdan with her. They backed into the forest, the wolf following at a distance, emitting a low growl. Eyvind struggled to his knees, then collapsed to the ground. He mustered all his strength and crawled after them. The forest itself seemed to obstruct him. The thick undergrowth scraped his face and tangled his limbs. Blood seeped from his wound, sapping his strength. At last he could go no further. He lay still, his head swimming.

He'd lost Åsa's son to her worst enemy. He'd tried to protect them and instead put them both in mortal danger.

The foliage rustled, and he opened his eyes to see Åsa gazing down at him. His vision swam. A hallucination.

"Eyvind! You're alive!" Her eyes lit on the blood that soaked through his tunic. "But you're hurt!" She knelt beside him. Searching under his tunic, she found the wound he'd reopened. She unwound the length of red fabric from his belt and bound it around his wound. "I'm so glad to see you. I thought you were dead."

With a groan, Eyvind eased himself into a sitting position. Every time he moved, blood oozed and his head swam.

Åsa eyed him with concern. "Can you walk?"

"I can try."

"Here, let me help," came a man's voice. A stranger emerged from the undergrowth. He wore a slave's ragged tunic, but he looked young enough and strong. Eyvind bristled at the sight of him beside Åsa.

"This is Cian, a fellow prisoner," Åsa said. "He helped me escape."

The man bowed to Eyvind. "At your service."

Eyvind still didn't like the man, but he had more urgent concerns. "We must find Halfdan," he blurted.

"Halfdan!" The shock in Åsa's voice struck him like a blow.

Eyvind rushed on. "He's here. I went to Vestfold to enlist Olaf's help to find you, and the boy must have overheard our plans. He stowed away on *Far Traveler*. When I discovered him, it was too late to turn back. I thought he would be safe with my crew, but he followed me today, determined to rescue you. He's been taken."

"Taken? By whom?" Åsa's voice rose in panic.

"By a woman—a witch."

"Groa," Åsa growled. She turned to Cian. "She has my son. We must go after him."

Cian shook his head. "Lady, that's impossible. She'll have taken him to the fortress. We can't go back there."

Åsa set her jaw. "I'm not leaving without my son."

"But this man cannot walk," said Cian. Eyvind flushed with shame.

Åsa tucked the seax into her belt and leaned the spear against the tree. "You will stay here with Eyvind. I'll go fetch my son."

Eyvind interrupted. "King Olaf is fighting Horik in the channel."

Åsa whirled on him. "Olaf doesn't have enough ships to take on Horik."

Eyvind nodded. He explained as quickly as he could. "Olaf and Olvir have attacked Horik with their combined fleet to draw him and his warriors away from the fortress. He's creating a diversion to give me a chance to free you. My ship is waiting about six miles overland to the north. I was on my way to find you when I ran into the sorceress and her man-at-arms. Olaf is waiting for my signal to retreat. Horik's fleet is twice the size of theirs. They can't hold him for long."

"What's the signal?" Åsa asked.

Eyvind indicated the length of red fabric that bound his wound. "I'm to fly this banner from the headland above the Little Belt."

"Give it to me," Åsa demanded. "When I get Halfdan back, I'll fly it."

"Lady, you can't do this," Cian protested.

"I give the orders," she said, taking the blood-soaked sash from Eyvind. She tied it around her own waist, then cut a strip of fabric from his tunic and rebound the wound. "Wait here for me. If I don't come by morning, head for the ship without me."

Cian and Eyvind watched her as she strode away.

CHAPTER 14

Åsa tracked Halfdan and the sorceress through the forest, but she headed toward the tunnel entrance. It was not far. Groa had undoubtedly taken Halfdan to the fortress to present her trophy to Horik. Åsa had to get there and rescue her son before Horik returned. Olaf was fighting a losing battle against the Danes, and she needed to give him the signal to retreat. She stepped up her pace.

When she reached the spot where the camouflaged entrance should be, she got down on her hands and knees to search the undergrowth. It was not hard to find. In her triumph at capturing her prey, Groa had not only left a trail of crushed and bent bushes, but she had left the cover open. Åsa climbed down without hesitation, pulling the hatch closed over her head. The tunnel held no terrors for her now. She forged ahead into the darkness, knowing it would lead her to her son.

Stormrider lay quietly, comforted by the contact with Åsa's body and the darkness inside her tunic. Åsa in turn was soothed by the bird's heartbeat against her chest.

In a surprisingly short time she reached the end of the tunnel.

In her haste, she ran face first into the rungs hard enough to make her curse. She stood hugging herself while the sting of impact wore off. As the pain faded from her nose and jaw, she ran her hands over her face. She would most likely have a black eye but nothing worse.

Gripping the rungs, she climbed up until her head bumped up against the cover. She stepped up another rung and lifted the cover silently with her shoulder, holding on tight to the top rung. She cautiously raised her head through the hatch. The cavernous room was a shade or two lighter than the utter darkness of the tunnel. Her eyes were well adjusted, and she eased the cover aside, peering into the gloom, straining to hear any noise.

All was silent in the narrow aisle behind the high seat. She climbed out and crept around the dais until she could see into the depths of the hall. There was no movement, no sound. She was alone.

Åsa slipped into the room and made for the side door. Once outside, she crossed the yard to Groa's chamber.

Fylgja lay outside the door, his head in his paws. At the sound of her footsteps, the blind wolf lifted his head. He sniffed the air and gave a faint whine. Åsa leaned down and gave his head a reassuring pat.

She pressed her ear to the door and heard the familiar voice of her son.

"I want Mama!" he demanded.

"Hush, child. She'll be here soon."

Groa's remark brought Åsa up short. Of course. The völva knew Åsa would come for her son. She was waiting for her.

Åsa hesitated outside the door. She longed for Heid. How could she take on this fearsome sorceress without her mentor?

She took stock of what weapons she had: a seax in her belt; Stormrider drowsed inside her tunic; the blind wolf moped at her feet.

Åsa brought the falcon out of her tunic and set the bird on her shoulder. Stormrider blinked and roused, digging her talons into Åsa's unprotected flesh. Fylgja got to his feet with a faint whine. She closed her eyes and sent her thoughts to Stormrider and Fylgja, hoping the creatures understood her plan.

Taking a deep breath, Åsa drew her seax and shoved the door open. The room was dimly lit by the guttering pole lamp. In the gloom she saw Groa, her hand clutching Halfdan's arm. White-hot fury flowed into Åsa.

She launched Stormrider at the sorceress, talons aimed for Groa's eyes. At the same time, Fylgja leaped for the völva's throat, jaws snapping.

Groa was ready for them. She dodged the blind wolf's attack, and the goshawk launched from her perch with a cry. Talons extended, she flew at Stormrider. The two raptors collided mid-air in a flurry of feathers.

It was not an even contest. Though Stormrider fought ferociously with beak and claw, the hawk's greater size enabled her to force the injured falcon to the ground. The hawk stood on her victim's breast, gripping Stormrider in her talons while she opened her beak to rip out the falcon's throat.

Åsa rushed the goshawk, shouting and slashing her seax until the raptor abandoned her prey and retreated to her perch. Åsa scooped up the inert falcon and tucked the bird into her tunic, then whirled to confront Groa.

The sorceress clutched Halfdan with one hand and a knife in the other. She dragged the boy back into the shadows. "I'll kill him." She poked Halfdan's throat with the tip of her knife, drawing a tiny drop of blood. The boy's eyes were wide. Fylgja whined and sniffed the air. "Such a waste of a great ability. This child possesses real power. He could have become a mighty king and sorcerer."

"Halfdan," Åsa said, biting back desperation and fortifying her voice with galdr. She reached out again with her mind, searching for the connection they shared. She concentrated on the time she'd been trapped in the dark valleys of Niflheim, when she'd called out and he'd answered. Åsa drew that feeling from deep inside herself and projected it to her son, letting it empower her voice. "Halfdan, come to me!"

"Mama!" The boy bit the hand that gripped him and broke away from Groa.

The völva reached for him. "You little bastard, I'll kill you."

Fylgja lunged, knocking Groa to the ground.

"Halfdan! Come here," cried Åsa. Halfdan ran to her.

The goshawk flew down off her perch and attacked the wolf in a flurry of wings. Fylgja snapped at the raptor, but his jaws closed on air. The hawk lofted up, away from the wolf's teeth. Fylgja swiveled his head, sniffing the air, trying to sense where the bird had gone.

Groa scrambled to her feet, brandishing the knife. Åsa shoved Halfdan behind her and rushed at the sorceress, seax in hand. The two women circled each other, blades flashing in the guttering lamplight. Groa rushed Åsa, and Fylgja leaped. The wolf hit the sorceress, slamming her into the flaming lamp and knocking it over.

In an instant the rushes on the floor caught fire. Groa screamed as her clothing and hair ignited.

Smoke filled the room as flames licked at the walls. Åsa took Halfdan by the hand and ran out the door, Fylgja bringing up the rear. She fought down the impulse to rush to the gate. She'd never be able to fight her way through even the few Danes left to guard the fortress, and soon the smoke and Groa's shrieks would draw them to the bower.

Instead, she led Halfdan and Fylgja to the side door of the great hall. "We have to be very quiet," she said to Halfdan. "There might be bad men in here." The boy nodded solemnly. Åsa eased the door open and slipped inside, pulling her son with her. Fylgja seemed to understand the need for silence, for he followed silent as a shadow.

The longfire had burned down to coals, leaving the room in near darkness. Dapples of light from the tiny amber glass squares set in the roof did little to light the huge room.

Åsa paused inside the door, listening and trying to sense any presence. After a moment she was certain the hall was deserted, and her eyes began to adjust to the gloom.

"Come now, we are going into a secret tunnel," she whispered to Halfdan. The boy nodded, his eyes huge.

She felt her way along the wall to the high seat, then skirted the dais. In the narrow aisle behind the high seat, she got to her knees and felt along the floorboards for the wooden trap door to the tunnel.

The cover was still ajar as she'd left it. Åsa crawled to the opening and put one foot into the hole, flailing around in the air until it contacted the first rung. Gripping the edge, she climbed partway down the ladder and reached up for Halfdan. "Come on, son. It's dark, but I've been here before." He got on his belly and lowered his legs inside. She climbed down the ladder, hanging onto the top rung with one hand and guiding her son with the other.

Once her son was securely in the tunnel, Åsa put her arms out to Fylgja. She could just barely reach the top of the hole.

The blind wolf put one foreleg into the opening. When his paw met air, he whined and backed away. It was obvious he wanted to follow Halfdan.

"Come, Fylgja," Åsa coaxed. He cowered in the shadows.

A whiff of smoke came down the hole. Shouts and footsteps sounded above. The fire must have spread to the hall. Åsa turned to Halfdan, struggling to keep her voice calm. "You'll have to get him to come, son."

"Come on, Fylgja, hurry," said Halfdan. The wolf whined again. "Come on, boy, it's safe. Mama will catch you."

The wolf crept forward on his belly, shivering.

Åsa grabbed him by the scruff of his neck and gently pulled him into the hole. "Easy, big fella," she murmured. He whined but let her pull him down. She staggered under the wolf's weight as she lowered him to the ground.

The smell of smoke was stronger now. Footfalls and voices grew louder. Åsa didn't even try to pull the heavy cover closed. "Hurry, son." She herded Halfdan gently ahead of her, hoping the fire would keep everyone too busy to discover the open tunnel.

They stumbled into the gloom. Åsa could hear the crackle of flames licking at the hall behind them. Whiffs of smoke tickled her nostrils.

The smoke thickened and the air heated up.

"Run!"

Coughing and struggling for breath, she pushed her son in front of her. He stumbled and fell. Åsa tripped over him and sprawled on the hard floor, skinning her hands as she broke her fall. Inside her tunic, Stormrider thrashed. Åsa put her hand against her chest, calming the bird. The falcon's heartbeat was thready and faint against Åsa's chest.

She scrambled to her feet and pulled Halfdan up with her. Behind them, Fylgja whined. His claws tapped on the tunnel floor.

She picked up Halfdan and ran.

The passage ahead was pitch-black, but she couldn't slow down. She could feel hot air in the tunnel behind her. She ran until she collided with the wall.

She rebounded, ignoring the pain. They were at the end of the tunnel. She set Halfdan on his feet and felt the wall until she found the iron rungs.

"I'm going to climb up the ladder and open the hatch," she said to Halfdan. "You wait here until you see daylight."

"Yes, Mama." His voice sounded small in the enormous blackness of the passage.

Åsa climbed up the rungs until her head contacted the hatch. She pushed. It held fast. "Halfdan, hold my legs. Can you feel them?"

Little arms encircled her calves. She shoved with all her might.

Suddenly, the hatch gave way and daylight flooded the hole. The force threw her backwards. She scrabbled for a handhold and missed. "Look out!" she cried as she fell.

She landed hard on her back, but fortunately she missed both boy and wolf. Inside Åsa's tunic Stormrider roused weakly. Åsa drew in gulps of fresh air, but behind her she heard fire roar down the tunnel.

"Halfdan, climb up! I'm going to hand up Fylgja. You have to help him."

She hefted the wolf. Fylgja let out a whine, but he let her lift him. He scrabbled with his paws, gaining traction on the wall to aid her. Pain shot through her shoulders and back as she heaved. Hot air seared her back.

Fylgja's head cleared the top. He scrabbled again with his paws, and Halfdan grabbed the wolf's ruff, pulling with all his might. The wolf cleared the hole just as the fire roared up on them. As she clambered up the ladder, Åsa felt the heat on her back. The hem of her tunic flared, and she smelled burning hair as the end of her braid singed. She threw herself out of the hole and rolled in the dirt as flames shot out of the opening.

She lay catching her breath, feeling for Stormrider, still nestled in her tunic.

Halfdan took her hand. "Mama, are you hurt?"

Åsa coughed a laugh and tousled his hair. "I'll be all right, son. Give me a moment."

Halfdan hung his head. "I'm sorry, Mama. Sorry I ran away, and sorry I followed that bad witch."

"It's all right, dear one. I know you were only trying to help me, and I appreciate it. And you saved Eyvind. You're a very brave boy."

Halfdan brightened at this. "I am?"

"Yes, and I'm proud of you." Halfdan broke out in a big smile. "Now, you must promise to do as I say from now on."

Halfdan nodded vigorously. "I promise."

Åsa got to her feet and took inventory of her injuries. Her tunic was singed, but she was not burned, and for that she was grateful. Bumps and bruises made her wince when she took a step, but she would make it.

She needed to signal Olaf that they were safe, but it was too risky to take Halfdan with her to the signal tower. Cian and Eyvind should be close by, and she could leave Halfdan and Fylgja with them. She prayed she could find her way back to them.

She forged through the woods as quietly as possible with a blind wolf and a small boy in tow. Each step was a little easier, reassuring her that she was not too badly hurt. Inside her tunic, Stormrider's heart still pattered.

Muffled voices filtered through the trees. She halted, listening, then recognized them as Cian's and Eyvind's. She hurried toward the welcome sound and was relieved to find the two men beside the stream where she'd left them.

On her approach Cian leaped up, hefting his spear.

"It's me," she said. He relaxed at the sound of her voice.

"Thank the gods you're all right," said Eyvind from his bed of moss. Åsa hurried over and knelt beside him. He reached up and stroked her sooty hair. "You look like you've just come from Hel."

Åsa laughed. "Not quite that bad, but close. When I fought with Groa, we knocked over a lamp and started a fire in her room."

Cian said, "We've been smelling smoke, but we thought it was from the signal fire."

"I must leave Halfdan and the wolf here while I signal Olaf that we're free."

"Let me go," said Cian. "I know the way, and I'm not injured."

Åsa was tempted. She hated to part with Halfdan and Eyvind, and she needed to rest. But it was her responsibility. "No, I'll go. I'm not hurt as badly as I appear."

Cian sighed but didn't argue. "Go back the way you came. After you reach the tunnel opening, head south. You'll come out of the forest onto the headland. The Little Belt will be below you. You should be able to see the battle from there. The signal tower is on that headland. That's the place Olaf will look for the banner. Hopefully it will be deserted."

With a final glance at Eyvind and her son, Åsa hurried off into the forest. She found the entrance to the tunnel, still emitting a tendril of smoke, took her bearings, then set out toward what she believed to be south. It was difficult to tell in the forest, for she could see nothing through the dense canopy. She fretted that she might be going astray, but at last she sighted the glint of the sea through the foliage.

She reached the forest's verge and jerked to a halt within the cover of the trees. Straining the limits of her vision, she scanned the landscape for the signal fire station. It was easy to spot. The huge logs still smoldered, and the air was still thick with smoke. Through the haze she counted half a dozen men guarding the watchtower.

She'd never get near it.

Heavy footsteps sounded nearby. Åsa gripped her seax with both hands, poised to thrust.

A warrior approached, close enough to touch. He spotted her, gaped at her a moment as if trying to understand what he saw, then opened his mouth to cry out.

Åsa thrust the seax with deadly aim. The blade sliced the warrior's throat and cut his shout off. The Dane sank to the ground, mouth open, blood welling from his neck. Åsa jerked her seax out and wiped it on the fallen man's tunic.

A breathtaking panorama spread below her. The vantage point gave her a bird's eye view of the battle. The Little Belt snaked through the terrain, its waters jammed with ships. Weapons flashed in the sunlight, and faint shouts rose from the struggle. Ravens and gulls shrieked in excitement as they plundered the corpses that bobbed in the water.

She stared at the spectacle, straining to see how the battle stood. She picked out Olaf, a head taller than the others. To her relief, he was still standing, but the Danes far outnumbered Olaf and Olvir. More Danish vessels poured through the bottleneck, threatening to overwhelm them.

OLAF FOUGHT DOGGEDLY in the center of the shield wall. Gripping his spear with a sweaty palm, he rammed the point between the shields while dodging enemy blades that snaked through. His spear bit flesh, and a Dane screamed as Olaf drove the point in deeper. Over the rim of his shield he saw the enemy fall, and Olaf jerked his spear back, ready for the next Dane who stepped over the fallen man and took his place.

On either side, Kalv and Olvir maintained their barricades with grim determination. Whenever one of the shieldmen fell, another snatched up their shield and filled the gap.

Olaf's gaze flicked toward the headland above them. Through gritted teeth he prayed to Thor for the red banner. They were taking a beating. They would have to retreat soon whether the banner appeared or not.

All around him men were screaming and dying. As warriors in the lead ships on both sides fell, crews in the rear vessels surged forward, clambering over the corpses of their mates to fill the front ranks and take up the battle afresh. The decks were slick with gore and the air reeked of blood and entrails.

~

WATCHING THE BATTLE, Åsa knew she had to give the signal now. The fleet had to retreat, or perish. She unwound the length of red wool from around her waist. It was stiff with Eyvind's blood. The signal tower was the only thing sufficiently high up for the banner to be seen from the water, but she'd never get past the half dozen Danes that guarded it.

She surveyed the area, searching for an alternative. The trees were tall, but the banner would be lost in their canopy. Åsa stared at the battle below, thinking. How could she get the banner high enough to be seen?

The only way was to fly.

Åsa reached out to Stormrider's mind. Inside her tunic, the falcon roused. Åsa could feel the bird's pain, her weakness. Her chest muscles throbbed. Could she fly?

The falcon's heart beat harder in reply.

Åsa drew the bird out and held her close to her mouth, whispering. Stormrider might aggravate her injuries beyond healing, or worse, be shot down.

It was a risk, but one she must take.

She held the length of red wool out to Stormrider, visualizing what she wanted in her mind. Åsa held her breath.

The falcon reached out a talon and gripped the banner.

"Fly!" Åsa commanded.

The wounded bird flapped her wings and lofted into the air. Åsa felt the searing pain in Stormrider's chest muscles as she spiraled up, higher and higher. The falcon's determination overwhelmed the agony, and she rose above the trees, trailing the length of red cloth.

For a moment the banner hung slack in Stormrider's talons,

and Åsa despaired. Then a breeze rippled the red cloth and it unfurled.

Åsa stared at Olaf's helmeted head among the others in the shield wall, willing him to see the banner. *Look up, Olaf!* she thought fiercely.

A shout went up from the signal tower, followed by arrows loosed at Stormrider. The falcon gave a powerful flap of her wings and lofted in the air, high above the missiles.

Åsa saw Olaf's head go up.

He stared at the banner.

An arrow struck Stormrider, knocking her from the sky. The wounded falcon dropped the banner and plummeted toward the ground with deadly speed.

Pull up! Åsa sent the thought with all the power she could muster.

The bird did not hear her. Stormrider was unconscious, hurtling to her death. Åsa rushed toward her. She threw out her arms and caught the falcon. Stormrider landed with a force that knocked Åsa to the ground.

She scrambled to her feet, tucking the exhausted bird into her tunic, then dashed for the forest's edge. Shouts and footsteps sounded behind her.

OLAF'S RANKS were down to two rows, and Kalv and Olvir were equally hard-pressed. A shout rent the air as Horik rallied his men. They crowded into the ship's prow to board *Sea Dragon*. With a roar, Olaf and his men beat them back, sending bloody corpses into the water. More Danes lined up, and Olaf locked eyes with Horik. The determined hatred he saw there chilled his blood.

His peripheral vision caught movement in the sky. A bird, but more than a bird. His gaze flicked to it, and he stared, processing the spectacle. High above the signal tower, a falcon hovered, beating its wings. Something long trailed from the falcon's talons.

A red banner.

Åsa was free.

Olaf filled his lungs to order the retreat. Just as he opened his mouth to shout, a sword bashed his helm. His ears rang with the blow and his vision went black.

He fell to the deck.

CHAPTER 15

Åsa dodged through the brush, trying not to make too much noise but not daring to slow her pace. The shouts of men crashing through the undergrowth sounded behind her. In open country she could never outrun them, but in the thickly grown underbrush she might be able to elude her pursuers. She had to lead them away from Halfdan, Eyvind, and Cian.

She forged a serpentine course through the forest in the opposite direction. To her gratification, she heard the men follow her away from their site. But she was tiring. Her injuries were draining her stamina. She couldn't go on much further.

She needed to hide.

Ahead she spotted a dense thicket. She ducked under a low-hanging branch and plunged into the foliage. Thorns tore her clothes, but she managed to burrow in. She was glad that her undyed linen tunic blended into the undergrowth. Once she was in as far as she could go, she squatted down and froze. Sounds of pursuit came closer. She held her breath as the men lumbered past her hiding spot.

When their noise had faded, she eased her way out of the thicket and set off in the opposite direction. She should find her way back to Eyvind and Halfdan soon. But as she wandered, the terrain became less and less familiar. In her twisting flight, she had not marked her location. In the dense forest she could not get a look at the sky to get her bearings.

She was lost.

Åsa slowed to a halt. Her frenzied wandering was only leading her further astray. She sat down on a fallen log and gathered her thoughts. She called upon the landvaettir and opened her mind to them. *You love my son. Help me get to him.*

As her breathing slowed, her thoughts became ordered. When she fled through the woods, she had left a trail like any deer or boar. She was skilled enough at hunting to be able to locate that trail and follow it to the spot where she had begun her frantic flight. Once she was back at the beginning, she should be able to find signs that would take her back to the stream where Eyvind and Halfdan waited with Cian.

She got to her feet and dusted herself off. Calling on the landvaettir for guidance, she scanned the area. First she spotted a broken branch, then a trampled fern. Peering ahead she saw a clump of crushed leaves. Before long her vision became trained and she could read the trail like a line of runes, following a string of disturbed leaf litter, imprints on the forest floor, broken branches, and bent grasses.

Åsa set off, hunting herself.

Eyvind lay on a bed of moss in the forest. Halfdan and his wolf sat next to him in silence. The boy was tired, so was the elderly wolf. Cian stood watch, his spear at the ready. The Irishman seemed to have endless strength in reserve. Eyvind wished Åsa had let Cian go to warn Olaf. He understood that she felt personally responsible, but he wanted her here where he could see her. This was all his fault. Everything he'd done was wrong. How on earth were they going to get back to the ship? It was a two-hour walk for a healthy person, but an insurmountable journey for one in his condition.

One thing at a time. First get Åsa back here.

As if in answer to his wish, the bushes rustled and Åsa emerged. A wave of relief flooded Eyvind.

"Mama!" shouted Halfdan, rushing to her. She wrapped her arms around him.

She was pale and dirty, but smiling. "He saw the banner," she reported.

"Good," said Cian. "Now we'd better head for the ship."

Eyvind knew he couldn't get up on his own, much less walk six miles through the forest. "Leave me here. I'll only slow you down."

"Don't be an idiot," Åsa said sternly. "I would never leave you behind."

Her words nearly brought Eyvind to tears.

She and Cian gripped Eyvind by the shoulders and pulled him to his feet. Eyvind gritted his teeth against the pain.

"Here, lean on me," Åsa said. She looked up at him with affection and gratitude that sent warmth coursing through his veins. He put his arm around her waist and felt new strength flow into him. He tightened his grip.

Åsa had her falcon inside her tunic. Eyvind could feel the bird's heart beating fast.

"We follow this trail through the forest. The ship is about six miles," said Eyvind, nodding toward the northeast. He knew he'd never make it that far.

The Irishman slung one of Eyvind's arms over his shoulder while Åsa took the other. On her free side, Halfdan maintained his death grip on his mother's hand, and Fylgja stuck to his young master like a burr.

Their progress was agonizingly slow, with Eyvind staggering along, leaning heavily on Åsa and Cian.

They had gone less than a mile when Eyvind stumbled to his knees. Åsa and Cian eased him to the ground.

"Halfdan." Eyvind called the boy to him. "Can you guide your mother back to the ship?"

Halfdan nodded vigorously. "I know the way."

"We won't leave you," Åsa objected.

"I can go no farther. I'll wait here. You can go to the ship and get help and come back for me."

"Not necessary," said Cian. "There are no sounds of pursuit. We are safe enough here, for a little while, at least. I hear a creek close by. Help me to get him to it."

The Irishman's words took Eyvind by surprise. He'd expected Cian to take the opportunity to abandon him.

Between them, Åsa and Cian helped Eyvind to the stream. They fell to their knees and scooped up great handfuls of water.

Wiping his mouth, the Irishman turned to Åsa. He stared down at her seriously. "Åsa, queen, now that I've rescued you, remember you promised to do the same for me."

"We will gladly take you with us," said Åsa. "You are a free man once again. When we make it back to my kingdom, I will reward you with the means to return to your home if you wish, or take you into my hird as a warrior if you prefer."

Cian inclined his head. "I thank you, Lady." He looked around, examining their location. "Please lend me your seax."

Eyvind held his breath as Åsa handed Cian the seax. He felt better when the Irishman gave her his spear.

"I'll be back as soon as I can." Cian tucked the seax in his belt and slipped away into the forest.

"You and Fylgja must be very quiet," Åsa said to Halfdan. "We are hiding from the enemy warriors. You understand?"

Halfdan nodded, his face serious.

"You can help me with Eyvind's wounds." She must have seen the apprehension in Eyvind's face, for she patted his shoulder. "Don't worry. We'll be as careful as we can."

Eyvind closed his eyes and nodded.

"Halfdan, can you fetch me some moss?" she asked. The boy scampered off and began to search the wet rocks in the creek.

"Rest now," Åsa said to Eyvind. She rinsed the length of bloodstained red wool in the stream until the water ran clean. She wrung out the fabric onto Eyvind's blood-encrusted bandage to loosen the stuck-on linen, and gently pulled the fabric away from the wound. Eyvind winced but stifled a groan.

She rinsed the linen strip in the creek, then used it to clean the wound as gently as she could. Halfdan returned with a fistful of damp moss, and she packed this on the wound. Then she wrapped the linen around Eyvind's waist once again to staunch the seeping blood. "This should stop the bleeding."

The cool damp moss eased the sting of the wound. Eyvind relaxed for the first time since he'd lost Åsa.

They rested on the bank, listening to the stream's soothing babble. Bees buzzed contentedly nearby. The day was warm, even in the shade and coolness of the creek. Fylgja laid his head on his paws and closed his eyes. Even Halfdan was subdued. He snuggled up to Åsa, and she gripped the spear on the ground beside her. Eyvind knew she would defend them with everything she had.

"I am sorry for getting you into this," he said miserably. "I'm sorry I've failed you."

Åsa stared at him. "Failed me? Eyvind, you nearly gave your life to save me. It was my choice to come with you. It was my enemy who's been waiting for years for a chance to capture me. He would have succeeded sooner or later no matter what I did. At least he hasn't attacked Tromøy to get at me."

"I'm not a hero like the others," he said. "Olaf, Olvir—even the Irishman is more of a warrior than I am. You deserve a hero."

She snorted. "I am surrounded by warlike men who want my kingdom, my power. They want to enslave me. Only you want me for myself." She touched the ring he'd given her and gave him a tender smile. "You're a good man. A man I can trust."

Her words sent a warm glow through him. He reached out his hand and clasped hers.

He must have dozed, for a crackling in the brush snapped him awake. Åsa's hand tightened on the spear shaft.

The foliage parted and Cian appeared. Eyvind and Åsa exhaled in unison.

The Irishman carried two stout saplings. He used the seax to trim off their branches, then wove the supple branches between the saplings, making a taut web.

"Come, now, let's get you on this," said Cian.

"You can't carry me!" Eyvind protested.

"We won't. I'm going to drag you. Now climb on."

Åsa and Cian helped Eyvind onto the stretcher and strapped him in place with the red sash. He hated Åsa to see him helpless as an infant. The Irishman by contrast was strong and confident.

Cian put himself between the ends of the two saplings and began to pull. The Irishman grunted and strained, and the makeshift litter began to move.

"Let me help," said Åsa. She positioned herself in front of Cian and they pulled together like a harnessed horse team.

Their progress was even slower than it had been walking, but they gradually gained ground. Eyvind rode over the rough terrain in a daze. He gripped the sides of the litter and ground his teeth to stop from crying out each time they hit a bump and pain jolted through him.

It seemed the journey would never end.

The sun was low in the sky by the time the ship came into sight, still riding at anchor. Tears of relief rose in Eyvind's eyes. He blinked them away furiously.

Halfdan ran on ahead, trailed by Fylgja, and brought back a team of sailors to help them.

"We are so glad to see you," shouted Svein.

"Not half as glad as we are to see you!" said Åsa.

Svein took over from Åsa while another hefty sailor took Cian's place. They hoisted the travois like a stretcher and set off toward the ship. Relief at not being dragged over the bumpy ground made Eyvind tear up again. He blinked in shame, but the release from pain was overwhelming.

The crew had warped *Far Traveler* into the beach. Eyvind had never been so happy to see his ship. His sailors gathered to haul him aboard, taking care not to jostle him. They unlashed him from the litter and helped him into his hudfat in the stern of the ship, next to the steering oar.

The boarding plank was lowered, and Åsa and Cian helped Halfdan coax his wolf aboard. Åsa hurried to Eyvind, fussing over him, while Dagny knelt to examine his injuries. The young healer nodded in approval. "The wounds are sound. He should heal well. I have honey and herbs to make a poultice to prevent infection."

Once Eyvind was settled, Åsa rose and beckoned the Irishman to her. "This is Cian," she announced to the crew. "He helped me escape from Horik's fortress, then brought us here safely. I owe him my life, as well as the lives of my son and Eyvind. I have promised him a place in my hird should he wish it."

The sailors crowded around the Irishman, thanking him, and pelting him with questions. Cian seemed to blossom under the attention, and he soon had them laughing. The Irishman seemed able to charm everyone, Eyvind thought sourly.

He hated to break up the party, but they had to depart. "Hoist the anchor," he ordered.

"We need to join the battle while we still have daylight," said Åsa.

Eyvind shook his head. "I must take you to safety. Olaf and the fleet will meet us there."

"We have to go to Olaf's aid," said Åsa.

"If it were only me, I would join the fight in a moment," said

Eyvind. "But I have you and Halfdan here. I can't risk your lives. And there is not much our little crew can do to help. The most likely outcome is that we will all be killed, and you and Halfdan will fall into Horik's hands. Then Tromøy will be lost, along with Vestfold."

"I owe Horik a bad death," said Cian. "But I fear Eyvind is right, and my vengeance must wait."

"Very well, I know you are right," Åsa said. "But it tears at my heart to leave Olaf to his fate."

As they got underway, the mood of the crew was solemn. Åsa's face was a mask of misery. Eyvind wished there was some way he could comfort her. He felt helpless in the face of her grief.

If Horik succeeded in destroying Olaf's and Åsa's fleets, Tromøy and Skiringssal would fall to him as well.

If the worst happened, where could he take Åsa to be safe? They could flee to Ragnhild. The shield-maiden would offer them shelter.

But would Åsa ever forgive him?

CHAPTER 16

The Little Belt

From the prow of *Ran's Lover* Olvir saw Olaf fall. He scrambled onto the gunnels and leaped for *Sea Dragon,* landing midships as the ships parted. He grabbed Olaf's shoulders and helped the crew drag him to safety in the stern.

The manhandling roused Olaf. He shook his head and tried to sit up. "I saw the banner," he croaked. "We can retreat."

Olvir didn't hesitate. "Retreat!" he shouted, forcing his way to the prow. He slashed the grappling lines that bound them to the Danish ship, then hefted a spear and joined the crew in fighting free of the Danes.

As the enemy lost their grip, the rowers put their backs into it, and the ship began to move.

Olvir shouted to his own rowers to retreat. They had already gotten the idea, and the ship started to move away. Kalv passed the word to the remaining ships. In a few strokes, the entire fleet went into full retreat.

But the Danes had regrouped quickly, and now they forged ahead in pursuit.

"Row!" Olvir prayed they could maintain their slim lead in the race to open water. Without that lead, once they emerged from the narrow waterway of the Little Belt, the enemy would have the sea room to flank the Norse fleet and surround them. With the Danes' superior numbers, the battle would be over in no time.

"Thor help us elude the bastards," said Olvir.

"We can't lead them back to Tromøy," said Olaf.

"What's to stop them from going there whether we lead them or not?"

"We are. We have to regroup and fight them off before we get into open waters."

"They'll annihilate us, and Vestfold and Agder will be defenseless," Olvir pointed out.

"We can't let them get through." Olaf's face was set. "We must take as many out as we can now to give Tromøy a chance if they come."

The Danish ships were bigger and carried more rowers, and it soon became clear they were gaining. By the time the headland of the Little Belt hove into sight, the enemy had caught up with them.

Olaf's ears still rang, his stomach was unsettled, and his vision blurred. He shook his head to clear it. "Stand and fight!" His ships rafted up to each other and formed a hasty shield wall that stretched across the entrance to the Little Belt.

"Archers," Olaf bellowed. The archers snatched enemy arrows from shields and gunnels to supplement their dwindling stock. An echo of his command came from the enemy. "Nock! Draw! Loose!" A storm of missiles rose from Olaf's ships and met the Danish volley in mid-air.

The Danes closed in, and Olaf called for casting spears. The spearmen hefted their javelins and waited for the order. Olaf watched the Danes draw closer until he could make out their features. "Heave!" he cried.

The warriors hurled their javelins, but so did the enemy. A hail of spears whickered into the Norse fleet. This time cries rose as some found their marks, and the wounded thudded to the decks. But by the screams of the Danes, they also suffered losses.

From the center of the shield wall, Olaf stared as the enemy advanced. "Tighten up!" he shouted. The crew rallied their remaining warriors across their thinning ranks.

The ships closed in, and Olaf braced for combat. His own warriors scrambled for weapons, drawing axes and seaxes and yanking enemy spears from the gunnels.

The Danes surged forward and engaged, thrusting spears into the Norse shield wall while the defenders jabbed back.

Olaf found himself staring into Horik's face. The Dane king's eyes were battle crazed. His beard split into a mocking grin. "I'll have your ships, I'll have your kingdom, I'll have your queen as well as the queen of Agder. And you'll be feeding the crows." Horik shouted over his shoulder to his crew, "Prepare to board!"

Olaf heaved his shield against the Danish king's, testing his enemy's strength. Horik looked to be in his mid-thirties, filled out and strong but not yet weakened by age. The Dane had many more years of experience in warfare than Olaf, and Horik had proven himself ruthless. All Olaf had was his youth and a few inches in reach. He had to make them count or die.

The two kings shoved at each other, blades jabbing between shields, seeking flesh. Though not as tall as Olaf, Horik was stronger. Olaf's hopes that he could tire the older man out waned. Olaf was still dizzy and nauseous from his head blow, and the Dane was far from decrepit.

Horik shoved hard and forced Olaf to give ground until he came up against the shield of the man behind him. Olaf braced against the shield and launched himself at Horik, spear held in front. Horik knocked the spearhead away with his shield and thrust his own weapon. Olaf dodged and drove his spear from the side, trying to get behind Horik's shield. The wily Dane leaped nimbly aside and countered. Both men were breathing hard. Olaf shook his head again, but he was unsteady on his feet. Sweat ran out from under his helmet and down his face. It prickled behind his ears and on his neck. Horik's face was red, but he appeared full of vigor. Despair churned in Olaf's gut, nauseating him. He bit back the bile that rose in his throat, willing himself not to vomit.

Grinning in triumph, Horik readied his spear for the killing thrust. Olaf raised his shield, whispering a prayer to the Valkyries to fetch him to Valhöll.

A shout went up from the bluff above them.

Olaf's eyes flicked toward Horik's fortress. Though the signal fire had gone out long ago, smoke rose thick in the air.

Above them the fortress flamed, the air filled with smoke and the distant cries of men.

For a moment all was still while both sides gaped at the fire. The hall was fully engulfed, flames raging on the rooftop. Sparks shot high in the air.

A tremendous crack rent the air. They all stared, open-jawed, as the massive roof of the hall buckled. The sound was horrific, unlike anything Olaf had ever heard.

Horik froze, gaping as his fortress collapsed. A horn blast shattered the silence. In the rows farthest back from the battle, orders were shouted. Dane oarsmen woke from their shock, reversed in their seats, and rowed toward the fortress, away from the battle.

Olaf recovered first and attacked with renewed vigor. The men alongside him seemed to gain energy as well. They broke out of the shield wall and charged their enemies, sending Danes thudding to the floorboards or splashing into the water.

Horik seemed stunned. He barely fended off Olaf's strikes. It was the men flanking him who kept him alive against Olaf's onslaught.

Horik's warriors seemed to lose heart along with their king, and the Norse attacked with increased ferocity. As Horik's ranks thinned, Danes began to retreat to the remaining rear ships until Horik and his vanguard were all but alone. As Olaf closed in for the kill, the Danish king's gaze fixed on him, eyes wide.

Before Olaf's blade hit home, the Danes formed a shield fort around their king and hustled him over the rail and onto a ship in the rear guard. The enemy commanders barked an order, and the last ships pulled away, rowing toward the burning fortress.

Olaf checked his urge to pursue his enemy. They couldn't get past the abandoned ships that clogged the waterway. "Nock!" he shouted. "Draw, loose!" His crew sent a last volley of arrows after the Danes.

They had to flee before the Danes recovered. Olaf braced his legs and shouted, "Retreat!"

His order broke the spell, and the Norse rowers dug their oars into the waves. The oarsmen put their backs into it and pulled away from the carnage.

The Norse ships made for the entrance to the Little Belt. They snaked their way toward the open sea.

Sea Dragon rounded the last bend, and Olaf breathed a sigh of relief. The Norse ships forged into the Kattegat, where a favorable breeze welcomed them. Olaf signaled the fleet to set their sails and turn north toward Sandbjerg Vig, where they hoped to rendezvous with *Far Traveler*.

Olaf glanced over his shoulder, but there was no pursuit. He could hardly believe their luck. Or maybe it wasn't luck. The falcon carrying the banner had signaled that Åsa was free. It was possible that she and Eyvind had set the fire.

His head cleared and his nausea abated. Soon he would see Åsa and Halfdan, escort them safely back to Tromøy, then sail for home where Sonja and Rognvald waited.

The ships rounded the point and continued up the coast,

putting as much distance as possible between themselves and pursuit before dark. The crew treated the wounded as best they could, though they lost half a dozen more during the journey. Olaf regretted they couldn't give the dead the funeral pyre they deserved. Instead, they were sent over the side with a prayer asking the sea goddess, Ran, to welcome them in her halls.

The fleet reached Sandbjerg Vig in the early evening. Hope flared when Olaf spotted *Far Traveler* at anchor, but he kept scanning the shore until he saw the late afternoon sun glint on Åsa's red-gold hair. Beside her stood the black-haired boy and his wolf. Relief buoyed his spirits, and he ordered the sail lowered. As he maneuvered *Sea Dragon* into shore, his gaze kept returning to the mother and son.

As soon as *Sea Dragon* nosed onto the beach, Olaf vaulted over the side. Halfdan dropped his mother's hand and raced to Olaf, Fylgja hot on his tail. The boy pelted into Olaf's legs, and he reached down and picked up his son.

"Oof, you're heavy!" said Olaf. Åsa arrived and grabbed Olaf's arm to keep him from toppling over.

"Steady, son," she cautioned. Her eyes met Olaf's and she smiled. He fell into her gaze, unable to look away. "Come," she said. "We have food and drink ready."

The fleet nosed into the long, sandy beach and discharged their wounded. *Far Traveler*'s crew helped carry the injured ashore and made them as comfortable as possible in hastily pitched tents. Dagny examined each one and sent people hunting cobwebs and seaweed to treat punctures and lacerations.

Once the injured were settled, the crews of each ship gathered for a meal. They had no cooking fires for fear that the enemy might be hunting them.

Olaf sank gratefully down on a driftwood log beside Åsa. Eyvind, wrapped in a hudfat, leaned against the log on her other side.

"How do you, brother?" Olaf asked.

Eyvind gave him a wan smile. "Much better, now that I see you are safe and well."

Several of *Far Traveler*'s crew made the rounds with washing bowls and towels while others distributed cups of ale and dried meat. Åsa withdrew Stormrider from her tunic. The bird roused, ruffling her feathers. Åsa poured a bowl of water for the falcon, letting her drink and bathe, then perched her on a dead branch and tied off her jesses. She fed the bird tidbits of dried meat.

Åsa turned to Olaf. "We were so worried about you. How did you manage to get away?"

"Horik's hall was on fire. Was that your doing?"

"In a way." Åsa smiled and told him of the fight with Groa, the lamp getting knocked over, and their escape.

"It's been a busy day," remarked a man from across the fire.

Olaf stared at the stranger. His accent was Irish, and he wore the rags of a slave, but his proud bearing spoke otherwise.

"Olaf, this is Cian, a fellow prisoner," said Åsa. "He helped me escape, and saved Eyvind's and Halfdan's lives."

"At your service," said the Irishman.

"I am grateful to you, Cian," said Olaf.

"Congratulations, Lord," said Cian. "It appears that victory was yours today."

Olaf shook his head. "We managed to fight off the Danish fleet, but I am sorry to report that Horik seems to have escaped."

"I owe Horik a great deal," said Cian with a wolfish grin. "Part of my debt is paid, but I still must give him a horrible death."

"Not if I get to him first," said Olaf.

"I have offered Cian a place in my hird," said Åsa, "or restoration to Ireland, should he wish it."

"And I thank you, Lady. If you don't mind, I will take a bit longer to decide."

"Of course," said Åsa. "You've barely met us, and you have yet to see Tromøy. Take all the time you need." She scanned the crowd with a worried frown. "How many were lost in the battle?"

Olaf took a sip of his ale. "Olvir lost one ship and twenty-three of Tromøy's crew. Forty of mine were killed, and two ships lost."

Åsa got to her feet and announced, "I will hold a proper ceremony in their honor when we return to Tromøy, and a full roster of the dead will be recited. But for now, let's remember them with the minni cup."

All up and down the beach, each ship's commander stood in turn and named those lost from his crew. They drank in remembrance of each one. The toasts went on for a long time, for there were many to remember.

Afterwards, the crews sat in the gathering twilight, recounting their deeds, until one by one the exhausted warriors wandered off to their hudfat. Olaf set a watch, though he doubted Horik would be able to pursue them so soon.

He gazed at Åsa, asleep beside Eyvind, Halfdan and his wolf on her other side. A yearning for Sonja and Rognvald filled his heart.

He went in search of his sheepskin among his crew.

As THE SUN filtered through the trees, Åsa woke. She lay wrapped in a hudfat beside Eyvind. On her other side, Halfdan snuggled up with Fylgja. Stormrider slept, tethered to her makeshift perch. The falcon was recovering from her ordeal, but she needed rest.

Åsa studied Eyvind. His color was better, his breathing steady. Satisfied, she rose. Olaf was already up. She waved, and he returned the gesture. Warmth suffused her at the friendly exchange. Even after all that had gone between them, she could still rely on him to come when she needed him. As she would for him.

Halfdan and Fylgja scrambled out of their hudfat, instantly awake. Eyvind moaned and opened his eyes.

"Good morning," said Åsa. "Why don't you rest a while longer, and I'll bring you some breakfast."

"Nay," he said, sitting up. "I'll get up. We need to get underway in case the Danes come after us."

"I would think they're still busy with the fire. I doubt they'll catch us today. Let me help you."

"I can dress myself. Let me be, I'll be up shortly."

Åsa nodded sympathetically. He needed to do for himself. She left him with his pride and joined Cian.

The crews stumbled out of their hudfat one by one. They gathered at the ship, where they ate a cold breakfast, then struck camp and loaded the ships.

Eyvind joined them, dressed and armed. He hobbled to his ship and accepted a cup of small beer and a piece of flatbread. Åsa watched him with concern, but he seemed to be managing on his own. That was important. She sat beside him and bit off the solicitous words that rose to her tongue. He needed to be treated as if he were hale.

Breakfast done, the crews boarded their ships. *Far Traveler* was warped into the beach to take on the critically wounded. The cargo ship provided better shelter for them and a more comfortable ride than the longships.

Eyvind accepted help climbing up the knarr's boarding plank, and took his seat beside the helm, white-faced and exhausted from the effort of boarding.

Åsa took the tiller as the crew manned their sweeps and rowed away from the beach. Halfdan looked at her askance. "Don't worry, son," she said. "I think you have proven you can see over the gunnels. No harness for you, as long as you behave yourself."

His face lit up, and he scampered among the rowers.

All the ships were ready to go, afloat in the cove, rowers

waiting at their oars. Olvir in *Ran's Lover* led the Tromøy fleet. Olaf followed in *Sea Dragon,* his ships falling in behind him.

Once out into the open sea, a breeze filled in from the southeast. They hoisted sail and ran north toward home.

CHAPTER 17

Tromøy

The fleet arrived off Tromøy in the deep twilight. Though Åsa might have navigated the entrance in the uncertain light, she signaled them to heave-to offshore and await the dawn. She was exhausted, like everyone else, and she didn't want anyone to make a mistake and run aground on the bay's many rocks and skerries.

At first light she led the way in. Though the longships were faster than Eyvind's knarr, Olaf's and Olvir's fleets were worse for wear, with empty seats at some of the oars and others manned by the wounded. Only *Far Traveler*'s crew was unscathed. The wind was light, but they proceeded under sail, saving their rowers' strength for maneuvering.

Eyvind lay propped up against the ship's side beside the cowering Fylgja. He stroked the blind wolf's fur. Halfdan scampered about the ship, trilling with excitement at arriving home. Stormrider drowsed safe inside Åsa's tunic.

As the shore came into view, tears of relief welled up in Åsa's eyes. She was home. Halfdan and Eyvind were safe.

The watch had sighted them before the sun rose, and the folk of Tromøy were already preparing for their arrival. A crowd had gathered on the beach. Jarl Borg sat his horse proudly at the head of a small herd of horses waiting for the leaders to ride. Heid waited in her wagon, her apprentices lined up, ready to receive the wounded. More carts waited to transport those who could not walk.

Far Traveler's crew handed Eyvind over the side, strapped to his makeshift stretcher. Heid took charge of him, commandeering four burly men to carry him up the trail to the bower, a gentler mode of conveyance than bumping along in her wagon. Stormrider perched on her shoulder, Åsa led Gullfaxi, preferring to walk with Halfdan beside Eyvind's stretcher. The blind wolf shambled along, nose in the air, scenting home.

The ship commanders rode, while those sailors who were ambulatory helped each other hobble up the hill. The wounded who could not walk were loaded into wagons and brought to Tromøy's guesthouse, which once again served as an infirmary. Those of Olaf's crew who were able pitched tents in the meadows.

Brenna was waiting at the bower door. At the sight of Åsa and Halfdan safe, she broke into a broad smile, whisking Halfdan and Fylgja away to be fed and coddled.

Åsa took Stormrider to her chamber. After the falcon had fed and bathed, Åsa tethered her on her perch and let the bird rest in the dim quiet.

Exhausted as she was, Åsa made her way to the guesthouse where the apprentices were tending the wounded. Soapstone cauldrons steamed on tripods over the longfire, some heating clean water while others simmered various concoctions of herbs that scented the air with an evil smell.

Several women were trying to get Eyvind's bloody clothes off without reopening his wounds. The blood had dried, and the garments stuck to his skin. The women were soaking the clothes and carefully prying them away from the injuries. Despite their efforts to be gentle, his face turned white and he ground his teeth.

Heid dipped a wooden cup in a cauldron containing an odiferous potion. "Drink this," she ordered, holding the cup to his lips. "It will dull the pain." He wrinkled his nose and sipped at the brew.

Once he had downed the concoction, he settled back, color returning to his face. Heid looked at Åsa. "What happened?" she demanded. "I tried to reach your mind, but my way was blocked."

Åsa replied, "I was guarded by Horik's völva, Groa. She was very powerful, and she invaded my thoughts. I learned a few things from her—like how to keep her out of my mind."

"You say 'was,'" said Heid.

Åsa nodded. "I fought her when she took Halfdan. We knocked over a lamp in the struggle, and her clothes caught fire. The whole fortress burned. I didn't kill her, but it's hard to imagine that she survived the conflagration. I have no doubt I'd still be a prisoner if she were alive."

Heid gave her a look of regret. "I'm sorry I failed you."

"You didn't fail me."

"Yet when you sent out a cry for help, I heard nothing though I was searching for you. It was Halfdan who heard you."

"My connection with him is strong, stronger than Groa's spell to prevent it."

"It goes far beyond the bond between mother and child. Halfdan is truly gifted."

Åsa agreed. "I am glad Ulf will be teaching him."

Heid eyed her. "You need to rest. I can tell you're exhausted. Eyvind is in safe hands with us."

"I know he is. Thank you."

"Go let Brenna coddle you. We can manage without you for now."

"I need to visit the wounded first," Åsa said. She walked the narrow rows between the pallets where the injured lay and listened while the apprentices reported on the prognosis for each sailor. If the patient was conscious, Åsa thanked them for their courage and wished them well. The guesthouse was full and overflowing with wounded. So many had been lost. She dared not dwell on them for fear she'd lose heart. She hid her inner dismay at how many of those that had been injured would never recover their full abilities. Some had axe wounds, others had been hit by arrows or spears. Some lay unconscious, others moaned and writhed in pain.

Heid came alongside her as she stared at the ranks of wounded.

"This is all my fault. If only I'd listened to you and not ventured to Sebbersund," Åsa said.

"Nay. Horik has lain in wait all these years, looking for his chance. It was only a matter of time. You could not have prevented it. Remember, I told you disaster would occur no matter what you did. Now you must prepare. He'll not let this pass."

The völva's words were small comfort. When Åsa had walked the length of the guesthouse and checked on each of the wounded, she stepped out the door. Once outside, she let her shoulders sag.

So few left to face the war that was coming.

Åsa called a council of war that afternoon in the great hall, before Olaf left for home.

"I plan to send to Ragnhild asking for reinforcements," Åsa said.

"Thora is our fastest rider," said Olvir.

"Good," said Åsa. "We'll send her today."

Jarl Borg looked up at the ceiling, calculating. "It will take her three days to get to Ragnhild, and a week for her fleet to get here."

Åsa sighed. "I know. And I doubt that Horik will be so considerate as to give us that much warning." She wished she could send her mind out to Ragnhild, but the shield-maiden had never been receptive to such things. For Ragnhild all that was real was what she could touch with the edge of her sword.

Thora set out that same day, riding fast over the mountains to Ragnhild in Gausel.

Åsa sent other riders to carry the war arrow throughout the hinterlands of Agder, commanding all the minor lords and freemen who owed her allegiance to make their arrangements and bring their fighters to Tromøy.

That evening, those who were able gathered in Tromøy's hall. Åsa scanned their ranks. If Horik attacked now, they would be lost. She prayed to Thor that it would take him time to recover from the battle and the fire before he could ready an assault. She needed as much time as she could get to muster a defense.

Olaf rose, and silence fell in the hall. In his poet's voice, he related the tale of the battle to a rapt audience. "We never would have gotten away alive, but Horik's hall caught fire."

Åsa took up the narrative. "The fire started when I got Halfdan away from Horik's sorceress. But I would never have escaped in the first place without this man, Cian." She gestured toward the Irishman, who stood. "He was a prisoner like me, a slave of Horik's. When Olaf attacked, Cian came for me and led me out through a secret passage. When Eyvind was injured in a fight with Horik's warriors and could not walk, Cian all but carried him back to *Far Traveler*. I owe him much. I have given him the option of returning to his homeland or joining my hird." Åsa raised her glass to toast the Irishman.

Cian approached her. He knelt before her and bowed his head. "My lady, by your leave, I wish to be in your service for a time, though ultimately I want to return to my homeland."

Åsa laid her sword across her knees. "You may stay here as long as you wish. When you are ready, I will send you to Ragnhild, queen in Gausel. Her husband was formerly an Irish king, Murchad mac Maele Duin, and they will see you safely home."

Åsa thought Cian paled a bit at the mention of Murchad's name, but the Irishman laid his hands on Åsa's sword.

"Cian, do you swear to serve me and defend me and my kingdom?"

"I swear to serve you, Lady, to defend you and your kingdom with my dying breath."

"I accept your oath. You are bound to me until I release you."

Cian stood and returned to his seat on the benches, smiling.

Olaf raised his horn and solemnly recited the names of Skiringssal's dead. As he called each name, their shipmates recounted their deeds, and a minni cup was drunk in remembrance of each. When Olaf had finished, Åsa took up the cup and named the dead of Tromøy. The drinking went on late into the night, until all the dead had been honored.

Åsa was among the last to leave. She forsook her lonely bed in the hall and made her way to the bower, where she crawled in beside Halfdan and Brenna. Fylgja guarded the foot of the bed, and Stormrider kept watch from her perch on the headboard. Even so, Åsa's sleep was restless.

War was coming.

CHAPTER 18

Olaf departed the next day, taking Halfdan and Fylgja with him.

"Light the signal fire as soon as Horik's sails are sighted," Olaf said.

"I will. Give my love to Sonja and Ulf." Åsa gave her son another kiss. Halfdan wriggled out of her grasp and scrambled over *Sea Dragon*'s gunnels to romp about the decks, chattering away while blithely interfering with the sailors' efforts as they tried to shove off. Poor Fylgja cowered in the stern as usual, one paw covering his nose.

Olaf vaulted aboard. He took the tiller and saluted Åsa. Dread filled her heart. She forced herself to smile and wave as she watched the ship depart, taking the father and son she loved. She reminded herself Halfdan would be safer in Skiringssal when Horik came for her.

She set her jaw and turned to face her future.

Over the next few days, Eyvind made progress under Heid's care. Åsa spent time with him whenever he was awake, which was more frequently each day. It helped keep her mind occupied and her heart full.

Cian visited the wounded and played his harp for them. Åsa listened raptly with the others. A longing grew in her, as if she could not get her fill of the music. Her mind cleared and her shoulders relaxed. Her sadness lifted and her chest filled with joy and strength.

When Cian's fingers stilled at last, no one spoke. The Irishman remained seated, eyes closed, as the sound faded.

Åsa felt light and peaceful. Her sadness was gone. Healed. Cian's music was healing.

EYVIND HAD RECOVERED ENOUGH to fret with the inactivity, and Åsa did her best to keep him entertained with endless games of hnefatafl. He had never taken the time to gain expertise with the game, but now he was becoming quite good, showing a distinct talent for strategy. He enjoyed playing either side, whether the attackers attempting to trap the king in his hall, or the defenders trying to protect their king and to open an escape route for him.

Cian came every day to play for the wounded. Healing was in the air.

But every morning Åsa woke in her solitary bed, Stormrider perched on the headboard. The falcon had recovered from her injuries. Each morning Åsa sent her hugr into the bird and flew out over the Skagerrak, surveying the sea for signs of Horik's fleet.

She longed to know how many ships he had, and the status of his preparations. The fire had set him back, she had no doubt. His hall was in ruins, and he had lost a significant number of men and ships in the battle with Olaf. It would take him some time to fill out the ranks, make repairs, and reprovision.

But how long?

She was tempted to fly farther, across the Skagerrak and

Jylland Peninsula to Horik's harbor, Gudsø Vig. The bay was hidden well enough he could gather an enormous fleet in secret. The trip to Erritsø was long and arduous, and Åsa could not risk being gone so long when she might be caught or injured, and trapped in the falcon's body at so critical a time.

Instead, she prepared Tromøy for the attack that was surely coming. With Jarl Borg and Olvir she drilled every person able to wield a weapon of any kind. Those who could not fight fletched arrows, sharpened blades, and repaired shields. The ships' crews were busy overhauling the longships. The shore reeked of pitch, and the sound of caulking irons rang throughout the day.

Åsa ordered the log boom deployed across the entrance to the harbor. She sent Olvir out with a work party at low tide to drive sharpened stakes just below the surface in the shallows in emulation of Horik's bay. With luck the Danes would not expect Åsa to have copied their ploy, and the stakes would rip the bottom out of any ships that got past the outer defenses.

If the enemy got that far, it would mean they had destroyed the combined fleets of Tromøy and Skiringssal. Åsa shuddered as an image invaded her mind of the smoking hulks of longships, the bloody corpses of Olaf, Olvir, and Kalv, and all their húskarlar floating in the water. She shook her head, banishing the vision of carnage to focus on the endless tasks to be done. Weapons, shields, armor—all must be readied. Everyone must be armed, down to the children.

Six days later as Stormrider flew over the sea, she sighted a dark swarm at the mouth of the Kattegat. The horizon was crowded with longships pouring through the straits and spilling into the Skagerrak. She lost count at thirty vessels, and still they came.

Horik had mustered a fleet in a shockingly short time, considering his hall must be a total loss. The Danish king had resources beyond imagining.

With no breeze to enable them to hoist sail, the enemy was forced to row for now. But wind could come up any time, fair or foul to him or to Tromøy.

She had one day, two at most. The falcon wheeled in the air, flying to the west in hopes of sighting Ragnhild's fleet, but the waters were empty of all but a few fishing boats.

Stormrider soared back to the chamber where Åsa lay entranced. The falcon perched on the headboard while her mistress's hugr slid back into her human body.

Åsa roused herself and hurried into the hall, where she sent a boy running to the signal fire.

She gathered her war council—Jarl Borg, Olvir, and Heid. "I sighted a fleet of thirty ships or more, crammed with warriors. There's no wind so they're rowing, for now, but he'll be here in a day or two. I estimate Horik is bringing nearly a thousand warriors. We have fewer than three hundred able fighters. I'll send for Olaf immediately. If he arrives in time, that will give us a little more than six hundred warriors, and eighteen ships."

"Any sign of Ragnhild?" asked Jarl Borg.

Åsa shook her head in despair. "I hope our rider reached her, but even if she's coming, her ships have not yet rounded the cape. She won't arrive before Horik."

She outlined her plans. "We'll form two battle lines in front of the entrance. Olaf's fleet will give us enough ships for a double line of nine."

Heid nodded her approval. "Not only is each line the auspicious number nine, but the sum of the two lines makes eighteen, another nine. Very lucky."

"Outnumbered as we are, we need all the luck we can get," Åsa said.

"I'll take the south end of the line," Olvir volunteered. A wave of dread filled Åsa as the reality of the battle hit home.

Aside from the center, where she and Olaf would fight, the ends of the line were the most dangerous places, with one side of each ship undefended. These two positions were critical, for if the Danes overcame them, they could run their way up the fleet.

She nodded in resignation. "You are the logical choice. If anyone can hold it, you can. I thank you for your courage."

"Who will hold the north end?" asked Jarl Borg.

"Kalv." Olvir named Olaf's second-in-command. "He's the only other logical choice."

"If he volunteers," said Åsa. The others nodded in assent.

"I'm sure he'll volunteer, but who else if not him?" Olvir said.

They discussed several of their best ship commanders as possibilities, but they all knew they needed Kalv in that position.

Åsa turned to Jarl Borg. "Of course, you'll be in charge of the shore defense in case the enemy breaks through our line. I'll leave you as many able-bodied fighters as possible. We'll deploy the log booms across the entrance behind us, and station archers on the promontories above to pick off the enemy. Hopefully the underwater stakes will slow them down." She heaved a sigh. "The odds are you'll have to fight."

Jarl Borg nodded his head gravely. Olvir jutted his chin. "Our warriors are worth ten of theirs."

Åsa smiled at his defiance.

"Tell Olaf to bring his bearskin," said Heid.

Åsa gave her a startled look. Years ago, Olaf had killed a bear when it attacked Åsa. Though Olaf had never gone berserk in battle, he was entitled to claim the title of a berserker. Olaf's father, Gudrød, had seen to it that his son choked down a bite of the beast's heart. Gudrød had the bear's skin and head preserved so that Olaf could wear it during ceremonies, though he had never done so.

"We must perform a full-fledged war ceremony," Heid said firmly. "We must summon all the power we can and gain the favor of the gods. We're going to need it, if we're to survive Horik's attack. We can't fight his forces with battle tactics alone."

Jarl Borg nodded in agreement. "I fear it's our only hope."

Åsa realized that Heid was right. The full favor of the gods and the land spirits would be required. Every warrior must find the wild beast within their hearts.

Including her. She wondered if she would be able to achieve that state. She never had before.

Åsa dispatched a boat to Skiringssal for Olaf. Heid assigned her apprentices to take turns on the seidr platform, chanting a vardlokkur continuously to beseech the vaettir to keep the winds calm in the Skagerrak.

While the other apprentices made preparations for the war ceremony, Olvir readied Tromøy's fleet, and Åsa worked with Jarl Borg to organize the shore defenses. A dozen of the wounded had recovered enough to join their numbers.

Cian found her. "Lady, in my country I was a warrior of some renown. I would fight by your side."

Åsa regarded the Irishman. He was armed only with his seax. The man had saved her life, and that of Eyvind. He'd proven himself enough to gain her trust. "Follow me." She took him to the armory, where he selected a long spear with a shaft of ash wood and a double-bladed war axe. He handled the weapons with a familiarity that told her he would be an asset in battle.

She found a shield, an iron helmet, and varnished battle-jacket that fit him well enough. Armed and armored, Cian stood proud as any Norse warrior.

Åsa cleared her throat. "Tonight we will hold a ritual to request the favor of our gods. I know you are a Christian, and I don't expect you to participate."

The Irishman smiled and shrugged. "It's true, I am a Christian, but in Ireland we are not above accepting help from all the gods. We still honor the old ways."

"I'm glad to hear that," she said.

When the defenses were in place, Åsa took to Stormrider once again to monitor the progress of Horik's fleet.

Out on the Skagerrak, the Danes still labored under oar, the breeze refusing to assist them. She mentally thanked Heid's apprentices for their constant chanting and whispered a prayer to the land spirits.

To the north, she glimpsed Olaf's fleet emerging from Skiringssal's harbor. They, too, were under oar, but Olaf knew how to play the back-eddies along the shoreline to boost their speed. Unless a breeze filled in soon, favoring the Danes, Olaf would arrive before the enemy.

Still no sign of Ragnhild.

On the shore, Tromøy's eight ships sat ready to launch. Olvir oversaw the last-minute preparations. Shields lined the rails of each ship; oars were neatly stacked in their racks; sea chests filled with armor and weapons had been loaded.

Stormrider soared over the steading, where the yard bustled with activity. The cooks prepared a meal to fortify the fighters while warriors burnished spear points and sharpened axe blades.

She flew into the bower chamber. The falcon perched on the headboard above the inert body on the bed, still enough to be a corpse. Foreboding flooded into her.

She sent her hugr into her human form, empowering it with life. Åsa clenched her fists and bolted upright. She was no corpse.

She hurried to the yard and asked the steward for a bowl of broth. As she sipped the fortifying liquid, her courage returned.

The lookout reported Olaf and his fleet at the harbor entrance. Åsa sent a pilot skiff out to open the log boom and guide them through the staked shallows.

She met them on the shore. "Did you bring your bearskin?" she asked Olaf.

"I did," he said. "I feel a bit foolish, but I do understand how badly we need the favor of the gods."

She lodged Olaf's warband in the second guesthouse, where

they prepared for the ceremony while the warriors of Tromøy made ready in the great hall.

The women outfitted themselves in the bower. For the first time, Åsa donned her falcon cloak. She had gathered each feather painstakingly over the years from Stormrider's molts and from falcon nests on the cliffs of Tromøy. The cape covered her shoulders, reaching to her waist, and she wore the beaked mask of a falcon fashioned from felted wool, adorned with more feathers.

Tonight she fervently wished she had some real berserkers or ulfhednar in her hird, but she had outlawed them years ago. The risk was too great to harbor their kind. She shuddered, remembering Hrafn and his ferocious warriors. When the fighting madness came over them, they had been impossible to control and even harder to kill. They had nearly overrun Tromøy and slaughtered them all.

She went out into the yard, where many had already gathered. Olaf towered over the other men, imposing in his skillfully fitted bearskin. The bear's head, its lower jaw removed, came down over his forehead, incisors gleaming white and pointed against his skin. The bear's body encased his. His arms were sheathed in bearskin, his hands gloved in the paws with their dagger-sharp claws. Even his leggings were covered with bear fur.

Åsa thought of the day Olaf had killed the bear, the day Halfdan had been conceived. She'd fallen in love with Olaf and come to hate him all in the same day. He'd saved her life only to betray her and bring her back to his father.

For years, she had struggled with conflicting feelings of love and distrust of him or any man. The two had drawn closer and then apart until, in despair, Olaf had married Sonja, and Åsa's world shattered.

That was all in the past now. They both had their beloved children, and Åsa had Eyvind to console her. Olaf truly loved Sonja. She was a special woman, and Åsa was happy for them both. They had all weathered the storms of youthful love, and now their lives were complete, save for a hollow ache deep inside her.

Åsa dragged her gaze from Olaf. Beside him, his second-in-command, Kalv, was dressed in the hide of an elk, his head crowned with an impressive rack of antlers. Thora wore a boar's head and hide, complete with tusks and a ridged back. She led the squadron of shield-maidens, dazzling in their best gowns, fully armed with shields and swords.

Jarl Borg emerged from the hall, leading the shore defense. They wore no costumes but carried spears and shields. Eyvind was beside him. He had risen from his sick bed a few days before, insisting on taking his place among them. Åsa regarded her lover with concern. His recovery had left him pale and thin, but his step was firm, and he hefted his weaponry vigorously enough. Still, fear for him coursed through Åsa. She would not let the Danes penetrate her lines and get at him.

Heid appeared at the bower door, resplendent in her midnight-blue cloak studded with gemstones. The völva looked as if she wore the night sky. She carried an iron pole lamp filled with seal oil to light the way as she led the procession to the sacred grove. Heid's apprentices walked behind her, chanting a vardlokkur, joined by four stout men leading an ox for sacrifice. The big animal was drugged with calming herbs that made him docile, though spearmen flanked him just in case.

Åsa and the other war leaders filed in behind, followed by all of Tromøy's people, from warrior to the youngest child. Their voices filled the twilight with a magical chorus. Åsa glimpsed Cian in the crowd, singing with the rest.

Heid entered the grove and staked the lamp in the ground before the images of the gods. The flickering light cast an eerie glow on the carved faces of Odin, Freyr, and Thor on their poles, towering above the hundreds of people who thronged the glade.

The men led forth the ox, and Åsa dispatched the animal with a precise slash to its throat, sending arterial blood gushing out, spraying those nearby. The men helped her ease the dying animal to the ground while Vigdis caught the blood in a brass bowl. When the bowl was full, Vigdis carried it to Heid while another apprentice took her place to catch the stream with another bowl.

The völva accepted the brimming vessel and a bundle of fir twigs. In her persona as the goddess Freyja, Heid dipped the bundle in the blood and sprinkled the images of the gods, beseeching them to give Tromøy the victory.

The völva turned to the war leaders. She anointed Åsa and Olaf first, then Jarl Borg, Olvir, Kalv, then all their warriors. Even Cian allowed a few drops to fall on him. The apprentices carried their bowls through the throng, sprinkling blood. The folk crowded in to ensure at least a drop or two touched them.

Once everyone had been blessed, the war leaders began their chant. Heid took up the iron lamp and led the way back to the yard, her apprentices behind her. The war leaders came next, followed by their warriors, and finally the rest of the crowd.

Outside the hall a huge bonfire blazed. Heid took up her Sami drum, painted with symbols of magic and war. With the leg bone of a reindeer, she began to beat a rhythm. The warriors raised their voices in a fierce chant as they circled the fire in a shuffling dance. Cian was among them, between Eyvind and Jarl Borg.

As she danced and chanted, Åsa felt an inner shift as the battle magic came over her. Power flooded into her limbs as if she were transforming into a falcon without leaving her physical body. Her arms unfolded like wings, and a falcon's cry vibrated in her throat. Her heart thumped in the rhythm of the drumbeat while her feet moved of their own accord. All around her, warriors danced in time to Heid's drum, faces turned to the sky. They moved as one, voices raised together in a war chant that resounded through the valleys and over the sea.

The dancing continued into the night, until the warriors began to drop to the ground. As the last dancer collapsed, Heid's drum went silent. The sorceress sagged in her chair; the drum and reindeer bone fell from her grip. Her apprentices bundled their mistress off to her bed. The dancers slept where they lay, utterly spent.

The ceremony had exhausted the warriors and calmed their fears. They slept like children.

CHAPTER 19

Åsa woke at dawn, the chant still singing in her blood. Beside her lay Eyvind, his hand on her waist. Though she'd slept on the ground, she felt strong and confident. She called Stormrider to her and took one final flight to see the Dane's progress.

Ships swarmed the sea. Though she had been expecting a mighty fleet, the sight shocked her. There were at least thirty vessels, crammed with warriors. They swept down on Tromøy like a plague of insects, ready to pillage and kill.

They would arrive before midday.

Åsa flew to the west, but the waters were still empty. They would get no help from Ragnhild that morning. She soared back and entered her sleeping form, where she lay trembling. Beside her, Eyvind stirred. He smiled and gathered her in his arms, stroking her hair until she calmed. Her arms went around him, and they held each other for what could be the last time.

"I hate to be left behind," Eyvind murmured. "I want to fight by your side."

"I know," she said gently. "But you are needed here with Jarl Borg to mount a defense if the Danes break through."

He sighed and nodded. There was no shame in shore defense.

Sleepy folk emerged from the hall and started the cooking fires. Soon the aroma of porridge wafted over the yard, and the warriors stirred. They rose and washed. After breakfast, they began donning helmets and armor, giving their weapons one last burnish. Cian shot Åsa a grin as he sharpened his axe.

Åsa's courage wavered when she compared their numbers to the fleet that was about to attack. Though she trusted Jarl Borg to defend Tromøy, she was thankful that Halfdan was safe in Skiringssal with Sonja, far from the battle.

Heid's apprentices helped their mistress mount the seidr platform, where she took her seat on her chair of prophecy and lit the brazier with trembling hands. The völva raised her voice in a chant to call the spirits to aid the defenders. Her acolytes surrounded the platform, chanting the vardlokkur. Heid's eyes closed, her head lolled on her shoulder, and her voice stilled. Heid would remain there in communion with the land vaettir throughout the battle.

Åsa worried about the sorceress's health in such an arduous feat, but with the odds against them, Tromøy needed her more than ever.

The ship's crews finished their breakfasts and made ready to depart. Åsa mounted Gullfaxi to lead the entourage down to the shore. Eyvind climbed on his horse with effort and took his place beside her. Olvir, Jarl Borg, Olaf, and Kalv rode behind, followed on foot by their warbands and those who would remain behind.

Ran's Lover lay on the beach among the eighteen other ships, her hull resplendent with freshly painted green and red strakes and shields to match. Åsa dismounted and handed the reins to one of the stable lads. Eyvind got down from his horse and took her into his arms. He kissed her, murmuring, "Come back to me."

The urgency in his voice kindled an overwhelming determination in her. "I will," she said. I must win. The Danes can never reach my people.

Vision blurred with tears, she gently pulled away from Eyvind's arms and climbed aboard *Ran's Lover*. She took hold of the tiller and swallowed hard while the ships crewed up. Cian took his place beside her, proud in his helmet and varnished battle-jacket. He gripped the long spear, his battle axe tucked in his belt. The lanky Irishman towered over her and nearly everyone else except Olaf.

The shore folk heaved the ships out into the water. The rowers on every ship took their seats and raised their oars straight up. At her signal, they brought the oars down in unison and began to row. The crowd onshore raised a cheer as the fleet surged into the bay.

The ships dropped the archers off at the harbor's entrance. They opened the log boom to allow the ships to row out to the open sea, then drew it closed again and scrambled to their places on the promontory.

The Norse fleet emerged onto a flat calm sea. Åsa ordered the ships to raft up in their two lines of nine ships, effectively blockading the entrance to Tromøy's harbor. *Ran's Lover* took the center of the line, flanked by Olaf in *Sea Dragon*. Olvir, in command of *Night Raider*, stationed himself on the far southern end where he would defend the end of the line, with no ship protecting his southern flank. As hoped, Kalv had volunteered to take the position on the northern end. The second-row ends were strongly manned to support Olvir and Kalv.

As the sun rose high in the sky, the Danes' sails filled the horizon. Åsa took a deep breath and calmed her stomach. She set her jaw and gripped her spear. They had to survive. They had to prevent the Danes from breaking through and reaching Tromøy.

The enemy fleet approached. "Shields!" Åsa called, her order relayed throughout the fleet. Half the rowers shipped their oars and plucked shields from the rail while the other oarsmen held the ships steady. Åsa called to the archers on board, and they strung their bows. "Nock!" On every ship archers set their arrows on their strings. When she could make out the enemy's figureheads, Åsa cried, "Draw!" Bows creaked throughout the fleet. She watched the Danes get a little closer—then, "Loose!" Two hundred arrows hissed into the air.

An instant later, the order to loose came from the Danes.

"Shields!" Åsa cried, and the rowers flung up their shields to form a roof, sheltering the rowers and fighters alike.

The missiles hailed down. The Danes had gotten their range right on the first try. Arrows thwacked into shields and gunnels, raising cries where they found their mark in human flesh. Three of Åsa's crew fell, and their shipmates dragged them out of harm's way.

Åsa watched their own volley hit home on the Danes' shield fort. From the screams, their arrows found a few marks of their own.

The enemy surged closer, and the time for arrows was past. "Ready spears!" Åsa shouted. The tallest and strongest among them, those with the longest range, hefted their javelins and prepared to throw. Beside her, Cian's spear quivered in his hand, poised in the air.

"Hold! Hold!" Åsa ordered as the enemy rowed down on them. When she could make out their faces, she cried "Loose!" and the spears soared through the air. The Danes flung at the same time, and the javelins crossed in the air.

The shieldmen yanked enemy spears out of their shields and sent them back to kill their owners.

The sun rose higher, and the day heated up. Sweat trickled under Åsa's helm and ran down her neck. Already her shoulders ached from holding the shield against the enemy spears that thudded into the boards. The wood shattered under the continuous onslaught. A spear point impaled her shield and split the central board. She tilted the edge toward Cian, and he yanked the javelin out, but the shattered wood rendered the shield useless. Åsa threw it overboard where no one would trip over it and snatched up another from the rail just as a new enemy volley landed.

As Åsa had feared, half a dozen enemy ships in the rear ranks sheered off and headed for the southern end, where Olvir was stationed. The Danes kept the rest of the line fully engaged, so no one could go to his aid. The ships were close now, shield wall to shield wall, jabbing spears and short swords between and beneath shields as they sought enemy flesh.

Between onslaughts, Åsa glanced to the south. Olvir held the line with his two ships against six. Grappling hooks flew from the enemy, catching *Night Raider*'s gunnel and his support vessel on their open sides. Åsa glimpsed axe heads and spear points flashing in the sunlight as Olvir's crew and the ship behind him put up a ferocious resistance. The sound of wood splintering mingled with screams of rage and pain.

The Danish vessels gradually wore *Night Raider* down. Blades ceased to flash. The enemy overwhelmed Olvir's ship while Horik's front line kept up their attack on the center, preventing any chance of rescue. The Danes swarmed aboard *Night Raider* and cut the crew down. Screams and splashes sounded as sailors were slain and thrown overboard.

Åsa saw Olvir go down in the melee. She could not see what happened to him after that. Dread threatened to overwhelm her until a spearhead snaked past her shield and forced her attention back to the battle.

She shrank back, and the spear narrowly missed her side. She gave a roar of rage and rammed her own spear between the shields. Her blade met the hard surface of a varnished battle-jacket and threatened to slide off. She shoved the point harder and felt it pierce the coats of varnish. A scream told her she'd found flesh. Putting her whole body behind one final thrust, she felled her opponent.

With a shout of victory, she jerked her spear out of the varnished jacket. By now the air was seething with gulls and ravens. They wheeled over a sea of red foam, their raucous cries drowning out the screams of men. Corpses bobbed, and the carrion eaters swooped in to pick off the choicest tidbits of eyes and lips.

The Danes cleared the two end ships of warriors, cut them loose, and boarded the next two vessels in the battle line. More Danish ships joined from the rear ranks, and the enemy poured in like ants on a carcass. They cut down the crews of one ship after another, working their way toward the center where Åsa and Olaf fought, while Horik's main force pressed the line of defense hard with a continual barrage of spears and axes.

Then from the south, sails appeared. Åsa's heart thumped hard and her hopes surged as she recognized the familiar blue and white sail of the lead ship.

"Ragnhild!"

A cheer rose up from Tromøy's beleaguered fleet as the shield-maiden's ships descended on the Danes.

From the corner of her eye, she saw more of Horik's ships peel off from the rear and swarm the northern end of Skiringssal's line. Kalv appeared to hold them off as they tried to overwhelm his end and work their way to the center where they would meet up with their counterpart.

Åsa gritted her teeth and held her position, blinking away the sweat that stung her eyes. Her left shoulder and arm had long ago seized up and were now locked in position, gripping her shield before her, right arm jabbing her sword in and out between the shield wall.

She risked another glance toward Kalv. Her stomach dropped as she saw the Danes mob his ship. The enemy vessels poured in behind the defensive lines, rowing for the entrance to Tromøy's harbor—and the log boom. The boom was nearly submerged, barely visible on the surface of the water.

Åsa nodded to Cian and stepped out of the front line. He took her shield and slid into her place. She stared behind her at the enemy speeding toward the entrance.

As Åsa had hoped, the leading Danish ships hit the logs full speed. The shudder jolted through the front lines. Ships in the rear rammed the vanguard. Chaos and confusion reigned in the enemy fleet.

Åsa signaled the attack, and the rear line of her ships swarmed the Danes. The archers stationed high above the blockade rained arrows on the enemy as the Norse ships bore down on them. Caught off guard, the Danes were slow to mount a defense. Some tried to escape through the shallows, where Olvir's stakes ripped their keels out. Those ships sank and further clogged the entrance, while their warriors were picked off by the archers on the promontories.

The arrows took a fearful toll on the Danes, and the Norse ships closed in. They hurled grappling hooks onto the enemy gunnels and made them fast.

"Board!" cried Åsa, and her warriors leaped onto the Danish ships, slashing and stabbing the distracted foes, reaping a bloody harvest.

The Norse cleared the warriors from several enemy vessels, but the Danes had plenty of reserves. More Danish ships poured into the gap and soon surrounded the Norse, who scrambled back to their ships as the enemy cut loose the unmanned ships to get to them. Now Tromøy's defenders were caught between two lines of the enemy.

To the south, Ragnhild's ships were hidden by Danes. Åsa couldn't tell how the battle went there.

She stole a glance at the shore. Jarl Borg had rallied the shore defense, and they watched helplessly as the enemy overwhelmed the Norse fleet.

Åsa nudged her way back into the shield wall beside Cian. She found herself staring into the eyes of her enemy. Horik leered at her, his eyes alight with battle-lust. "There you are, little queen.

Soon I'll have your ships and your kingdom, and next I'll take Skiringssal since I see that all their forces are gathered here. I'll take Olaf's queen instead of you, and the Shining Hall will be under Danish rule once again. Then I'll find your son and bash his brains out. You will be my thrall."

Åsa's throat was so dry her retort came out as a croak. She glared at her enemy.

Horik turned his head and shouted over his shoulder to his crew, "Prepare to board!"

Olaf and Åsa rallied their surviving warriors to form a shield fort around the dwindling fleet.

The Danes surged in on all sides, grappling their prey and thrusting blades between their shields while the Norse jabbed back from behind their defenses. Her warriors had long since run out of their own missiles and had been yanking spears from their shields to fling them back at the enemy.

A javelin shot through the shield wall to strike Åsa in the thigh. She staggered as the pain sent fury burning in her veins, and Cian caught her before she fell. Battle rage surged through her, revitalizing her exhausted body. Shrieking a battle cry, she ripped the spear from her thigh and hurled the bloody missile back at the enemy. The javelin struck its owner full on the chest, piercing his varnished battle-jacket and felling the man.

She snatched up an axe and whirled it in a flurry of blows, chunking meat off the boarding Danes. Beside her, Cian worked his own axe, his long reach punishing anyone in range. The battle fever caught among her crew, and they attacked the enemy with fury.

The boarders fell back under the onslaught. Åsa caught her breath and elbowed the sweat from her eyes. What she saw stopped her heart.

From the north, more ships closed in. Was there no end to the Danish fleet? Beside her, Olaf was still holding his own against the Danes, but now he was sure to be overrun. Åsa braced for the arrows and spears to fly. "Ready shields!" she rasped.

Åsa shoved her shield against the warrior next to her while Cian sheltered them both beneath his. From under the roof of shields, she saw a volley of arrows fly from the new ships.

She frowned. Their range was too short. She knew the enemy needed to test their distance, but this flight was going to hit Horik's ships.

The arrows hailed down on the Danes from behind. Fully engaged in fighting Åsa's warriors, none of them raised a shield, and the missiles reaped a deadly harvest. Shrieks rose from the enemy. Over the rim of his shield, the king of the Danes stared, mouth open.

The newcomers grappled Horik's ships from behind. They clambered over the gunnels, axes in hand, and began to harvest Danes.

"Who are they?" shouted Åsa. The ships looked no different than the Danish ships. The warriors wore helmets exactly like Horik's men, and her own crew for that matter. All she could tell was that the newcomers were slaughtering her enemies.

Hope gave new strength to Åsa's arms, and she attacked Horik with renewed fury. The men alongside her gained energy as well. Cian windmilled his axe while the others jabbed their spears into the Danish ranks.

Horik and his húskarlar fought on against Åsa's and Cian's onslaught. Still the arrows from the north hailed down on the Danes, decimating their numbers.

With a cheer, the newcomers overran Horik's northern ships, cutting them loose as they went. Ragnhild's fleet emerged from the melee to the south, clearing the decks of Danes. As the ranks of enemy ships thinned, Horik screamed, "Retreat!" His ships formed a fortress around his flagship and began to back oars.

"Shoot them!" Olaf shouted. Spears and arrows followed the enemy ships as they tried to flee. Danes screamed and fell.

The newcomers surged forward to join the defenders. Their leader faced Olaf, breathing hard. From beneath his helmet his eyes twinkled.

"Greetings, Grandson. Sorry it took us so long," Alfgeir huffed. "The tide was against us."

"Grandfather!" Olaf stuttered. "You said you wouldn't come. What changed your mind?"

Alfgeir shrugged. "I need the exercise. My wife says I'm getting old and lazy. When my patrol saw the Danish fleet attack, I couldn't resist joining in the fun."

Bodies bobbed in the red water, but none of them were the Danish king. In the distance, the decimated enemy fleet retreated, maintaining their defensive formation. Horik's pennant flew from the mast of one of them.

"Horik's getting away," said Åsa. Her head felt strangely light. Cian was behind her, gripping her arm.

"There are too many of them for us to vanquish," said Alfgeir. "We would only waste our warriors and Horik would still get away. They could defeat us. Best to save our strength for the next time." He turned to Åsa and Olaf. "Hurry, children. We need to salvage those ships we can and get back to shore. It's getting late. I'm an old man and I need a pot of ale and a soft bed."

Åsa's vision swam and the world spun. Cian caught her as she fell.

"Åsa!" Olaf cried.

Cian was on his knees beside her, binding her leg with a length of linen. Åsa felt the pain come on for the first time as her battle fury wore off.

"We need to get her to shore," said Olaf. "Take on the wounded and head home. We'll cruise the waters to pick up survivors and gather what ships we can."

Åsa heard someone call out that they'd found Olvir. "Does he live?" she cried, but got no answer.

CHAPTER 20

As the Norse fleet approached the harbor entrance, the archers scrambled down from the overlooks and opened the log booms. The surviving ships rowed into Tromøy's harbor, towing several Danish ships, as well as their own vessels that had lost their crews. The wounded littered the decks, their groans mingling with the shrieks of the carrion birds that hovered above them, watching for death.

Åsa sat propped against the gunnels while one of her crew members steered the ship. Over the rail she glimpsed Eyvind on the shore, craning his neck to search the ship anxiously. When he saw her sitting on the deck, his face wrinkled with concern.

He was waiting in the shallows when the prow of *Ran's Lover* touched the shore. As the ship's keel ran up the beach, he reached in to pull her over the side.

He gaped at the blood-soaked linen tied to her leg. "You're wounded!"

"I'm all right," she said. "I've lost a little blood."

Cian helped her up and delivered her to Eyvind's waiting arms. The Irishman vaulted over the side to help carry her. Åsa gritted her teeth against the pain and clung tight to Eyvind as he sloshed through the shallows.

They laid her in one of the wagons that awaited the injured. Eyvind climbed in beside her and wrapped her in sheepskin.

"What of Olvir?" she said. "I heard he's been found, but I don't know if he lives."

"I'll find him. But now let's get you to a healer."

Soon Åsa's cart was overflowing with wounded. Some were conscious, their faces set in grim lines. Others moaned in a trance of pain. The cart reeked of blood and vomit.

The driver clucked to the horses, and they set off up the trail. Those who could walk made their way wearily behind, supporting each other.

Åsa clutched Eyvind's hand as the wagon lurched up the trail. Every rut sent pain shooting through her leg. Cian's wrap had stopped the blood seeping, but her head swam and her vision blurred.

The cart jerked to a halt before the guesthouse that served as an infirmary. Cian was there to help Eyvind lift her down and carry her inside. Brenna met them at the door. Clucking, the old fóstra directed the men to lay Åsa on a pallet. She ground her teeth to keep from crying out as the healers peeled away her blood-soaked trews and cleaned and dressed her wound.

"You'll do fine, my brave lamb," her old fóstra murmured, plying her with a cup of foul-smelling brew.

Åsa held her breath and gulped down the potion. The hot liquid sent new strength flowing through her limbs.

She gently pushed Brenna aside and rose. "Take me to Olvir."

"She won't rest until I do," said Eyvind. Brenna nodded her assent.

Eyvind took her arm and helped her limp over to where her second-in-command lay on a pallet in the corner. The young healer, Dagny, knelt by his side. The girl examined him with an anxious look on her face.

Olvir was pale and unmoving. He looked like he was dead. For an instant, Åsa could not breathe. He was her right hand, the man she had relied upon for so many years. He'd stood with her against Gudrød. Once, before she had made her agreement with Sonja, Åsa had considered making him Halfdan's foster father if and when he married. If he died, what would she do without him? There were promising warriors among her hird, but none she had known all her life, none who had been such a friend through so much. Olvir could never be replaced.

"How does he?" Åsa asked, worry gnawing at her gut.

"He breathes, but his wounds are grievous." Dagny choked on the words. She pulled back the covers.

Olvir's whole body seemed to be bandaged. His arms, chest, and legs were wrapped in bandages stained pinkish with blood. The most worrisome was an abdominal wound. His body was scrupulously clean, his injuries bound with linen from which Åsa scented honey and herbs. Dagny was a skilled healer. What's more, the girl appeared to care for Olvir. If it were possible for him to survive, she would ensure it.

Åsa swayed on her feet and the edges of her vision darkened. Eyvind gripped her elbow. "You need to rest."

She shook her head. "I have guests I must see to. Help me, please?"

In the yard, a throng of folk awaited her. She suddenly felt overwhelmed and wobbled on her legs. The world swam. Eyvind caught her.

"Åsa!" cried a familiar voice. She looked up into Ragnhild's face.

"Am I glad to see you," Åsa murmured.

"Let's get her to her chamber."

She let Eyvind and Ragnhild half-carry her to her chamber off the hall, where they pulled off her padded jacket and battle-grimed tunic. They washed her then helped her into a clean linen underdress.

"You've lost too much blood," said Eyvind. "You must rest awhile. I will see to your guests for now." He kissed her on the forehead and departed.

"I'll stay with you," said Ragnhild. "We have some catching up to do."

The shield-maiden unbraided Åsa's hair and carefully combed out the sweat-soaked tangles.

"I've never known you to be so gentle," Åsa said.

Ragnhild snorted and gave the hair a yank. "It's motherhood. It makes you soft."

Åsa yelped. "I'd hardly call you that. A little compassion is a nice addition to your character. Tell me, how is your son?"

Ragnhild grunted and tied off a neat braid. "Herolf is wonderful! I never wanted children, but now that I have one of my own, my opinion is completely changed. I wish I could have brought him with me, but even I won't bring a baby to war."

Åsa marveled that the shield-maiden had taken to motherhood with such enthusiasm. But Ragnhild did everything with gusto.

"And Murchad?"

"He is well. He's getting used to Gausel, and he is respected by my people. It's taking him some time to get accustomed to the fact that I rule there, not him. He's kept busy initiating trade with Ireland. We'll make a voyage there soon. You wouldn't believe their goldsmithing, and their linens are even finer than ours." Ragnhild chattered away about crops and cattle and ships.

Åsa's eyelids began to feel heavy. They seemed to be stuck together. "I'm listening," she murmured. "Keep talking."

ÅSA BLINKED AWAKE in the dimness of her chamber, alone. She must have fallen asleep while Ragnhild was talking. Well, she felt much the better for it. Her wound was little more than a dull ache.

She hoisted herself out of bed and pulled a wool apron dress over her linen undergown. Fastening the straps with bronze oval brooches, she stepped into her shoes and limped out the door.

A throng greeted her as she strode into the yard. She spotted Eyvind in a knot of men, including Olaf and Alfgeir.

Ragnhild saw her and smiled. "You look much better now."

"I feel much better," said Åsa. "Ragnhild, I have someone I'd like you to meet. One of Murchad's countrymen. He helped me escape from Horik's fortress, and I owe him a great deal." She scanned the crowd. Cian was nowhere to be seen. "He must be resting. You'll meet him tonight at the feast."

One of Heid's apprentices hurried to Åsa. "Lady, you're needed. It's the völva."

Something in the apprentice's tone put her on alert.

"I must go to her." She hurried after the apprentice. Eyvind pulled away from the men and trailed along behind her, a look of concern on his face. The women looked at him askance as he entered the bower, but no one told him he couldn't be there.

Åsa entered the völva's chamber, where apprentices clustered around Heid's bed. They stepped aside to let Åsa through.

The völva lay in her bed, obviously still in a trance. Her arms and legs twitched in spasm.

Vigdis caught Åsa's eye with a worried look that sent a shard of fear through her heart. "She should have come out of it hours ago," said Vigdis in a strained tone. "We've tried everything possible to bring her back. I fear she has become lost in the Otherworld. You must search for her on the paths of the dead."

Åsa nodded, tamping down the terror that welled up at the thought of returning to the Hel road. But even worse was the possibility of losing the völva again.

Eyvind clutched her arm. "Åsa, you're exhausted. This is too dangerous."

"Not as dangerous as losing Heid," she said.

"You're wounded. Let Vigdis do it."

Åsa looked into his worried face. "I have to be the one to go. I'm the only one who's been there before." He did not look reassured, but he released his grip on her arm.

Her stomach curdled with fear, Åsa climbed onto the bed beside Heid. She rummaged in the völva's pouch and took a seed of henbane from it. The apprentices gathered around her and began to croon the vardlokkur. Åsa cast the seed on the brazier that burned beside the bed. She leaned back against the headboard, drew in a deep breath of the intoxicating smoke, and sent her exhausted mind to search the paths of the dead.

Her vision swam. Darkness whirled, then gradually steadied and resolved into a forest landscape. A trail led into the woods, and she followed it until she came to a clearing where an immense ash tree stood. Its branches stretched into the heavens and its roots disappeared into the earth. This was Yggdrasil, the World Tree. Its name meant Odin's Steed, and on its limbs the adept could travel through the nine realms.

Beneath the tree three jotun women worked at their loom. They were the Nornir, the three sisters who wove the web of life. As Åsa approached, they looked up from their work.

"Hail, Åsa, queen of Agder," said Skuld, the veiled one. "We have been waiting for you. You seek the völva Heid."

"Is she here?" asked Åsa.

"She wanders the paths of the dead, but she cannot linger there. She has much yet to do in Midgaard before she earns her rest."

Urdr, the eldest sister, nodded toward the World Tree's third root. "You must fetch her and bring her back."

Åsa swallowed and stared at the immense tree. Beneath one of the three roots a dark hole yawned.

She approached the root, fighting panic with every step.

Taking a deep breath, she got to her hands and knees and crawled headfirst into the hole.

She slithered into the muddy passageway. Below her she heard the gnashing teeth of the serpent Nidhogg as it chewed on the roots. The tunnel twisted and turned, down and to the north. The earth was chill, and moisture dripped from the overhead. As she crawled down, the air grew colder, but ahead a kind of daylight glimmered.

Shivering, she worked her way toward the light and spilled out into the gray of Niflheim, the land of freezing mist. Beside the root flowed the icy waters of the spring, Hvergelmir.

Before her lay the road to Hel, a way she knew well and dreaded. At least her leg no longer hurt, here in the land of the dead. She got to her feet, squared her shoulders, and set off into the mist at a jog, hoping to catch Heid before she reached the dark valleys.

In the foggy distance a figure wandered. Åsa hurried her steps. As she drew near, the figure resolved into that of the völva. Åsa breathed a sigh of relief and called her name.

The völva did not look up at her approach. Heid clutched her shawl around her head, muttering into it.

"Heid!" shouted Åsa. "Heid! You must come back with me!"

The sorceress raised her head, glaring at Åsa. "No!" she snarled.

"This is not where you belong," said Åsa.

"I've done enough. I have given everything I have."

"The Nornir say otherwise. They say your work in middle-earth is not complete."

The völva turned away.

Desperation overwhelmed Åsa. "You are needed. I need you. Halfdan needs you. Your apprentices and all of Tromøy need you. Don't abandon us, I beg you."

"I am old. I'm worn to the bone." Heid's voice was raw with despair.

"I know," Åsa said softly, taking the sorceress's arm. Gently but firmly, she pulled the völva back toward the root of Yggdrasil. Her heart ached for Heid. "Come with me. I will take care of you. I promise."

To Åsa's relief, Heid shuffled along, grumbling plaintively. Her voice chilled Åsa to her marrow. Heid sounded like an old woman who had lost her wits. What if she brought the völva back in body, but not in mind?

She had no choice but to follow the Nornir's command.

They reached the muddy passage beneath the root. Åsa boosted Heid's frail body up into the tunnel and climbed up after her, pushing her along, murmuring encouragement as they scrabbled their way toward daylight. At last, covered in muck, they crawled out from beneath the tree. Åsa's leg began to throb again.

The Nornir were busy at their weaving and did not look up as Åsa approached the sisters of fate. Åsa cleared her throat. "Good ladies, I have found Heid, but her mind is ailing. What must I do to heal her?"

Verdandi, the middle sister, spared her a sympathetic glance. "It may be that you cannot."

"What?"

"It may be too late to heal her mind. The damage is great."

"Then why must I bring her back?"

Verdandi shrugged. "It is woven," she said.

"What do you mean, 'It's woven'?" Åsa shouted. She wanted to rip the tapestry down and tear the threads apart.

Urdr fixed her with a stern gaze. "Mortal, take your old woman back to Midgaard and live your lives. The pattern is set. You'd better fetch her."

The three sisters turned their backs and resumed their weaving.

Åsa glanced over to see Heid wandering back toward the roots of Yggdrasil.

She limped to the völva and took her arm. Heid stared at Åsa as if she'd never seen her before.

"I want to go home," the völva said plaintively.

"This way, Heid. Home is this way." Heart breaking, Åsa pulled her gently away from the World Tree. To her relief, the sorceress followed obediently.

~

Åsa jerked awake, dread pooling in the pit of her stomach.

Heid lay on the bed. The völva's arms and legs had stopped twitching, and her eyes were open. Her gaze met Åsa's.

Relief washed over Åsa. The völva was alive, if not quite well.

"Who are you?" said Heid.

Alarm shot through Åsa, shaking her to her core. "You know me. I'm Åsa."

A claw-like hand snaked out from the covers to clutch her arm. "Where am I?"

"You're home!"

"This isn't home. Where is my husband? Where are my children?"

Guilt darkened Åsa's spirits. She'd brought Heid back against her will. Damn the Nornir!

Vigdis arrived with a bowl of broth. She looked down at Åsa's leg. "You've opened your wound. Go to the guesthouse and have someone bind it."

"She doesn't know me," Åsa said as she got up and made for the door. "She doesn't know where she is."

Vigdis shook her head. "She has been through far too many strains. She's had no time to fully recover. Perhaps with rest…"

Åsa bowed her head and limped out the door, simultaneously relieved to get away from the horror, and guilt-ridden for abandoning Heid. She tried to convince herself the völva would be better off in Vigdis's care, but she didn't believe it.

The guesthouse overflowed with wounded. Their moans sounded a chorus of pain. The cauldron simmered over the central fire, and the scent of healing herbs permeated the air with its undertone of blood and vomit.

All the able-bodied women and men of Tromøy were busy binding wounds, stitching gashes, and setting limbs. In the far corner, she glimpsed Olvir. His eyes were closed and his face was very pale. The young healer, Dagny, still tended him.

The girl was so engaged in her ministrations that she did not look up at Åsa's approach. Åsa caught her breath as she realized the girl loved Olvir. Her feelings were declared in the gentle way she bathed his wounds, the expression of devotion on her face. Åsa prayed fervently that Olvir would survive, for both their sakes.

Dagny looked up at her, startled. "Lady," she said, hastening to rise.

"Any improvement?" Åsa asked.

The girl's eyes were liquid with emotion. "There's no sign of infection, but he's lost so much blood. I've fed him the leek soup —soon we'll see." A tear spilled down one cheek.

Åsa took her hand. "Olvir is very dear to me. I don't know how Tromøy could survive without him. I am most grateful for anything you can do for him. I will wait with you while the leek soup finds its way."

The girl met Åsa's gaze, and an understanding passed between them. Åsa took her hand, and they sat, waiting for what seemed an age.

"I think enough time has passed." Dagny looked at her inquiringly, and she nodded.

The girl put her nose to Olvir's stomach wound and sniffed. She sat up and looked at Åsa with a face full of hope. "You try."

Åsa's heart skittered as she leaned over the wound and took in a deep breath. She smelled blood and soap. But no leeks. She sat up and met Dagny's gaze. "No odor," she affirmed. "Under your care, I'm sure he'll do fine."

Joy lit Dagny's face. Satisfied, Åsa rose and walked among the rows of wounded on their pallets. Cian came in, carrying his harp. He nodded to Åsa, then took a seat on a stool and began to play. The healing music resounded in the room, its rhythm pacing that of a heart at rest. The moaning stopped as wounded and healer alike listened raptly. Åsa stood transfixed, her anxiety lifting and hope rising in her heart.

Brenna caught her by the elbow. "Come here and let me tend to that leg." Keeping a firm grip on Åsa's arm, Brenna led her over to a bench, where she unwound the blood-soaked bandage from Åsa's thigh. The old fóstra murmured as she cleaned and bound Åsa's wound with fresh linen. "You need to stay off this leg, Lady. If you let it heal, soon enough you'll be running with the best of them."

Åsa patted Brenna's shoulder, wishing she felt as young as the fóstra perceived her to be. She hated to leave while Cian played, but she had something else she must do. Walking slowly to please Brenna, she left the guesthouse and crossed the yard to the stable. Gullfaxi whinnied a greeting. Åsa brought out a withered apple and a knife and cut pieces for the mare. The horse nuzzled her and lipped her hair. Åsa picked up a curry comb and groomed her, then saddled her and led her outside. She mounted and rode down the trail to the beach, her heart a lead ingot in her chest.

The dead had been laid out in the boathouse, awaiting the proper ceremony. Åsa dismounted and pushed open the door. The stench of death hit her like an evil storm. She squared her shoulders and stepped into the dim, cavernous structure, now transformed into the realm of Hel.

She walked the rows of corpses, looking into each bloodless face, each one once a friend, now frozen forever in death. Dismay and grief overwhelmed her, and she sank to her knees. Tromøy had survived, and sent Horik packing, but so many had been lost.

She spent an hour in silent communion with the dead. At last she rose, shoulders stooped, and went outside.

Eyvind was waiting. "Brenna told me you were down here."

Åsa nodded glumly.

He put his arm around her. "We're alive. We owe it to the dead to make the most of the lives we have left."

His words rang true. Åsa lifted her head and met his gaze. "You're right. Let's do them proud."

In the evening those who were able gathered on the beach where the dead had been laid upon a bed of logs, every crevice stuffed with tinder and kindling. The pile rose high as a burial mound.

The living gathered to toast their victory and remember the dead. Eyvind took his place beside Åsa, while Alfgeir stood next to his grandson.

Åsa turned to Olaf. "King Olaf, I thank you for coming to our aid," she said formally.

Olaf inclined his head and raised his horn in return. "We are forever allies."

They drank. Next Åsa saluted Olaf's grandfather. "King Alfgeir, if not for your timely arrival, I fear this would be a Danish hall."

Alfgeir took a huge swig of his ale and said, "In truth, you owe your thanks to my wife. Had she not shamed me into it, I would never have come. I had forgotten how much fun it was to kill Danes." The old warlord looked at Olaf. "You have grown into a great warrior. I am proud to call you my grandson."

Olaf smiled and toasted Alfgeir. "Long have I waited to hear you say those words, Grandfather."

Åsa raised her cup to Ragnhild. "Dear friend, I thank you for answering our call."

The shield-maiden raised her cup in return. "I will always come when you call, my queen."

"And should you ever call for my help, I will come as well," said Åsa. She spotted Cian and waved him over. "Ragnhild, I'd like you to meet the newest member of my hird, Cian. I owe him my life and the lives of many others."

The Irishman swept a bow. Ragnhild smiled and toasted him. "I'm sorry my husband could not be here to meet you. I'm sure it would have been a happy meeting of two countrymen."

"I'm sorry he's not here, Lady. I hope one day to meet him."

There was an odd note in the Irishman's voice. Åsa reminded herself that Norse was not his native tongue, and his accent gave his speech strange inflections.

Heid was still not able to rise from her bed. Vigdis presided over the rites of the dead. While the acolytes chanted, the senior apprentice circled the pyre with a torch, lighting the tinder and kindling as she went.

As the bonfire flamed, Åsa named each of the Tromøy dead, and the friends and family of each rose and spoke of their loved ones. She raised her horn in a toast to them all. When they had drunk the minni cup to Tromøy's deceased, Olaf rose and named those he had lost. Their shipmates praised the fallen, and he raised his horn in a salute. Lastly Alfgeir rose and toasted the five warriors he'd lost that day. Ragnhild kept her head bowed. Her crew had come through the battle with no losses, only a few wounded.

When all the dead had been remembered, Cian brought out his harp. The moment his fingers plucked the wire strings, a bell-like chord resonated and everyone fell silent. A heavy, sodden mass weighed in Åsa's chest as sorrow overcame her. Tears fell as the crowd mourned their dead.

CHAPTER 21

Åsa's leg throbbed, waking her in the night. She eased out of bed, trying not to disturb Eyvind, and fumbled for the willow-bark potion Vigdis had given her. She took a big swallow, then wandered outside. It would take a while to bring relief. She limped about the yard, easing the stiffness in her leg.

The steading was bathed in the pale light of the waning half-moon, giving it a ghostly appearance. She glimpsed another figure hobbling over near the byres. Someone else's injuries kept them awake. She made her way over to commiserate.

The person was bundled in a hooded cloak. As Åsa drew near, something familiar in the figure's movements alerted her. The figure turned to face her.

"Heid!"

"Good evening, Åsa, queen." The völva's tone was strangely formal.

Åsa reached out to hug her. "I'm so glad to see you're feeling better."

The figure vanished.

Åsa's heart hammered. What had she just seen? She hurried to the bower. There lay the völva, still and white under her down comforter. Vigdis was slumped on her stool, her head resting on the mattress. As Åsa entered, she startled up from her doze.

"I saw Heid outside, walking," Åsa gasped.

Vigdis's mouth formed an O. She looked toward Heid's sleeping figure, touched the völva's forehead and listened to her breath. "She has not moved."

She rose and motioned Åsa outside. "This is an affliction unknown to me. You have brought her back from the Otherworld, yet she is not wholly with us."

Åsa pondered. "She did not return willingly. I know she's exhausted. Perhaps she is trapped between the worlds, unable to fully manifest in either."

"If she doesn't come back to this world soon, she'll die of thirst and starvation," said Vigdis.

"We must give her a reason to live."

Vigdis nodded agreement. "But what?"

What indeed. Åsa cudgeled her brain. She knew Heid cared for her, and for her apprentices, but the völva's heart lay in Helheim with her dead husband and child. Only the Nornir's commands kept her among the living.

There was nothing for her here.

Åsa thought back over the years to Heid's actions and motives. The völva had been instrumental in Gudrød's proposal of marriage, goading his attack on Tromøy when Åsa refused him. Yet once Åsa became his wife, Heid allied with her. In the end the sorceress helped her kill Gudrød to save Halfdan's life. Perhaps now that Åsa was queen and Halfdan growing up, the völva felt she had fulfilled her purpose.

There was no doubt that Heid was worn out. She'd borne the pain of her crippled back since she was a young woman. As she aged, the pain worsened. The völva had never fully recovered from the sickness and her journey to Hel. Her spells and trances no doubt drained her. Heid needed to be restored to health.

But what cure was there for age and wear?

Åsa's mind drifted to Cian's music. It had made her feel younger, stronger, full of vigor and hope.

Perhaps it could do the same for the völva.

It certainly would not make her worse.

Åsa hurried back into the hall to find the Irishman.

She found him asleep on a bench near the longfire. His harp in its leather bag hung above him on the wall. Åsa didn't have the heart to wake him, so she returned to her chamber to await the morning.

Eyvind was awake. "I wondered where you'd gone," he said.

"My leg was bothering me," she said.

He smiled. "Let me take your mind off it."

Åsa woke late to find Eyvind already gone. She'd slept well and felt refreshed. Pulling a wool apron over her linen gown, she hurried out of the chamber to find Cian.

The Irishman was sitting among an admiring group, regaling them with a tale. As Åsa approached, a respectful silence fell over them all.

"Cian, may I speak to you privately?"

"Indeed, Lady, I am at your service." He rose and followed her into the empty hall.

She turned to him. "Your music has a healing quality. It has done wonders for the injured and for those of us wounded in spirit."

Cian smiled. "I'm so glad to hear that. That is one of the abilities my instructors tried to instill in us. At school I was deemed competent, but I feared I had lost it during my years of captivity."

"Your training must have been very special."

A sad expression flitted across the Irishman's face. "That it was. I had completed eight years of the twelve required to become a master harper when the Danes took me. My instructors had high hopes for me as a harper. They called me gifted." He stared disconsolately into the hall's gloom.

"I would agree with them. I'm so sorry you were taken from your life. But it seems to me that your music has retained healing qualities." She gave him a searching look. "I have a favor to ask you."

Cian put his hand on his heart. "Anything, my queen." His voice was fervent.

Åsa struggled with a pang of guilt. "I don't want to ask you to do anything that may go against your Christian beliefs, so if what I ask is wrong for you, I release you from your promise." It hurt her to give him the right of refusal. So much was at stake.

"We are all sinners," he said. "God forgives us. Please tell me what you need."

A glimmer of hope rose in Åsa. "The völva Heid is lost in the Otherworld."

Cian nodded gravely. "In Ireland, we have those who stray into the Otherworld and become trapped there by the Sidhe."

"We've done everything we know of to bring her back. The trouble is, she doesn't completely want to return."

"How so?"

"Long ago, her child and husband died. When Heid took sick last year, she entered the land of the dead and was reunited with them. She did not want to leave her loved ones, but the Nornir decreed that her work among the living was not complete. They sent her back from the dead. She was much weakened by her ordeal. When Horik attacked Tromøy, Heid sent her hugr to the Otherworld to help us in battle. Without her efforts, Tromøy would not have survived. After the battle, she did not return to her body. I journeyed into the Otherworld and fetched her back, but she did not come willingly. Now she seems to be only half in this world. The rest of her remains in the land of the dead."

Cian stroked his chin. "You are very skilled to have traveled in the Otherworld and come back whole. In my experience, the living do not return unscathed."

"Your music...Cian, when you played last night, my soul was healed after all the death I'd seen. I believe Heid is wounded in spirit and lacks the will to fully reenter the world of the living. If you can play for her...your music might heal her as it did me."

"That's a tall order," said the Irishman.

"I won't hold you responsible. I only ask that you try."

"I will do my best, my lady."

Cian fetched his harp from the wall above his bench. They emerged from the shadowy hall into bright daylight. Åsa stopped at the cookfire to dish up a bowl of porridge for Vigdis. The apprentice had not left Heid's side in days.

They crossed the yard to the bower. Cian hesitated at the door, his eyes full of doubt.

Åsa put a hand on his shoulder. "Don't fear. You are my protected guest. There is no evil here, only healing."

The Irishman squared his shoulders and stepped across the threshold. Åsa led him through the bower hall to the völva's chamber.

As they entered, Vigdis rose. "No change," she said, her voice choked with despair. She accepted the bowl from Åsa, stirring the porridge listlessly. They watched the sleeping sorceress for any sign of awakening. Vigdis shook her head. "She's too far gone."

"I won't give up," said Åsa. "I've asked Cian if he can try to heal her with his music."

Vigdis sighed. "We've tried everything else." She gestured to her stool beside the bed. "Please."

Cian sat and brought his harp out from its leather bag. "A master's cláirseach is larger, and has more strings," he explained. "This is a student's harp, the instrument of a wandering bard. I fear that is the highest level I achieved. But I will do what I can with this poor instrument and my paltry ability. In Ireland, we believe our ancient god, the Dagda, played magical music on his cláirseach. All those who heard him fell under his spell. He created three kinds of music: Goiltai, which filled people with sorrow, as I played for you last night. Another kind of music, Geantrai, filled them with joy, and Suantrai, to send them into a deep and healing sleep." He regarded Heid's still form. "To bring this lady's spirit back to the mortal world, I believe we need all three."

"Please, do whatever you feel you must."

The Irishman closed his eyes and took a deep breath. With his strong, curved fingernails he struck one brass string, and a high, clear, bell-like note rang out. He stopped it with the flat of his hand. Then his fingers flew over the strings, pouring out a melody that reverberated in the chamber.

The longing rose in Åsa once more. Potent emotions rolled through her like a storm followed by the sun. Tears came to her eyes and the next thing she knew, she was laughing.

Sweat poured down Cian's face, but the Irishman kept playing. Heid began to mumble under her breath. She twitched restlessly. Åsa and Vigdis looked at each other in alarm.

Suddenly the völva rasped in a breath. Her eyes flew open, and she began to speak. "I went under the cloak for three days, and there I had a vision. The gods spoke to me." Her voice deepened with the resonance of prophecy. "From Gudrød the Hunter and Harald Redbeard will spring the greatest king of all. The lords will unite under this king, and cease their strife. This I saw in the darkness."

Heid reached out a claw-like hand and gripped Åsa's arm. "I must stay a little longer, though I begrudge each day."

Åsa threw her arms around the völva. "Oh, my dear. I promise to do everything I can to make your stay a happy one." She looked up at Cian. "Ask what you will as a reward."

The Irishman had stopped playing. He gave her a hesitant look. "My lady, I do have a boon to ask."

"Ask, Cian. If it is something within my power to give, you shall have it."

His eyes glinted with determination. "Åsa, queen, I am very grateful to you for taking me from captivity. You have treated me well here, accepted me into your household, but I find in my heart that I long for my own country. I ask that you release me from my oath, my queen. And that you ask the Lady Ragnhild to take me with her when she departs, and restore me to my homeland."

Åsa said, "If Ragnhild agrees to take you, I release you from your oath, though with regret."

The völva gazed at Cian. "I suppose I owe you my thanks, Irishman," she said grudgingly. "Your music has real power. You are right to return to your land and continue your studies, and fulfill your potential to become one of the great harpers of all time." Heid's gaze turned piercing. "But you must think long and hard about what else you plan."

At her words, Cian's face paled.

"Go now," said Heid. "I need to rest."

"I'll stay with her," said Vigdis.

"Come now," said Åsa. "Let's speak to Ragnhild."

They found the shield-maiden on the shore, readying her ships to sail. The beach was crowded with ships in various states of repair, quite a few of them Danish. Ragnhild's fleet had sustained no real damage in the battle. Her crews scurried back and forth from the carts, loading casks of fresh water and ale, as well as food for the voyage home.

"Must you leave so soon?" asked Åsa.

"I have longed to see you," said Ragnhild. "I'm so glad I've had the opportunity. But I miss my husband and our son. It's hard to be away from them."

Åsa smiled in sympathy, thinking of Halfdan. She nodded toward Cian. "Ragnhild, I have a favor to ask you. Cian wishes to be restored to his homeland. I owe him so much, and I hoped you would be willing to take him back with you, and on your next voyage to Ireland, bring him home."

Ragnhild smiled at the Irishman. "We would be more than happy to honor the request of such a brave and honorable warrior. I'll gladly reward you for saving my dearest friend and mentor. You're welcome in my hall while you await our next voyage to Ireland."

"Then it's settled," said Åsa. "You will sail with Lady Ragnhild when she departs."

"I'm sure my husband will be thrilled to meet a countryman with whom he can speak his native tongue, and to hear your enchanting harp music."

Cian smiled and swept a low bow. "I look forward to meeting him."

As he spoke, Åsa thought a shadow passed over him. But Cian straightened out of his bow, smiling with happiness. This was the man she'd come to trust and like.

~

THE NEXT MORNING AT BREAKFAST, Åsa said good-bye to Olaf and Ragnhild. Cian was ready to depart, with a sea chest Åsa had filled with armor and weapons and silver. His harp in its leather case was strapped to his back.

King Alfgeir appeared with his men, and Åsa gestured him to the bench beside her. "I owe you much, my lord. You and your crew are welcome to stay as long as you wish."

"I thank you, Lady. You need time to put your kingdom back to rights. I move slower these days, but my húskarlar are all hale enough, and our ships have sustained little damage. We will depart today with the others."

"Very well. My shore crew are at your disposal should you need anything."

When breakfast was finished, she led Olaf, Ragnhild, and

Alfgeir to the stables. They mounted up and led their crews down to the shore, crowded with ships ready to depart. Olaf and Alfgeir each chose from among the twenty-one captured Danish vessels to replace those they'd lost in battle.

"I will have to leave them with you until my wounded recover enough to man them and bring them home," said Olaf. Kalv had agreed to remain behind with Skiringssal's húskarlar who were unable to travel, and sail the ships home when the wounded were well enough to man them.

Åsa offered Ragnhild one of the captured ships, though the shield-maiden had not lost ships or warriors in battle. "It's the least I can offer to repay you for coming to my aid."

"Another ship is very welcome to my small fleet," Ragnhild said. She chose a longship and assigned a crew, since she had filled her ships with extra warriors to fight the Danes.

Åsa stood by as her allies boarded, and the shore crew shoved them off the beach. As she watched Olaf's fleet sail away, her blood simmered with eagerness to see Halfdan, but first she must restore order to Tromøy.

Åsa ventured to the infirmary to find Olvir sitting up on his pallet, playing hnefatafl with Dagny.

"I see you are feeling much better," Åsa teased.

Olvir blushed and grinned. This was so different than the sober, practical Olvir she'd grown to depend on. He exchanged a look with Dagny and cleared his throat. "Lady, we have something to ask you."

Åsa raised her eyebrows. "Do you, now?"

Dagny nudged him. Olvir rushed on as if he feared his courage would fail him. "Yes, Lady, we'd like to marry."

Åsa suppressed a grin and gave the couple a stern look. "So, much has been going on behind my back."

The two of them looked so distressed she had to relent. "Of course you may marry. But I have one condition."

They both looked alarmed. "Anything, Lady," Olvir said cautiously.

"Let me build you a house here on Tromøy."

Olvir and Dagny stared at her, then at each other, expressions of joy dawning on their faces.

"Well?" said Åsa with mock impatience. "What say you?"

"Yes, Lady! Thank you!" Olvir said.

Åsa closed her eyes in bliss. Her home was safe, for now. Heid was alive, Olvir was alive. Now she could go and visit her son.

She embraced the two and made her way to the yard to find Eyvind.

AUTHOR'S NOTE

The places in Denmark in this book actually existed, as did Horik and his rivals.

Sebbersund was a big international trade market during the Viking Age, situated in the calm waters of the Limfjord, which provided a safe channel between the North Sea, the Skagerrak, and the Kattegat, avoiding the treacherous Skagan Point at the tip of the Jylland Peninsula. The area was a crossroads for European and eastern trade.

Excavations have turned up more than one hundred fifty pit houses in Sebbersund dating from the Viking Age, which were most likely workshops or animal byres. Fish bones, as well as remains livestock of all kinds, have been found in the pit houses.

Artifacts from the site include raw materials from Norway such as soapstone and slate, belt buckles from England, as well as handicrafts from the Middle East. Spindle whorls are a common find, along with warp weights and looms. It is likely Sebbersund had an early industry in cloth production. There is evidence that jewelry was mass produced here as well.

The water level in Viking times was higher than it is today, enabling passage for the shallow draft longships and knarrs. The sandy shores have shifted since those days, and the passages have silted up.

To the south, Erritsø is an archeological site that has been investigated fairly recently. Its name can be translated as Horik's fortress.

Though Åsa's kidnapping and the battles with Horik are fictitious, they are plausible. There is evidence that the Danes controlled portions of eastern Norway along the Skagerrak at times during the ninth century. The Frankish annals mention that two Danish royal brothers, Harald Klak and Reginfrid, traveled to Vestfold in 813 to put down a rebellion. The rebel would likely have been Olaf's father, Gudrød.

Horik was one of five sons of King Godefrid, who ruled the Danes until his murder in AD 810. Some sources suggest he was murdered by one of his sons, possibly Horik. The names of Godefrid's other sons are not known, though I have named one Rorik. Horik ruled from about 813 to 854, at times jointly with his unnamed brothers until he and one brother drove the other two out.

The relationship between the Danes and the Franks was fraught from the time of Charlemagne and Godefrid and continued after their deaths. Harald Klak, the uncle of the sons of Godefrid, allied with the Franks and attempted to use their power to gain the throne. He was joint ruler with his nephews for a time, but Horik eventually drove him out for good. Harald took refuge with the Franks, adopted Christianity and was given his own kingdom.

In Åsa's day, Erritsø was an imposing fortress with commanding views over the surrounding approaches, including the serpentine waterway known as the Little Belt. The landscape was primarily treeless marshland, though there was some forest land.

The fortress's extensive palisade may have been as tall as ten feet, and was fronted by a deep moat. The palisade enclosed a hall and other buildings dated to the ninth century.

The great hall measured forty meters long, ten meters tall, and thirteen meters wide. Other buildings were located within the palisade, including a small, fenced-off cult house similar to the one in Tissø. The size of the hall and the extent of fortifications identify it as a royal fortress, the residence of a king beset by powerful enemies. Horik fits the bill perfectly. The hall was burned to the ground at least once during the Viking Age and was rebuilt several times.

To this day, place names in the surrounding countryside of the Elbo valley suggest that this area was a major royal center. A nearby settlement bears the name "Kongsted" or King's Place. Other place names throughout the Elbo valley indicate the existence of army barracks, a smithy, and other craft shops, as well as a shipyard. This shipyard was located near a lake whose tributaries may have been navigable in the Viking Age, and linked to Gudsø Vig, a harbor near the fortress. The harbor shows evidence of posts driven into the waterway to impede hostile ships.

The Irish slave Cian is a fictitious character, but in Ireland at the time, harpers were high-ranking counselors of kings. The harp is the national symbol of Ireland. Ancient Celtic harps were strung with brass wire and plucked with long crooked fingernails. The Gaelic word for a wire-strung harp is cláirseach, while instruments strung with sinew were called harps.

Ancient Irish harpers were professionals of the highest order, and their training was long and rigorous. Children began their training before the age of ten, and the student had to master Irish music, the history of the harp, its care and, of course, playing. The title of harper was not hereditary but earned in competitions. The excellence of Irish harpers was recognized throughout the world, and other cultures learned their methods from the Irish.

According to ancient Irish manuscripts, harpers were so highly respected that Irish kings competed to attract the best to their courts, where they were seated in places of honor at banquets and adorned with gold and jewels. Harpers were said to have led troops into battle, singing of victory.

Such was the power of harpers that, centuries later, Queen Elizabeth I commanded her lord in Ireland to "Hang harpers, wherever found, and destroy their instruments."

CHARACTERS

Tromøy—an island off the east coast of Agder, Norway

- Åsa, age 22, queen of Tromøy, daughter of the murdered King Harald Redbeard
- Stormrider, Åsa's peregrine falcon
- Gullfaxi, Åsa's horse
- *Ran's Lover*, Åsa's flagship
- Gudrød's Bane, Åsa's sword
- Halfdan the Black, Åsa's 6-year-old son (turns 6 in June 825)
- Fylgja, Halfdan's blind wolf
- Brenna, Halfdan's nurse (fóstra)
- Olvir, head of Åsa's household guards
- Jarl Borg of Iveland, Åsa's military advisor
- Ulf, blacksmith of Tromøy
- Heid, a famous völva (sorceress), Åsa's mentor
- Vigdis, Heid's senior apprentice
- Other apprentices: Halla, Mor, Liv
- Eyvind, a Svea trader and Åsa's lover, age 28

Far Traveler, Eyvind's ship
Crew of *Far Traveler*

- Svein, second-in-command
- Thora, shield-maiden
- Dagny, a healer

The Deceased

- Svartfaxi, Murchad's horse, killed in battle
- Harald Redbeard, King of East Agder, Norway, Åsa and Gyrd's father
- Gunnhild, his queen, Åsa and Gyrd's mother, a noblewoman of Lista
- Gyrd, their son, Åsa's brother
- Estrid, Åsa's ancestress, The Queen in the Mound

Vestfold
Skiringssal, the Shining Hall of Vestfold, Norway
Borre, another stronghold of Vestfold, north of Skiringssal

- Olaf, age 23, king of Vestfold, son of King Gudrød
- Sonja Eysteinsdottir, age 21, Olaf's wife
- Rognvald, their 3-year-old son
- Kalv, captain of Olaf's guard

The Deceased

- Gudrød, king of Vestfold, Olaf's father, formerly Åsa's husband
- Alfhild, Gudrød's first wife, Olaf's mother
- Halfdan the Mild, Gudrød's father—Olaf's grandfather
- Hrolf, Gudrød's natural son

Danes

- Horik, king of the Danes
- Rorik, deceased, one of Horik's four brothers
- Harald Klak, their uncle, brother of the murdered King Godefrid
- Groa, Horik's völva
- Ingebjorg Roriksdottir, age 17, Horik's niece
- Cian, age 20, an Irish harper enslaved by Horik

Others

- Alfgeir, king of Vingulmark, Olaf's maternal grandfather
- Gudrun—age 16, his queen
- Knut, a famous traveling skáld (poet and historian)

Gausel—a farming settlement in southwest Norway

- Ragnhild Solvisdottir, age 19, leader of Tromøy's shield-maidens, daughter of the deceased King Solvi of Solbakk
- Murchad mac Maele Duin, age 32, Ragnhild's husband, deposed king of Aileach of the Northern Ui Neill—Cenel nEoghain
- Herulf, their son, born April AD 825
- Einar, Thorgeir, Svein—warriors formerly of Solbakk, now sworn to Ragnhild
- Jofrid, headwoman of Gausel
- Thyra, Gausel's healer
- Unn, age 18, shield-maiden and healer, sister of deceased shield-maiden, Helga
- Ursa, age 17, Unn's younger sister, also a shield-maiden

- Tova, age 16, their younger sister
- Ylva, age 15, their younger sister

NORSE TERMS

Aett—(pl. aettir) groups of eight runes in the elder futhark
Álf—elf, male, often considered ancestors (plural álfar)
Berserker—warriors said to have superhuman powers. Translates either as "bear shirt" or "bare shirt" (also berserk)
Bindrune—three or more runes drawn one over the other
Blót—sacrifice. i.e., Álfablót is sacrifice in honor of the elves, Dísablót is in honor of the dís
Bower—women's quarters, usually a separate building
Breeks—breeches
Brisingamen—Golden necklace belonging to the goddess Freyja
Brynja—chain-mail shirt
Dís—spirits of female ancestors (plural: dísir)
Distaff—a staff for holding unspun wool or linen fibers during the spinning process. About a meter long, usually made of wood or iron, with a bail to hold the wool. Historically associated with witchcraft.
Draugr—animated corpse
Ergi—a serious insult meaning unmanly, particularly a man who practices seidr or other magic considered the province of women
Fylgja—a guardian spirit, animal or female

Fóstra—a child's nurse (foster mother)
Flyting—a contest of insults
Galdr—spells spoken and sung
Gammelost—literally "old cheese"
Hafvilla—lost at sea
Hamr—"skin"; the body
Hamingja—a person's luck or destiny, passed down in the family
Haugbui—mound-dwelling ghost
Haugr—mound
Hird—the warrior retinue of a noble person
Hnefatafl—also Tafl, a chess-like board game found in Viking graves
Holmgang—"isle-going"; a duel within boundaries, sometimes fought on small islets
Hudfat—sleeping bags made of sheepskin
Hugr—the soul, the mind
Húskarl—the elite household warriors of a nobleman (plural: húskarlar)
Jarl—earl, one step below a king
Jól—Yule midwinter feast honoring all the gods, but especially Odin
Karl—a free man, also "bonder"
Karvi—a small Viking ship
Kenning—a metaphorical expression in Old Norse poetry
Knarr—a merchant ship
Lawspeaker—a learned man who knew the laws of the district by heart
Longfire—a long, narrow firepit that ran down the center of a hall
Minni cup—a toast in remembrance of the dead
Odal land—inherited land
Ørlög—personal fate
Primstave—a flat piece of wood used as a calendar. The days of summer are carved on one side, winter on the reverse.

Runes—the Viking alphabet, said to have magical powers, also used in divination
Saeter—a summer dairy hut, usually in the mountains
Seidr—a trance to work magic
Shield-maiden—female warrior
Shield wall—a battle formation
Skáld—poet
Skagerrak—a body of water between Southeast Norway, Southwest Sweden, and Northern Denmark
Skerry—a small rocky islet
Skjaergarden—a rocky archipelago on the southern cape of Norway
Skyr—a dairy product similar to yogurt
Small beer—a beer with a low alcohol content, a common drink
Sverige, Svea—Sweden and Swedes
Swinehorn—a v-shaped battle formation
Thrall—slave
Ting, Allting—assembly at which legal matters are settled
Ulfhed—"wolf head," another warrior like a berserker (plural ulfhednar)
Urdr—(Anglo-Saxon wyrd) the web of fate, the name of one of the Norns
Utiseta—Sitting out at night to call the spirits
Vaettir—spirits of land and water, wights (vaettr singular)
Valhöll—"corpse hall," Odin's hall
Valknut—"corpse knot," a symbol of Odin
Valkyrie—"choosers of the slain." Magical women who take warriors from the battlefield to Valhöll, or Freyja's hall Sessrumnir
Vardlokkur—a song to draw the spirits
Völva—a sorceress. Literally, "wand-bearer"
Wergild—the value of a person's life, to be paid in wrongful death
Wootz—crucible steel manufactured in ancient India

NORSE GODS AND HEROES

NORSE GODS AND HEROES

- Angrboda—a jotun, wife of Loki, mother of Hel, Fenrir, and Jörmandgandr
- Loki—a trickster jotun who becomes Odin's blood brother
- Nidhogg—a serpent who gnaws at the roots of Yggdrasil. When he gnaws through, Ragnarok will occur
- Muspelheim—world of fire
- Niflheim—cold and misty land of the dead, ruled by Hel
- Norn—(plural nornir) three sisters who spin the lives of men and gods, also known as the Weird Sisters or three fates: Skuld, (future) Verdandi, (Present) Urdr (past)
- Ragnarok—twilight of the gods, end of the world
- Yggdrasil—"Odin's steed," the World Tree, by which Odin travels between the nine worlds

HELHEIM

- Hel—daughter of Loki and Angrboda, queen of Helheim, also referred to as Hel.
- Fenrir—a giant wolf, son of Angrboda and Loki.
- Jörmungandr—the Midgaard serpent, son of Angrboda and Loki. .
- Gorm—the hound of Hel who guards the Gnipa cave at the entrance to Helheim
- Ganglati—Hel's steward
- Fjolsvith—jotun guarding Hel's gate
- Modgud—shield-maiden guarding the bridge

ASGAARD

—home of the Aesir gods

- Odin—lord of the Aesir gods, of many names
- Valhöll—Odin's hall—literally, "corpse hall"
- Einherjar—heroes slain in battle who come to Valhöll
- Gungnir—Odin's spear that marks an army for Valhöll
- Sleipnir—Odin's horse
- Baldr—Odin's son, most beautiful of gods
- Thor—Odin's son, god of thunder, preserver of mankind
- Mjölnir—Thor's hammer
- Tyr—one-handed god of war
- Freyja—"Lady" originally of the Vanir gods. Goddess of love and magic. She gets first pick of the slain heroes
- Sessrumnir—Freyja's hall in Folkvang.
- Brisingamen—Freyja's magic necklace.
- Freyr—"Lord," Freyja's twin brother, fertility god of peace and plenty

- Idunn—goddess with the golden apples of youth
- Ran—goddess of the sea
- Njord—Vanir god of the sea, father to Frey and Freyja
- Skadi—a jotun shield-maiden
- Thjazi—Skadi's father
- Valkyrie—"choosers of the slain." Magical women who take warriors from the battlefield to Valhöll, or Freyja's hall Sessrumnir

ACKNOWLEDGMENTS

I have so many people to thank in bringing this novel into being: My beloved mother who first introduced me to Åsa and the Viking world; my wonderful fellow writers at Kitsap Writers, each of whom contributed so very much and kept me going; and to critique partners DV Berkom, Chris Karlsen, and Jennifer Conner. Thanks to my dear husband Brian who is always on my side and eager to read more, and beta readers Colleen Hogan-Taylor and Linda S., each of whom gave me priceless insights. I owe many thanks to editors Kahina Necaise and Sarah Dronfield. Any errors that exist in this book are entirely my own.

ABOUT THE AUTHOR

Like her Viking forebears, Johanna Wittenberg has sailed to the far reaches of the world. She lives on a fjord in the Pacific Northwest with her husband, whom she met on a ship bound for Antarctica.

Thank you for reading! If you enjoyed this book a review would be appreciated.

If you would like updates of forthcoming titles in the Norsewomen Series, as well as blog posts on research into Viking history, visit www.JohannaWittenberg.com and join the mailing list to receive a free short story, *Mistress of Magic*, the sorceress Heid's origin story.

Join fellow author, K.S. Barton, and me on our podcast, Shieldmaidens: Women of the Norse World. Available on most platforms: https://linktr.ee/womenofthenorseworld

Follow me on Facebook

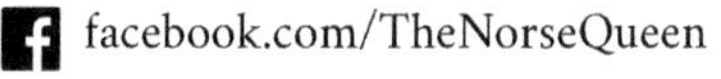

Printed in Great Britain
by Amazon